# PRAISE FOR MARY HIGGINS CLARK

'I **ADORE** Mary Higgins Clark'
**Karin Slaughter**

'Clark plays out her story like the **pro that she is . . . FLAWLESS**'
*Daily Mirror*

'The **"QUEEN OF SUSPENSE"** is renowned for her fast-moving prose and dazzling plot twists'
*Good Book Guide*

'Mary Higgins Clark's **AWESOME gift for storytelling** has always been the secret of her strength as a suspense novelist'
*New York Times*

'**Teeming with TANTALIZING twists**, Clark's cracking tale . . . is a tempting and thought-provoking thriller'
*Booklist*

'There's **something special** about Clark's thrillers . . . the **compassion** she extends to her characters'
*Publishers Weekly*

'Should come with a warning: start in the evening and you'll be reading **LATE INTO THE NIGHT**'
*USA Today*

**Unmissable thrillers by the QUEEN OF SUSPENSE**

# Have you read them all?

**WHERE ARE THE CHILDREN?**

A woman is falsely accused of murdering her two young children . . . and the real killer is still out there.

**A STRANGER IS WATCHING**

An innocent man awaits the inevitable on death row, while the man who put him there waits and watches . . .

**THE CRADLE WILL FALL**

What seems to be a straight-forward suicide leads a prosecutor down a dark and harrowing road – one which ends in murder.

**A CRY IN THE NIGHT**

Jenny MacPartland has just married the man of her dreams. But her husband is hiding a terrible secret.

**STILLWATCH**

While investigating the woman who might become the first female Vice President of the United States, a young journalist is drawn into a deadly world of secrets and intrigue.

**WEEP NO MORE, MY LADY**

Elizabeth Lange escapes to a seaside sanctuary after the death of her sister – but paradise hides deadly secrets.

**WHILE MY PRETTY ONE SLEEPS**

An innocent witness in a murder investigation becomes trapped in a sinister web of greed and ambition, which will put her in mortal danger . . .

**LOVES MUSIC, LOVES TO DANCE**
A killer is on the loose, using personal ads to lure his victims to their deaths . . .

**ALL AROUND THE TOWN**
University student Laurie Kenyon is accused of murdering her English professor, but she has no memory of the crime. Her fingerprints, however, are everywhere.

**I'LL BE SEEING YOU**
When a reporter sees a sheet-wrapped corpse, she feels as if she's staring into her own face: the murdered woman could be her twin sister.

**REMEMBER ME**
A killer turns a young family's dream holiday into an unfathomable nightmare . . .

**LET ME CALL YOU SWEETHEART**
When Kerry McGrath visits a plastic surgeon, she sees a woman with a hauntingly familiar face. On her next visit, she sees the same face again – on a different woman . . .

**MOONLIGHT BECOMES YOU**
With her stepmother brutally murdered and the police stumped, Maggie Holloway decides she'll have to solve the case herself.

**PRETEND YOU DON'T SEE HER**
While showing a luxurious penthouse flat, estate agent Lacey is the only witness to a murder – and to the dying words of the victim . . .

**YOU BELONG TO ME**
A radio talk show host tries to discover the identity of a killer who is stalking and murdering lonely women.

**WE'LL MEET AGAIN**

They're best friends: but one has just been convicted of murder, and the other may have committed it . . .

**BEFORE I SAY GOODBYE**

A desperate wife searches for answers to her husband's death, but the nearer she comes to learning the truth, the nearer she is to becoming the next victim of a ruthless killer . . .

**ON THE STREET WHERE YOU LIVE**

A young woman is haunted by two murders that are closely linked – despite the one hundred and ten years that separate them.

**DADDY'S LITTLE GIRL**

Seven-year-old Ellie's testimony put a man behind bars for the murder of her sister. Twenty years later, the murders start again . . .

**THE SECOND TIME AROUND**

A wealthy man disappears but his wife seems bafflingly unaffected. Is he in hiding, or dead? Or is something more sinister going on?

**NIGHT-TIME IS MY TIME**

High school reunions: the perfect time to catch up with old friends . . . and enact vengeance against the women who once humiliated you.

**NO PLACE LIKE HOME**

Ten-year-old Liza Barton accidentally shot and killed her mother while trying to protect her from her violent stepfather. Twenty-four years later, she's the target of a ruthless killer.

**TWO LITTLE GIRLS IN BLUE**

When her twin daughters are kidnapped, a mother's nightmare is about to become her reality.

**I HEARD THAT SONG BEFORE**

Peter seems like the perfect husband, until police show up with a warrant for his arrest . . . for murder.

**WHERE ARE YOU NOW?**

Her brother vanished when she was a child . . . now Carolyn's pursuit of the truth plunges her into a world of unexpected danger and unanswered questions.

**JUST TAKE MY HEART**

Broadway star Natalie Raines accidentally exposes the killer of her former roommate – but that's just the beginning of the story.

**THE SHADOW OF YOUR SMILE**

Eighty-two-year-old Olivia Morrow has a horrible choice: expose a long-held family secret, or take it with her to her grave.

**I'LL WALK ALONE**

What do you do when you're falsely accused of kidnapping your own child?

**THE LOST YEARS**

When a well-respected academic in possession of a priceless artefact is found murdered, his wife becomes the main suspect. But she has Alzheimer's . . .

**DADDY'S GONE A-HUNTING**

Two sisters' lives are under threat when a dark secret from their family's past comes to light.

**I'VE GOT YOU UNDER MY SKIN**

A father murdered in cold blood – and his widow intent on revenge.

**THE MELODY LINGERS ON**

Parker Bennett has been missing for two years – and so has billions of dollars from his company. Did he commit suicide or was his disappearance staged?

**AS TIME GOES BY**

A woman is on trial for the murder of her wealthy husband – but is she a cold-blooded killer or an innocent victim?

**ALL BY MYSELF, ALONE**

A glamorous cruise on a luxurious ocean liner becomes a nightmare when an elderly woman with a fortune in jewels turns up dead . . .

**I'VE GOT MY EYES ON YOU**

Kerry Dowling is found dead at the bottom of her family's pool. She threw a party the night before, but no one saw anything . . .

**KISS THE GIRLS AND MAKE THEM CRY**

Allegations of sexual misconduct rock a television news network, but somebody will go to any lengths to bury the story . . .

**(with Alafair Burke)**

**WHERE ARE THE CHILDREN NOW?**

The thrilling sequel to *Where Are the Children?*, with the children of Nancy Harmon all grown up, but once again in peril.

# The *Under Suspicion* series

## (co-authored with Alafair Burke)

**THE CINDERELLA MURDER**

Laurie Moran investigates the murder of a college student, where everyone is a suspect . . .

**ALL DRESSED IN WHITE**

A destination wedding goes awry when the bride disappears the day before the ceremony.

**THE SLEEPING BEAUTY KILLER**

Casey Carter was convicted of murdering her fiancé fifteen years ago. But Casey claims she's innocent. Now Laurie must try and prove it . . .

**EVERY BREATH YOU TAKE**

The Met Gala: the world's most glamorous fundraising party. People would *kill* for an invitation . . .

**YOU DON'T OWN ME**

Kendra Bell is suspected of killing her own husband. But she knows the real killer is still out there. Laurie will have to prove it before it's too late.

**PIECE OF MY HEART**

A child has vanished. Long-buried family secrets may hold the key to finding him . . . but the clock is ticking.

MARY HIGGINS
CLARK
& ALAFAIR BURKE

# IT HAD TO BE YOU

SIMON &
SCHUSTER

London · New York · Sydney · Toronto · New Delhi

First published in the United States by Simon & Schuster LLC, 2024

First published in Great Britain by Simon & Schuster UK Ltd, 2024



1 3 5 7 9 10 8 6 4 2

Simon & Schuster UK Ltd
1st Floor
222 Gray's Inn Road
London WC1X 8HB

Simon & Schuster: Celebrating 100 Years of Publishing in 2024

Simon & Schuster Australia, Sydney
Simon & Schuster India, New Delhi

www.simonandschuster.co.uk
www.simonandschuster.com.au
www.simonandschuster.co.in

A CIP catalogue record for this book
is available from the British Library

Hardback ISBN: 978-1-3985-2542-9
Trade Paperback ISBN: 978-1-3985-2543-6
eBook ISBN: 978-1-3985-2544-3
Audio ISBN: 978-1-3985-2888-8



Printed and Bound in the UK using 100% Renewable
Electricity at CPI Group (UK) Ltd

FSC
www.fsc.org
MIX
Paper | Supporting
responsible forestry
FSC® C171272

*In memory of Jerome "Jerry" Derenzo,*
*the beloved grandson of Mary Higgins Clark*

*And for librarians everywhere, who open*
*a world of possibilities with each book*

# IT HAD TO BE YOU

# Prologue

Ten Years Ago

As the moonlight painted a glistening path across the water behind the Harbor Yacht Club, fifty-four-year-old Sarah Harrington's eyes scanned the outdoor party, a serene smile gracing her lips. It was the kickoff of Memorial Day weekend and she was looking forward to having the family together for another summer. The unseasonable chill in the air was the only possible hint of the deadly turn this night of celebration might take, but Sarah's thoughts were focused instead on her children and how quickly life was moving.

How was it even possible that her baby boys—her twin sons, Simon and Ethan—had graduated from college? A sense of awe washed over her as she watched Simon twirl his girlfriend, Michelle, expertly on the dance floor. Ten feet away, Ethan and his girlfriend, Annabeth, danced hand in hand, ring-around-the-rosie style with Sarah's third child, twelve-year-old Frankie.

A flicker of memory transported her back to the days when motherhood seemed like an elusive dream. She and Richard had married fairly young, right after he graduated from law school. He was twenty-six at the time. She was twenty-four. They both knew they wanted children, but they were in no hurry. He was building his career in Boston. She was a budding artist. Their family would grow when it was meant to happen. Seven years later, he was a successful law firm partner. She had landed a regular spot with an art gallery in Manhattan.

They were more than ready for a child. More than ready to stop waiting patiently. She was so devastated when the first round of in vitro failed that Richard wanted to stop trying, to spare her another heartbreak. Father Hogan from Saint Cecilia suggested an adoption consultant another couple from the parish had used.

But the second try at the clinic worked and then some. The first ultrasound showed two eggs sharing a single placenta. Identical twins. Not as common as fraternal twins, but still an increased possibility with fertility assistance. Just like that, she went from having no babies to two. And ten years later, when Sarah was forty-three, little Frances gave them a delightful surprise. Then the Harringtons were five, as Sarah had always wanted.

The twins, such proud and doting big brothers, were the ones who quickly decided that their beloved baby sister wanted to be called Frankie. Sarah wasn't certain about allowing it. She assumed the boys said it because they wanted a little brother instead. But the name managed to stick for good, even though Frankie never became the tomboy her brothers may have yearned for. Tonight, she wore a dress she had selected from the department store herself after Sarah told her that the theme was a "summer white party," meaning everyone would be wearing white. Sarah had never seen a dress with so much satin and tulle outside of a wedding. Frankie could not have been more thrilled.

Oh, how happy Sarah was that this party to celebrate Simon and Ethan's accomplishments had turned out so splendidly. The boys were strikingly handsome, their dark hair and tanned skin contrasting with their matching white outfits—collared shirts, linen blazers, skinny jeans. The clouds that had threatened to move the entire affair indoors had cleared. And though Simon and Ethan weren't exactly exuding brotherly love, there were no outward signs of the conflict they'd been having the last couple of days over that ugly business about Annabeth. From the smile in Ethan's eyes, Sarah was fairly certain that the girl wasn't going anywhere. Maybe Richard would eventually see that, too, and come around. Maybe seeing how sweet she was being with Frankie tonight would change his mind.

"A candy for your thoughts."

Sarah had been so overcome by sentiment that she hadn't even noticed her best friend Betsy approach. They had met at an art camp in the ninth grade and were instant friends. They'd known each other so long that they couldn't remember which one of them had decided that a penny wasn't enough to trade for your innermost thoughts. Candy it was.

They weren't twins, but they had both managed to buy the same tailored white pantsuit for the party. Rather than flip a coin to see who had to return the purchase, they decided to embrace the fact that they obviously both had impeccable taste.

Even in matching outfits, no one would ever confuse the two friends. Betsy was five-foot-six, with an athletic build, and frequently referred to Sarah, small-boned and five inches shorter, as her *pint-sized pal*. Sarah, as usual, had opted tonight for an understated but refined look, choosing a white silk tank and classic pearls to coordinate with her pantsuit. Her chestnut hair, already slightly kissed by the sun from their time at the beach house, was swept back in a loose bun with a few playful tendrils to frame her heart-shaped face.

Betsy, always the gutsier of the pair, had gone with a white tuxedo-style vest instead of a blouse. Her gold statement necklace arguably violated the all-white dress code, but Betsy always knew which rules to follow and which to bend. Her blond hair, streaked with threads of silver, cascaded in gentle waves around her shoulders.

Watching her boys, Sarah thought about how they, too, might appear very similar—physically identical, in fact—on the surface, but were so completely different. Simon the Harvard graduate would start Columbia Law School in the fall.

He'd had his life planned for as long as she could remember.

He announced in sixth grade he wanted to be a lawyer, just like his father. When Sarah and Betsy had proposed, half jokingly, that perhaps one of the twins would like to take Betsy's daughter, Michelle, to a ninth-grade dance, Simon had leapt at the suggestion. The two had been together ever since.

Ethan was more of a free spirit like Sarah. *Or at least the free spirit I used to be*, Sarah thought. He finished U Mass Amherst on time, but not without a stern talk or three when he wanted to quit. He was a talented guitarist who dreamed of being a working musician. Richard told him he may as well buy lottery tickets for a living.

As for girlfriends, Sarah suspected there were many, even though she never met any of them—not until Ethan met Annabeth in Harbor Bay last June. She and Richard assumed it would be a few weeks of Cape Cod flirting until Ethan resumed his senior year, but instead, Ethan had developed a focus for the young woman that he'd previously shown only for music. *It will all work out for them*, Sarah told herself. *For all of us. Of course it will.*

How could she sum up all of these thoughts for Betsy and her offer of candy?

"Look at them, Betsy. I know I'm biased, but they're just perfect. When I think about how much I love my children, and how quickly they've grown up, I think my heart might literally burst."

"Well, let's certainly hope it's not literal. Bad for your health and would be quite a mess to clean."

"Perhaps an overly graphic choice of words," Sarah conceded.

Betsy wrapped one arm around Sarah's shoulder and gave a quick squeeze. "I know exactly what you mean. It goes by so fast. I still think of Dennis as my little boy, but he told us today he's planning on law school. He's starting to study for the entrance exams already. So we'll both have another generation of lawyers in the family."

"Where is Dennis by the way?"

"With my notorious early-bird of a husband. Don't be upset, but Walter was practically falling asleep at the table, so I gave him permission to go home. If I had to guess, Dennis would have stayed longer if the bartenders hadn't carded him when he tried to get a drink. His twenty-first birthday is in October, and I can tell he's counting down the days."

"Hopefully the day will come and go with less fanfare than the twins stirred up." Simon and Ethan had asked to spend their birthday weekend at the beach house alone with two friends. Sarah and Richard only found out about the raging party of almost a hundred college students when they got a call from their neighbor about a group of kids who had snuck into their backyard to jump in their hot tub. "Look at your Michelle out there with Simon. So smart and beautiful and grown-up already."

"If I had to guess, we two birds might have a wedding to plan in the not so distant future."

"It's certainly only a matter of time," Sarah said. "But knowing Michelle, we won't have a single bit of sway. That girl is even more stubborn than her headstrong mother."

Sarah noticed Betsy's gaze move from the Harrington children on the dance floor to Sarah's husband, Richard. He was talking to Howard Carver, one of Richard's two law partners at the small firm he founded when he walked away from big-firm practice. The other was Betsy's husband, Walter. Richard and Sarah were the first to announce thirteen years ago that they were building a vacation house on the Cape, only two short hours from Boston in Harbor Bay. Sarah soon convinced Betsy and Walter to do the same. Howard, seeing a good investment opportunity, soon followed.

Richard and Howard both held martini glasses half-filled with a dark liquid. Manhattans, if Sarah had to guess.

"Have you made any progress with him?" Betsy asked.

"Not tonight, Betsy, of all nights. Look how happy they all are. That's all I wanted out of this weekend." Richard's eyes connected with hers as he registered that they were looking in his direction. He smiled, his blue eyes gleaming with energy even at this distance. She felt herself returning his admiring gaze instinctively—the way she always did, the way he expected.

To any outside observer, it would look like a scene from a fairy tale. The perfect graduation party for the perfect twins from the perfect family.

Two hours later, as thirty-six-year-old Jenna Merrick drove past the Harbor Yacht Club, she could see the twinkling white lights from the party. She rolled down her car window to take in the sounds of laughter and music soaring above the coastline. The Harringtons, always so kind, had invited her to attend. She had been tempted. She'd worked the yacht club before as catering staff, but had never actually been a guest. But how would it look for the local diner waitress to show up at a fancy summer party with the vacation-house crowd? And what would she possibly wear?

Maybe it would be a Cinderella story. She'd find her future prince at the ball. Or maybe not and she'd end up standing alone in a corner or, worse, handling requests from people who assumed she worked there. If someone asked her how she knew the twins, what would she even say? *From the diner and then somehow ten years ago, I became their family's summertime dog walker and sitter?*

Jenna had declined the invitation, offering instead to give Bacon a nighttime walk during the party as her graduation present to the boys. She was actually there nine years earlier when the kids had named the boxer puppy. The family's previous dog, Picasso, had passed away the November before, and the grief had passed enough for the Harringtons to welcome a new canine friend.

Continuing prior tradition, Sarah wanted to name the puppy after an artist. She narrowed the list to Warhol, O'Keeffe, and Pollock. Simon, the same kid who had mastered at a young age the fine art of requesting a menu substitution politely, asked his parents if he and his siblings could research other options. Onto the Internet they went. As Simon read aloud a list of artists the children had never heard of, he reached Francis Bacon. Sarah explained that he was an Irish-born portraitist known for his dark, unsettling paintings of the human figure, but all the kids cared about was his funny last name. Their delighted giggles were even louder than the sound of tonight's graduation party. Bacon the Boxer it was.

When Jenna reached the Harringtons' house, she stopped at the gate and entered her personal passcode into the keypad. As the gate slid open, she took in the grandness of the house that awaited. It had a traditional rambling Cape Cod shingle exterior with a gable roof but was three times larger than the neighboring homes. The lush, manicured gardens burst with color. The nights she spent alone in the home with Bacon were like a luxury vacation.

Her key was in the front door when her stomach tightened with a sudden unease. Something felt different.

The night was completely silent. Even when she closed her eyes to try to hear something—anything—all she came up with was a faint thump in the distance, likely music bouncing off the water from the yacht club.

Instead of turning the key in the lock, she rang the doorbell. She heard the resulting chime clearly, even from the front porch. And yet, the night silence returned immediately.

*Where was Bacon?*

Bacon had an uncanny ability to sense who was at the other side of a door. And to Bacon, all humans fell into two camps—friends and strangers. Strangers were assumed to be home invaders and were greeted with a thunder of deep-throated barks that would send the toughest of criminals running for dear life. But with friends, Bacon was pure joy, whining with the anticipation of an imminent playdate.

Bacon was a nine-year-old dog, which was getting up in years for his breed. Maybe he had lost his hearing or his magic people-detecting skills. But it might be worse. She didn't want to find him that way. And how would she possibly break the news to the Harringtons about their sweet boy, Bacon?

She had no choice. She couldn't exactly call the police because of a dog's silence. She turned the key and pushed the door open slowly, steeling herself to find him if the worst had in fact happened.

She saw the blood immediately, and then the bodies. A broken strand of pearls was spilled in the blood. Richard was facedown, but Sarah's eyes were open, frozen in death with confusion. It wasn't until Jenna began to scream that Bacon joined her, howling in anguish from the back of the house.

The dog knew his mom and dad were gone.

# Almost Ten Years Later

# Chapter 1



Thirty-two-year-old Michelle Ward heard the clatter of scampering feet above her, a sure sign that the children were up and that her two and a half hours of early morning solitude were coming to an end. The words were flowing quickly onto her screen and she wanted to finish this chapter while she was on a roll. The sound of her husband's voice telling the kids to brush their teeth assured her that he had everything under control, and she found herself smiling as she finished writing the scene where her novel's two main characters first met in the cutest way.

She knew Simon's legal career wasn't the one he'd dreamed of when he first went to law school. While his father thrived in the elbow-rubbing culture of small-firm practice, Simon had wanted to clerk for the Supreme Court and then become a complex commercial litigator with one of the largest law firms in the world. He was the guy who planned out his entire life from a young age until life decided it wasn't going along with his plans.

He was in no condition to begin law school after the gruesome murders of his parents, so Columbia promised to hold his place in the following year's entering class to give him time to grieve. By the time he felt ready to focus on his studies, a group of current students and alumni had petitioned the dean to revoke his admission in light of what they called "more than probable cause to believe he either committed or was complicit in a double murder." Michelle had wanted him to sue when the school pulled its offer, but her parents advised that a lawsuit was unlikely to prevail and would only call more negative attention to Simon and his brother. Instead, her father called his own alma mater, Suffolk Law School, and got the son of his deceased law partner quietly enrolled.

Even when Simon sat for the bar, two lawyers who didn't know him at all had contacted the state bar's character and fitness committee trying to ban him from being sworn in. Their efforts failed, but employers weren't exactly pounding on the door to hire one of the notorious "Deadly Duo."

So instead of the big, flashy career at a big, fancy firm, Simon worked at the same little law office his father had, accepting a job offer from Michelle's father to join the practice. When Michelle's brother, Dennis, graduated from Boston College Law School the following year, he joined the firm, too, and now Dennis and Simon were partners. In truth, Simon was a far brighter attorney than her brother and did most of the actual legal work behind the scenes, but Dennis was the face of the firm, lest Simon make any potential clients flinch. Where Simon's father had been the unquestioned leader at Harrington, Ward & Carver, the tables had turned at the newly formed Ward & Harrington LLC.

Maybe it was her natural disposition toward optimism, but Michelle chose to believe that, despite the utter horror of that awful night, in some ways their life was happier than if Simon's professional dreams had come true. His hours were routine, he rarely traveled, and he was home to have dinner every night with her and the kids.

And unlike most of her writer friends, who complained about husbands who didn't understand how hard they worked, Simon made a point to help her carve out time when she could write in peace and quiet. That's why she was currently in the kitchen in her PJs, writing a smile-inducing meet-cute scene. These early morning hours were for her to work while Simon got the kids dressed and ready for a breakfast that he would cook for them all before heading to the office. She'd written four successful romance novels so far, using a pseudonym to avoid any whiff of notoriety.

Her laptop was closed by the time her children, Daniel, six, and Sophie, four, came thundering down the stairs.

"I'm hungry," Sophie said, her cherubic face still sleepy-eyed.

"You're always hungry," Daniel teased. "You're an eating machine."

"No, *you're* an eating machine."

Simon soon trailed them into the kitchen wearing a fluffy white robe, his hair damp from a shower. "You're both eating machines, which is why I'm going to make a giant stack of pancakes."

Sophie clapped, and Daniel let out a satisfied "Yesss." Where did they pick these things up?

As she was clearing their breakfast plates while Simon finished getting ready for work, the shrill ring of the house phone startled her. These days, they usually used their cell phones, and it was so early for an unexpected call.

"Hello?" Michelle said, her voice tinged with curiosity.

"May I speak with Simon Harrington?" a voice on the other end inquired. The caller was female with a hint of a Southern accent.

"May I ask who's calling?"

The voice on the other end was calm, almost detached. "My name's Lydia Martindale. I have a podcast called *Deadly Secrets*."

Michelle's heart quickened, and she felt a chill run down her spine. "Why do you want to talk to my husband?"

"You probably know that it's been almost ten years since his parents were murdered. We'll be talking about the case to mark the anniversary. We'd like him to come on our show."

It had taken so many years for them to settle into a new kind of normal. Simon, worried what his own future would look like, almost hadn't proposed to her, even though they had both known in high school that they would spend their lives together. Then after they were married, they weren't sure whether it was prudent to have children in the event Simon was ever formally charged. All these years later, she had trained herself not to fear developments they could not control. Their life was their life. Time moved on.

Michelle tightened her grip on the receiver. "I'm going to hang up now—"

"If he doesn't talk to us, but Ethan does, how will that look?" The question sounded to Michelle like a threat. "Does Simon still speak to Ethan? What about Frances? Is she on good terms with her brothers?"

Michelle hesitated at the mention of Simon's sister, Frankie. After the murders, Frankie had moved in with Michelle's parents. She was only twelve years old at the time. Although she was told that her parents had been killed, she did not know that her brothers were suspects until she overheard children at her school talking about them. When Frankie came home crying, Michelle's parents told her children could be misinformed and cruel, and assured her that her brothers were innocent, a position that both of Michelle's parents clung to, even to this day, despite the evidence. Michelle wasn't certain whether her parents actually believed someone else killed the Harringtons or if they simply loved Richard and Sarah's children too much to allow themselves to entertain the alternative.

With the encouragement of Michelle's parents, Frankie remained close to both of her brothers as she grew up, even as they became estranged from each other. But once she moved to California for college, her calls and texts became increasingly rare. Simon tried to tell himself that it was because she was busy, but even on her trips home to Boston, she seemed chilly, so different from her usually sunny and playful personality. When Michelle pressed her mother on the point, she finally explained that Frankie had been reading the details of her parents' murders and was now wondering if in fact her brothers were involved. Simon was devastated when Michelle broke the news to him.

"No comment," Michelle said, the sadness of their fractured family casting a shadow over her thoughts.

The podcaster continued, undeterred. "Ethan's wife, Annabeth, is having a child in three months. Will your children meet their new cousin?"

With a growing sense of unease, Michelle hung up the phone. She had an unfocused gaze when Simon returned to the kitchen, his robe replaced by a suit and tie. "Hey, did I hear the phone?"

She told him about Lydia Martindale and her prying questions.

"I guess we should have known that TV show that called your mother a few years ago wouldn't be the end of the media trying to profit from my parents' murders."

Almost three years ago, someone from a true crime program had inquired about the family's interest in appearing on her television show. Unlike this Lydia Martindale person, that woman had not called their home first thing in the morning. Instead, she had gone to Michelle's parents. As Michelle understood it, she had wanted to make sure Frankie was comfortable with the idea before approaching Simon and Ethan. Frankie was not, and that was the end of the discussion.

"Did you know Annabeth's pregnant?" Michelle asked.

He was silent as he shook his head, but she could see the pain in her husband's eyes. Until the murders, he and Ethan had been not only twin brothers, but best friends, confiding everything to each other.

But that was before Ethan killed their parents. Simon would never forgive him, and nothing could change that.

After Simon left for work, Michelle found herself watching her children, blissfully unaware of the phone call that had pulled their mother's thoughts into the past.

The murders of Sarah and Richard had left scars that might never heal completely, but Simon had worked so hard to make peace with the fact that the investigation had gone cold and the police would never prove Ethan's guilt, meaning the rest of the world would be free to wonder whether Simon had been involved, too. She and Simon had built a life together with the kids, far removed from those grim memories.

Had it really been almost ten years? There were days that had felt endless, but somehow the time had flown by so quickly.

When their children first asked why Grammy and Papa were their only grandparents, while many of their friends had two sets, they had explained that Daddy's parents had died when he was twenty-two years old. She and Simon did not know when and whether to tell the fuller story, but eventually it would be out of their control.

Those tablets in her children's hands. This morning, Sophie was using hers to tend to her plants on a game of the Very Hungry Caterpillar, while Daniel was mastering Candy Crush. It wouldn't be long before they learned how to use those miniature computers to Google information on the Internet. Eventually they'd type in their father's name.

How do you tell your children that strangers believe their father murdered their grandparents in a conspiracy with an uncle they didn't even know existed? Maybe some extra attention to mark the anniversary of the deaths could be a blessing in disguise if it might finally clear Simon's name.

She reopened her laptop and looked up the *Deadly Secrets* podcast with Lydia Martindale. She hit play on one episode and immediately recognized the voice. The audio was tinny, and the show only had seventeen online reviews. She should have known from the 8 a.m. phone call that it was not a professional operation.

She googled "true crime media" and found a flurry of articles about the boom of the true crime genre. She clicked on an article called "When Crime Solving Becomes Entertainment." She hadn't heard of any of these podcasts or television shows, even the popular ones. After everything that had happened with the murders and the investigation that followed, Michelle could not imagine using her free time to think about crime.

Her eyes widened at the claim that one television show, *Under Suspicion*, had managed to crack nearly every case it had covered. The narrator was a handsome man named Ryan Nichols, who looked more like a TV anchor to Michelle than a detective. Apparently sources at the studio attributed the successful case outcomes to someone behind the scenes, a producer named Laurie Moran.

Michelle Googled the producer's name and landed on a *New York* magazine profile. The journalist daughter of the NYPD's former first deputy commissioner, she was motivated to reinvestigate unsolved crimes after the murder of her own husband was unresolved for five years.

At the mention of the homicide, Michelle realized that Laurie Moran was the same journalist who had once contacted her mother and Frankie. According to her mom, the woman seemed serious and empathetic, not at all like the podcast woman who called this morning.

When Michelle got to the part of the article where Laurie described those years as "living in limbo," she found herself nodding along, tears forming in her eyes. Michelle couldn't help but wonder if it was finally time to confront the shadows of the past.

She found her phone on the kitchen counter and scrolled down to a name that was close to the top of her contact list. She had never been able to bring herself to delete it.

Annabeth. Annabeth, to whom Michelle had been so needlessly cruel. Annabeth, who was apparently expecting her first child in three months with Ethan.

She hoped the number hadn't changed.

# Chapter 2

Laurie Moran noticed that she was smiling in the mirror as she applied a thin layer of tinted moisturizer and a single coat of mascara, her only makeup on a typical day.

For as long as Laurie could remember, her early morning thoughts focused on how to get her son out of bed and both of them out the door. The nightmares she suffered for years after Greg's murder did not help, but the bad dreams became less frequent over time, and Timmy eventually grew into his own morning routine. As certain as she had been about marrying Alex, she had worried that blending their households would shake up the sense of order she'd worked so hard to achieve.

Now, six months into their marriage, Laurie was smiling to herself because she had woken up to the aroma of freshly brewed coffee in the air, the quiet sound of jazz music from Tim's bedroom down the hall, and the feeling of her husband's arms wrapped around her waist. No hint of chaos.

Her heart only soared higher when she made her way to the kitchen. Ramon was humming a tune she couldn't quite place while overseeing a griddle of French toast. At the breakfast nook, Alex and Tim sat side by side over the *New York Post*, hashing out where the national hockey teams ranked in the weeks since the all-star break.

They were completely at ease together. Even though Alex had dark, wavy hair, while Tim's own hair was sandy-blond and wispy, any stranger who saw them like this would assume they were father and son.

"Our team will be unstoppable once Tim Moran's at the net," Laurie said, hoping that her use of *at the net* was correct. At least she'd finally grown accustomed to calling her little boy Tim. Back when he was still Timmy, he declared he wanted to be the Rangers' goalie by the time he was twenty-one.

"Tim might be too busy playing trumpet in a jazz quartet for professional sports," Ramon said, proving that he never missed a beat of a conversation, no matter how hard at work he appeared.

Alex gave Tim a friendly pat on his shoulder. "This guy can do it all," he said.

"Just like my mom," Tim said with a satisfied expression. "We were waiting for you to come down, Mom." He looked to Ramon in anticipation and began to whisper a shared countdown: three, two, one . . . "Happy Six Month Anniversary!"

The same four words Alex had said to her that morning. She dropped a kiss on the top of Tim's head, still damp from the shower. "You two are so sweet to remember. Speaking of big days, Tim, your birthday is in two weeks and you haven't given us any hint at all about what you want." *How was he almost eleven years old already?*

"But then it wouldn't be a surprise."

Tim bounced from his seat at the sound of a knock at the apartment door. The doormen no longer called upstairs to announce the arrival of Laurie's father, but Leo still insisted on knocking instead of using the apartment key she had given him.

"Good morning, Grandpa! Ramon made cinnamon French toast! Do you want some?"

While Tim admired musicians, athletes, and YouTube stars like the other kids at school, he still looked at his grandfather like he was Superman. The former first deputy police commissioner of the NYPD, he might have been the city's next commissioner if he hadn't retired to help Laurie raise a child alone when Greg was killed. Leo Farley was indeed a real-life superhero.

"No thanks, buddy. I made myself a veggie egg white omelet this morning the way Ramon taught me," he said, patting his stomach lightly. "Got to keep the old ticker ticking."

It had been nearly three years since her father had been rushed to Mount Sinai for a cardiac fibrillation episode that led to the insertion of two stents in his right ventricle. Laurie felt like a broken record, always lecturing him about dietary restrictions while her father complained she was trying to make him a miserable gluten-free vegan. It wasn't until Ramon and his culinary talents got involved that her father began to accept some lifestyle changes. He still indulged in the occasional steak or his legendary "Leo lasagna," but not enough to worry her.

The list of requirements when she and Alex had been searching for an apartment had been long. Lots of space for a home office and at least one extra guest room. Thick walls to protect the neighbors from Tim's enthusiastic trumpet practices. A separate living area for Ramon, who insisted on being called a "butler," even though he was Alex's honorary uncle at this point, not to mention a kitchen that complied with Ramon's exacting demands. But top of the list was *location, location, location*.

Laurie's former apartment on 94th Street had been only a block from her father's and five blocks from Tim's school. Someday, maybe soon, Tim might announce that he wanted to walk to and from St. David's on his own, but until that happened, no apartment in the world was important enough to deprive her son and his grandfather of their cherished daily tradition. Laurie had worried that even the move to 85th Street might be too far, but her father assured her that he'd benefit from the extra steps.

While Tim grabbed his backpack from his bedroom, Laurie pulled her father aside. "Can I ask you to put on your former detective hat?"

"My detective hat is never off," he said dryly.

She smiled. "Of course not. *Tim* is apparently too grown now to drop his usually heavy-handed hints about what he wants for his birthday. Can you try to sneak it out of him?"

Her father's shoulders shook gently as he chuckled.

"What am I missing?" she asked.

"Oh, yes, Mr. Timothy tries so hard to be grown, but on our walks? For every old cop-on-the-beat story I give him, he mentions a new video game or concert he wants to see. Trust me, your old man's got a list. You may need to take a loan out on this place by the time we're done."

"I should have known Farley was hot on the case."

"Always."

It was the usual morning rush on the subway platform, another morning tradition that Laurie wouldn't change, despite Ramon's repeated offers to drive her. Laurie was a journalist. As grateful as she was to have other people's help, she couldn't completely remove herself from the real world.

She noticed a young woman seated on a bench, trying to type a text on her phone with one hand while holding onto the wriggling toddler on her lap with the other. The woman's eyes darted between her screen and the subway tunnel, anticipating the inbound train that could be heard in the distance.

"Is everything all right?" Laurie asked. "I'm sorry to pry, but you seem a bit overwhelmed."

When the woman looked up, Laurie could see that her eyes were tired. "It's just a rough morning. I've got to get this guy to daycare but we're running behind schedule, and if I'm late to work again . . . I can't lose this job. I've got to at least email my boss before I get on the train and lose the phone signal, but I can't let go of my son, not when you won't sit still, Jake, and with the train coming and all the horrible things you read about subway platforms." The woman's words were spilling out so quickly, Laurie thought she was close to tears.

"Let me help. Please." The woman shook her head immediately, but then she looked up at Laurie's face again. "I'm a mom, too.

Please. I can entertain Jake or type the text for you, whatever you want."

She hesitated for a moment, as if wrestling with the decision. Finally, she nodded and gave a grateful smile. "That's so kind of you." She handed Laurie her phone. "Jake, this is our friend . . ."

"Laurie. Hi Jake. It's nice to meet you." Laurie read the message the woman had started and then finished it on her own with two thumbs. When she was done, she read it aloud.

"It's perfect," the woman said.

"And sign it?"

"Tara. I'm Tara."

"She's not Tara," Jake said, sticking out his tongue. "She's my mommy."

"You don't know how much this means to me," Tara said. "It's just been so hard lately. Sometimes I wish I had family who could help out, but then I remember why it's just the two of us. Sorry, that's a lot—Let's just say that when a family no longer speaks to each other, there's usually a good reason."

As they stepped onto the train together, Laurie gave the woman a sad smile, feeling even more grateful for the support she and Tim had found in their lives.

Fifteen minutes later, she arrived to the sixteenth floor of 15 Rockefeller Center, home to the offices of Fisher Blake Studios. As she stepped from the elevator, she saw Ryan Nichols sauntering into the office of her boss, Brett Young. Within seconds, she heard her boss welcome the host of her show with an enthusiastic assurance: "My door's always open for Ryan!"

What were the two of them up to now?

# Chapter 3

Annabeth Harrington paused on the staircase landing, her eyes drawn to the mirror there. Her brown eyes were noticeably puffy. Between the changes to the shape of her body and the morning sickness, she was not getting enough sleep. She gently cradled her swollen belly with both hands. "Only three more months," she whispered. "I can't wait to meet you."

She felt a small kick against her right hand. "You can hear me, can't you, sweet pea?"

When she turned around, her husband, Ethan, was gazing up at her from the foot of the stairs. He wore a Bruce Springsteen T-shirt and workout shorts, his wavy brown hair damp from his morning run. "If I was as pretty as you, I'd check myself out in the mirror, too." He gave her a quick kiss when she had completed her trip downstairs.

"First of all, you are definitely as pretty as I am. And two, I was *not* checking myself out. I was gawking at my giant belly."

"Which is as beautiful as the rest of you," he said. "How's the little guy doing today?"

"Or girl," she said. They had decided not to learn the baby's sex, but she could tell in subtle ways that Ethan seemed convinced they'd be welcoming a boy. "Can't sit still. Just like daddy. How was your workout?"

She wasn't kidding when she said her husband couldn't stay still. If he didn't run a few miles in the morning, he'd pace and fidget all day long. He swore that his wake-up jogs were the only way to manage his excessive energy. If only they could bottle it, they'd be billionaires. He normally ran one of a few standard routes through their neighborhood, but he had bounced from bed even earlier than usual today, announcing that he wanted to run the Charles River Path. The river divides Boston and Cambridge and is lined by paths on both sides. With no elevation and views of both the river and city, it's considered one of the best running routes in the nation."Perfect. The sun's so bright out today."

"You weren't freezing?"

"Can't be cold when you're running seven-minute miles, babe."

"Show-off."

"When you're only good at a couple of things, you've got to give yourself credit when it's due."

Typical Ethan. "Funny how you manage to be self-deprecating even when you're bragging."

"It's a talent."

"So many talents," she teased, a smile spreading across her face. "I hope our baby is so modest."

As they shared this tender moment, Annabeth's cell phone rang in the back pocket of her maternity jeans. Ethan must have registered the confusion on her face as she looked at the screen, because he asked who it was. "I have no idea." She answered with a wary "Hello?"

The voice on the other end was unfamiliar. "Is this Annabeth Harrington?"

Annabeth's brows furrowed. She should have known it was some sort of telemarketer. "Who's calling, please?"

"My name's Lydia Martindale. I'm a podcaster trying to reach your husband, Ethan."

Ethan squinted as he made out the sound of his own name.

"How did you get this number?"

"I reached out to some of your friends on social media. I hope you don't mind."

"Of course I mind. I don't know you." She put her phone on speaker so Ethan could also hear.

Lydia Martindale's voice remained steady, almost unsettlingly so. "It's been almost ten years since his parents were murdered. We're marking the anniversary, and we'd like him to come on our show."

Ethan was shaking his head vigorously, waving one hand across his throat to signal her to end the call.

"I can assure you he's not interested."

"Does he ever speak to his brother, Simon? Will he and his wife, Michelle, meet the new baby?"

Annabeth hesitated, the complexity of their family dynamics weighing heavily on her. "We prefer to keep our family matters private."

The podcaster pressed on, her voice taking on a more sinister edge. "I just spoke to Michelle. They're likely to go on air with me. Aren't you and your husband concerned about what they might say?"

Annabeth's heart constricted at the sound of Michelle's name. Ethan's brother and father had been so icy toward her when she began dating Ethan, but his mother, Sarah, had always been kind. Michelle? Annabeth would have expected the girlfriend of Ethan's brother to rise to her defense. Surely she would see how controlling Richard was of his sons and want them to be free to live their own lives. Instead, Michelle almost seemed to revel in the knowledge that Richard Harrington approved of her perhaps even more than he disapproved of Annabeth. Michelle, after all, was the daughter of Betsy and Walter Ward, Sarah's best friend and Richard's law partner. The Wards weren't as wealthy or fabulous as the Harringtons, but Michelle went to the same fancy schools they attended and was the perfect girl for perfect Simon. They treated Ethan as the lesser son even before he fell for a local girl, one whose parents had to work for wealthy families like theirs.

How many times had she wondered what would have happened if Richard and Sarah had not been killed? Would Ethan have eventually yielded to his father and broken up with Annabeth? Or would he have stayed with her, even if it meant being estranged from his judgmental family? Or would Richard, as Sarah had assured her repeatedly, have ultimately come to accept Annabeth? Maybe with time, she and Michelle would even have become friends. She could imagine the four of them—Simon, Michelle, Ethan, and her—living in the same neighborhood and spending holidays together. But the murders ruined any chance of a happy ending together. If they went on that podcast, what would Simon and Michelle say about Ethan and her?

She had a vague idea, given Michelle's cruelty the last time they spoke, shortly after it became clear the police thought Ethan and Simon had conspired to kill their parents. *Ethan did this on his own,* Michelle insisted, *all so he could be with you and still get his inheritance. Their blood is on your hands.*

"Don't believe anything they say," Annabeth said firmly, "and don't you dare call here again." Her eyes were wide as she looked to Ethan after ending the call. "What are we going to do?"

"Keep living our lives," he said, seemingly unperturbed. "Don't let some crackpot ruin this gorgeous day."

With that, he galloped upstairs, two steps at a time. Seconds later, she heard their shower running.

She could still feel the sting of the podcaster's implicit threat to blame the murders on Ethan when her phone rang again. She expected to see the same number on her screen. Instead, she was surprised by a familiar name—Michelle Ward, still stored under her maiden name.

"This is Annabeth." She could hear the edge in her own voice.

"It's Michelle. I'm sorry to call so early, but I need to talk to you."

"About Lydia Martindale?" she asked. "She just called and said you and Simon are going on her podcast. Why would you do something so thoughtless? Why can't you leave it alone?"

"What? That's not true. She made it sound like you guys were the ones talking to her."

Annabeth allowed herself to exhale a sigh of relief. "So she was trying to manipulate us both."

"Apparently, but Annabeth, don't you think maybe it's time to finally find out what happened that night?"

"I know what happened. Because I know it wasn't Ethan."

"Well, I know it wasn't Simon. And yet, it had to be one of them, so . . ."

"I'm well aware you think it was Ethan," Annabeth said, "and his supposed motive. You made that clear."

"And you must think it was Simon," Michelle said, matching the sadness and resignation in Annabeth's voice. "I'm sorry I said what I said to you all those years ago. I admit I think it was Ethan, but I never really blamed you. I was just so angry. I still am. Simon not only lost his parents, but his life was ruined because he couldn't prove his innocence. You must feel the same way."

Ethan had a nice career working as a freelance sound engineer, and she worked in the marketing department of a family-owned chain of movie theaters. Most importantly, they had each other and would soon have a child. "Ethan and I are happy. My husband's life wasn't *ruined*."

"Fine, but until the world knows the actual truth, all of us live under a shadow of guilt. It's like we're in limbo, waiting for things to be normal again. And you have a baby on the way—"

"How did you know that?"

"The nosy podcaster," she said with small laugh. "Congratulations. I really am happy for you. Don't you wonder what you're going to tell your children someday about what happened to their grandparents?"

Annabeth thought about it all the time. It was another reason she couldn't sleep at night. It was part of why they had waited so long to have children, not sure they wanted to subject the next generation to the horrible speculation that Richard and Sarah's twin sons had collaborated to murder them for money. "So what are you suggesting?" she asked.

"Have you ever heard of a show called *Under Suspicion*? There's a producer named Laurie Moran."

Annabeth had been engrossed by multiple episodes of the show and knew that the producer had called Michelle's mother and Frankie years earlier, but listened patiently as Michelle summarized the premise and the series' success at resolving unsolved cases. She had no interest in sharing any more information than necessary with Simon's wife.

At the sound of Ethan's footsteps bounding down the stairs, she cut Michelle off abruptly. "Thank you for calling, but we're not interested."

"You won't even consider it, Annabeth?"

"He won't do it. I'm certain of that."

She was relieved when Ethan began pouring himself a cup of coffee without asking if she'd been on the phone again. Annabeth had learned ten years ago that they couldn't trust either Simon or Michelle. They weren't going to start now.

As she watched her husband settle in over the *Boston Globe*, she had a terrible feeling that the two phone calls this morning would not end the matter. A door was opening to the past and they might not be able to close it.

# Chapter 4

Laurie arrived at her office to find a chocolate croissant on her desk beside an envelope with her name on it. It was an anniversary card signed by her assistant, Grace Garcia, and assistant producer, Jerry Klein. The handwritten note inside read, *Some workplace romances lead to H.R. but some bring a lifetime of happiness. Glad you and Alex found the latter.*

Classic Grace and Jerry.

She heard the familiar sound of laughter from Jerry's neighboring office and made her way next door. Grace was wearing a jade-green mini dress, black stilettos, and gold hoop earrings that nearly touched her shoulders. Her thick black hair was pulled into a tight *I Dream of Jeannie* topknot. Jerry sported a green turtleneck, black pants, and a plaid blazer.

"No fair," Laurie said, joining them in Jerry's office. "You didn't send me the wardrobe memo."

"No advance planning," Jerry said, posing beside Grace. "We obviously both have excellent taste."

"And can a rock a jewel tone," Grace added. "How long have you been here? Sorry, I didn't hear you arrive."

"Because I'm a little ninja, but I just got in. I can't believe you guys got me an anniversary card. How did you even remember?"

"I wish we could take credit," Grace said. "Your son texted a reminder."

Laurie smiled and shook her head. "He should not be texting you about that. Or bothering you at all, in fact."

"Girl, you don't know we text all the time? He sends me music he thinks I'll like, and I send him funny dog videos."

She was going to have to get used to the fact that she might not know every single thing about her son now that he was getting older. It suddenly dawned on her that Tim might have a specific reason to be texting Grace.

"Oh my gosh. I guess he's old enough that he might have a little crush? I hope that hasn't put you in a bad spot."

"Timmy and a crush? No, he's still such an innocent little boy."

"And he texts both of us," Jerry said. "Just last week, he asked for wardrobe advice for his trumpet recital."

"The two of us are like his really fun auntie and uncle," Grace said, holding up a hand for a high five from Jerry.

It made sense. Grace and Jerry were her coworkers, but they were also two of her closest friends at this point, and Tim loved them like family.

"What were you two laughing about before I interrupted?"

"Grace's latest dating escapades," Jerry said, his face lighting up. "You arrived just in time for the good stuff."

Grace chimed in, her laughter still evident in her voice. "Okay, so like I already told Jerry, I finally linked up with a guy I'd been talking to on Bumble." Grace was an active participant on multiple dating apps, treating the search for love like a competitive sport. "Everything seemed great at first. He looked like his photos. Hadn't lied about his height. Picked a really nice French bistro, and you know I love me some escargot. Then he starts complimenting my outfit, and I'm thinking, yes, this man is nice to be around. But then he starts asking me what brand is my dress? Where did I buy my shoes? Suddenly I felt like I was being interrogated by the fashion police. When he asked me point-blank how much money I spent on everything I was wearing, I finally asked him why he had so many questions. Do you know what he said?" She waited the requisite beat for perfect comedic timing. "Because he could never be with a woman who made more money than him."

"I don't even know how you can laugh about that," Laurie said. "I would have given him an earful."

"Oh, I laughed directly in his face, right before I told him he was a ridiculous human and dropped cash on the table for my half of the check. At least the escargot was good."

Laurie was more than grateful that she'd never have to date again. She didn't know how Grace managed to keep a sense of humor about her notoriously bad dating luck, joking that she'd keep kissing frogs until she found her prince.

With the levity of the moment lingering, Grace's expression grew more serious. "Speaking of ridiculous men, we should probably tell you that Ryan was here a few minutes ago looking for you."

Ryan Nichols was the host of *Under Suspicion*, and he and Laurie had gotten off to a bumpy start when he joined the team about a year and a half earlier. It didn't help that Alex had been the show's original host, and in Laurie's eyes, no one could possibly fill his shoes. But Laurie's boss, Brett, had hired Ryan without her input, not even bothering to consider other candidates she suggested—all because Ryan was the nephew of Brett's best friend and former college roommate, a famous historian named Jed Nichols.

Ryan was certainly smart enough for the job, having graduated magna cum laude from Harvard and completing a Supreme Court clerkship before working as a federal prosecutor on white-collar cases. But unlike Alex, who had years of trial experience, Ryan had left the U.S. Attorney's Office while he was still green to become a part-time talking head on a cable news network, and it was clear to Laurie he cared more about being a celebrity than the actual work.

After months of butting heads when he first joined the show, they had finally reached a détente about a year ago, but the old Ryan had been rearing his annoying head in recent months, and Laurie could tell from Grace and Jerry's expressions that something about his visit to her office that morning had bothered them.

"Did he say what it was about?" Laurie asked.

"No, but he seemed frustrated that you weren't at work yet," Grace said.

Jerry barely disguised an eye roll. "Which is rich given the fact that he routinely saunters in late the morning after whatever high-profile event landed him on Page Six again the previous night."

"I just saw him going into Brett's office. I'll track him down."

"That's not all, though," Grace said. "When he stopped by, he looked in your office and saw the card we'd propped up on your desk. He asked about it, so I told him it was your six-month anniversary and maybe that's why you were running a little late. He sighed beneath his breath and said something snarky, like *Guess she has different priorities now that she's married.* I'm sorry. I shouldn't have even said anything to him. I wasn't sure whether to tell you, but Jerry said you'd want to know."

"You didn't do anything wrong," Laurie said. "I'll take care of it. You guys ready to go over case possibilities?"

She had been researching cold cases for their next special but didn't feel any of them pulling at her strongly enough to commit. An intriguing unsolved case wasn't enough. The case needed at least one identifiable suspect—someone who had been living for years "under suspicion," even though never officially charged. And the suspect or suspects had to be willing to go on camera to proclaim their innocence. Laurie had a practice of not reaching out to possible suspects until she was confident that her show could find new evidence. She had asked Grace and Jerry to review the three cases she was considering so they could brainstorm possible avenues for re-investigation this morning.

"Absolutely," Jerry said, "but we've got a fourth case to add to the mix. You tell her, Grace. You answered the phone."

Grace rubbed her palms together in anticipation. "A call came in this morning, nine a.m. on the dot. Does the name Frankie Harrington ring a bell?"

Laurie bit her lip. Something about the name tugged at a corner of her memory, but she couldn't quite place it.

Grace added another hint. "You spoke to her and a woman named Betsy Ward a couple of years ago when you were looking for a case for our second special."

Laurie remembered the pressure she'd been under at the time. The first special had been a huge success, solving the high-profile murder of a wealthy socialite who was smothered in her bed after a luxurious gala to celebrate the graduation of her daughter and three friends. But the production had taken an emotional toll on Laurie personally. Five years earlier, a man had shot and killed her husband, Greg, in front of Timmy when he still a toddler, leaving her son with a terrifying threat—"Tell your mother she's next, then it's your turn." By the time she had gone back to work, in charge of her own show, she had started to believe that the killer Timmy had dubbed *Blue Eyes* wouldn't actually come back for them. How wrong she had been. While they were filming, Blue Eyes returned, and he came not for Laurie first, but for Timmy. Her son had escaped, and Blue Eyes would never hurt anyone again, but the trauma of seeing her son in danger made her wonder how she could ever focus on work again.

Reflecting back on that period of her life helped her remember the case Grace was referencing.

"The Deadly Duo," she said.

"Bingo!" Jerry said.

"The sister actually called?"

Laurie had thought at the time that the case would be a perfect follow-up to her first special. Like the wealthy socialite, Richard and Sarah Harrington were also killed in their home after celebrating a graduation—the college graduations of their identical twin sons.

The Harringtons' Cape Cod vacation home had a gate at the driveway entrance that could be opened in one of two ways: a keypad code or from inside the house. A recent storm had dislodged the gate's camera, and the family's handyman had not yet remounted it. As a result, the camera footage showed only the exterior of vehicles coming and going rather than the occupants' faces. Richard Harrington's black BMW returned from the party at 9:12 p.m and the key code was entered to open the gate. Four minutes later, at 9:16 p.m., the code was used again, this time by someone driving the family's white Range Rover, which they kept at the Cape and which the twins had used that night to take their girlfriends to the party. Another ten minutes later, the dislodged camera captured the sounds of two gunshots, only moments apart. And seven minutes after that, the Range Rover departed. Shortly thereafter, one of the twins—unclear which—was seen walking away from the Range Rover, left on the outskirts of an overflow parking lot, and walking back toward the party. The car keys were subsequently found left in the ignition.

Based on the evidence, the police believed that one of the brothers snuck out of the party after their parents went home, shot them both, and then snuck back to the beach club, while the other twin remained at the party, switching roles as necessary to make it appear as though neither of them had left. The twins, in contrast, each insisted that they'd remained at the party that night, until the police arrived to tell them that something terrible had happened at their house. It was at that point, they claimed, that they realized their car was no longer in the valet-parking lot. The Range Rover was not located until the police found it the following day.

It was a perfect case for *Under Suspicion*.

Before approaching the sons, Laurie had contacted Sarah Harrington's best friend, Betsy Ward. Betsy and her husband, Walter, had taken in the Harringtons' daughter, Frankie, after the murders. She was an innocent girl who found herself orphaned at the hands of at least one of her brothers. Whether she chose to appear on screen or not, Laurie could not imagine doing the show without her blessing.

Frankie was an adult by the time Laurie contacted her through Betsy, but barely past her eighteenth birthday. Betsy and Frankie had both given Laurie a chance to make her pitch, but after a week of consideration, Betsy notified her that Frankie did not want to renew attention to the case. She was focused on her studies at Chapman

College in California and didn't want to revisit the gruesome night that had changed her life forever.

"I guess she kept your number all this time," Grace said.

"And she changed her mind about the show?" Laurie asked.

"I'm not sure. I didn't know why she was calling. I simply said you were out of the office and asked to take a message. But when she told me she was calling about her parents, I got a chill up my spine, realizing it must be about a case. I didn't want to press her for details, but I Googled the name afterward and figured it out."

Laurie was at her desk, about to dial Frankie Harrington's phone number, when another call came in from an internal number. It was Dana Licameli, Brett's secretary. Brett, who had welcomed Ryan into his office with an open door. Ryan, who had made the snarky comment to Grace about Laurie's priorities.

She picked up the call. "Good morning, Dana."

"Oh good. You're in." Her voice was low with an apologetic tone. "Brett wants to see you. As in, right now."

"Sure thing. Let me guess: He's not alone?"

"Nope."

"Okay. Thanks for the heads-up."

# Chapter 5

As Laurie entered Brett's spacious office, her eyes immediately fell on the man sinking a seven-foot putt on the boss's newly installed indoor putting green, the two of them seemingly oblivious to her arrival.

"Nice one," she said.

"Ah, Laurie, glad you could make it," Brett said, taking the putter from Ryan and leaning it against the adjacent floor-to-ceiling windows overlooking the Rockefeller Center ice skating rink. He was in his early sixties with a full head of iron-gray hair. His expression was sealed in permanent displeasure, but he was nevertheless handsome, and she knew from their years working together that he favored other attractive people. Laurie was by all accounts nice-looking, yet how many times had he suggested that she get some tips from Jennifer Marciano, whom he referred to merely as the studio's "makeup girl"?

Laurie offered her best smile. "Of course, Brett. Dana indicated it was urgent." She resisted the urge to give a knowing glance to the golf putter.

Brett gestured for her to take a seat on the sofa, and she obliged. He took his usual spot in one of the two modern black leather chairs across from her. Once Ryan occupied the other, she felt like a suspect being interrogated by two detectives, albeit in much more luxurious digs.

"Glad to see you're in the office despite your six-month anniversary," Brett said pointedly.

"That was something my son arranged."

Brett mustered a small smile, which was always unsettling. "Sweet kid, that one. Did you find a case for your next special yet? I'm eager to hear the pitch."

"We're close, but not quite."

Brett leaned forward, his fingers steepled, his gaze focused on Laurie. "We're at a crossroads, Laurie. The true crime space is more crowded than ever, with streaming shows, podcasts, and a new generation of armchair detectives. We need to stay relevant, and we need to do it fast."

Laurie nodded. She was thirty-nine years old and had worked as a journalist for seventeen years, twelve of them as a producer. She understood the pressure of the media industry. "I agree, Brett. But I still believe in the unique approach of *Under Suspicion*. We're not just rehashing old cases or speculating about crimes. We're actively involved in solving them. That sets us apart."

She noticed Ryan let out a puff of air as he looked up at the ceiling.

"You don't agree?" she asked.

"That just feels a little dramatic. Are you saying the other true crime shows don't chase leads or do real journalism?"

Laurie felt her patience wearing thin, but she maintained her composure. "Of course many of them do, but not all. What I'm saying is our show has a different investigative approach, and we have a track record of making a difference. I don't want to break our streak."

"Well, I don't want to miss our earnings projections," Brett said pointedly. "The problem with your show is that the concept is too narrow. Why do we need someone who's under suspicion? Plus you're focused entirely on cold cases. And to younger viewers, *cold* means *old*. Your demo is a bunch of gray-hairs." She chose not to remind him of his own hair color. "Sometimes I wonder if I made a mistake green-lighting the idea, but given your family situation at the time, I thought it was just what you needed to get back in the saddle. But now we're saddled with this very narrow concept."

When Laurie had gone back to work after Greg was killed, she had been distracted. Her shows flopped, and her position at Fisher Blake was on thin ice. The success of the first *Under Suspicion* special had been her comeback. Now Brett was making it sound like a liability.

"So what exactly are you suggesting?"

"We need to be more current," he said. "We could shift into cases ripped from today's headlines instead of a decade ago. Tell her your idea, Ryan."

And there it was. First he mentioned Laurie's six-month anniversary. Now Ryan had a suggestion. She had run a few minutes late, and he had seen an opportunity to undermine her with Brett while the two of them played pretend golf.

"The Sorority Sister Slaughter," he said.

"Please don't call it that," she said. "Seven innocent women lost their lives to some maniac who broke in at night with a gun."

Ryan gave Brett a glance that said, *See what I'm dealing with?*

"A scandalous tag line means ratings, Laurie," Brett said, his tone straddling a line between patience and frustration. "I appreciate your passion for the show, but we need to start thinking outside the box. In retrospect, we should have had cameras on you last year when your nephew went missing."

"You can't be serious. His life was in jeopardy."

"All right, fine. Bad example. But Ryan's on the right track with these sorority murders. It's a high-profile case with a lot of media buzz. It could be a game-changer for us."

"It only happened two weeks ago. The police are actively investigating. By the time we finished our special, there could be no new information or the case could be solved."

"Or we could change the model entirely," Ryan said. "Have a new episode every day that viewers could stream on demand."

"So now we're saying hot cases instead of cold ones. No identified suspects. No deep-dive investigation. We'd be replacing everything that is special about *Under Suspicion* and creating a completely new show."

Laurie couldn't shake the feeling that something was off. Last year, it had seemed like she and Ryan had fallen into a good working relationship, and her show's success had finally convinced Brett to trust her instincts. But lately, it seemed as though her ideas and contributions were being pushed aside. She glanced at Ryan, who was watching her with a smug expression.

Brett was looking at the ceiling, deep in thought. "I hadn't thought of it that way, but it wouldn't be the worst idea. Maybe get Ryan more involved behind the scenes instead of only on camera. It would certainly lighten your load so you can focus more on your home life."

And then she saw what was happening. She flashed back to the day Ryan told her in this very office that, unlike Alex, he would be working full-time at the studio, leaving behind his law practice to focus on Fisher Blake Studios. In addition to hosting her show, he'd be pitching in on the other news programs, giving legal opinions on the pop culture shows when celebrities got into trouble, and serving as a legal consultant to the scripted shows. "If it works out," he had said, "I may produce a show of my own," as if creating a news-based show was a cute little skill he could pick up along the way. *If I take to playing in the sand, I may even build my own castle*, Laurie had thought at the time.

Now that day had come. But instead of doing the work of creating his own show, his plan was to take over hers. And he had clearly been using his buddy time with Brett to create a false narrative that her "home life" was somehow interfering with her work.

"If I can speak candidly, Brett, I'm surprised by the tone of this conversation. If Ryan is so interested in being involved behind the scenes, he might know that the reason I haven't chosen one of the cases we've been bouncing around is because we're very close to getting the family on board to reinvestigate the murders of Richard and Sarah Harrington."

"Never heard of them," Ryan said flatly.

It was exactly the response she had expected . . . and wanted. "Twins long suspected of killing their parents," she said.

Brett's eyes lit up as he recognized the case. "The Deadly Duo? Now *that* would be huge. They'll go on camera?"

Laurie was constitutionally incapable of lying, but under the circumstances, she was willing to let Brett believe what he was eager to believe. "I need to nail it down, but their younger sister has been in touch. She was opposed to the idea when I first suggested the case for our second special, but"—she gave Ryan a knowing look—"sometimes the hard work takes time to pay off." Every word of it was true. "If we work quickly enough, we could go to air by the tenth anniversary of the killings."

"I love it!"

The quick turnaround in her boss's attitude felt like Laurie's version of sinking a thirty-foot putt. Now that Ryan realized what case she was pitching, she could see him scrambling for a way to sway Brett back to his side.

"Everyone knows those boys did it together. Two identical twins at their well-attended graduation party. When the parents went home early, one drove back to the house and shot them. The other one stayed behind and pretended to be both brothers depending on who he was talking to. That's why they wore identical outfits."

"We don't know that," Laurie said. "It could have been because the dress code was summer-white, and it would be fun for twins to match. Those are the things we'd ask them."

"What *I* would ask them," Ryan said.

"Of course," she said. "As always." *You have your job, and I have mine.*

Brett was already out of his chair, ready to move on to the next unfortunate person who caught his ire. "Sounds like a plan, Laurie. Go lock it down. And quick. And tell Alex I said hi and happy mini-anniversary. You've got a good man there."

"And he's got a pretty good woman," she added.

"Touché."

Ryan said nothing to her in the hallway as they turned to go their separate ways.

Grace glanced up from her workstation as Laurie approached her office. "How'd that go?" she asked. "You look upset."

"Old Ryan is back with a vengeance. I'll fill you guys in, but I need to make a call first."

Frankie Harrington's phone went directly to voicemail. "Frankie, it's Laurie Moran from *Under Suspicion*. I'm so glad you kept my number. Let's talk soon."

Laurie was updating Grace and Jerry, invoking her best impersonation of ratings-hungry Brett, when a new call came in on her office phone. She recognized Frankie Harrington's number from the message Grace had taken.

"This is Laurie," she said.

"Ms. Moran, this is Frankie Harrington calling you back. You might remember we spoke a couple of years ago—"

"Of course I remember. I've wondered many times since then how you've been, and please call me Laurie."

"I've been well. I mean, mostly. As good as can be, I guess. But I've been thinking about your show. Do you have time to meet with me? In person? Soon, if possible?"

She and Alex had tickets that night for a Broadway show, and Tim's school had a science fair the following afternoon, and then she was supposed to meet her friend Charlotte for dinner. But she knew Brett and Ryan would view any sign of delay as a problem with her *priorities*. "Of course. I can take the next train up to Boston."

"No, I'm in New York City. I'm at work now, but I get a lunch break at noon."

"Tell me where to meet you."

# Chapter 6

The scent of cured meat and warm rye bread greeted Laurie as she stepped inside Katz's Delicatessen. The walls were adorned with photographs of satisfied customers, some famous, some not, each one celebrating the rich history of the city's most venerable name in pastrami and pickles. The sounds of lunchtime chatter and clinking dishes filled the air. She hadn't been here in years, but the place felt instantly familiar. This had been one of her father's favorite places to take her as a child whenever it was only the two of them. She hoped that Frankie's suggestion that they meet here was a sign of good things to come.

She searched the sea of midday patrons waiting for tables and spotted the turquoise-and-yellow paisley dress that Frankie had told Laurie she'd be wearing. Her long dark hair cascaded past her shoulders.

As Laurie approached, Frankie turned in her direction. Laurie fought back a gasp. Other than her darker coloring, Frankie Harrington looked exactly like her fairer-skinned mother—petite with high cheekbones and long lashes.

Frankie's eyes lit up with recognition. She must have looked up photographs of Laurie online. Laurie had tried to do the same but had failed to locate a single picture. Frankie had a LinkedIn profile for professional networking, but it did not include a photograph. And though someone named Frankie Harrington had an Instagram account, it was not visible to the public.

"You must be Frankie," Laurie said.

Laurie was surprised when Frankie pulled her into a brief hug. "I feel like I know you after all those conversations we had. We've had a lot of reporters bother us over the years, but you were so kind."

Her words were a comfort after the way Brett and Ryan had dismissed her show's unique approach that morning. "The last thing I ever want is to add to a family's pain," Laurie said.

"I could tell, and that's why I called. Thank you so much for coming down here on short notice. It's my turn to bring lunch back for the judge I'm working for, and he had a hankering for his favorite sandwich. I figured we could meet and then I could get his food to go, but I didn't realize there'd be so many people."

A man in a white shirt and a butcher's apron was rushing from a dining table toward the takeout counter when he did a double take as he passed Laurie. "Well how about that?" he said, his face breaking into a broad smile. "Long time, no see. You meeting the old man here?"

"No, but I may need to bring home some pastrami or he'll be jealous. I'm here to meet this young woman," she said. "Frankie, this is Hank. He's good people."

"Eh, only sometimes. Just two of you?"

Laurie nodded, holding up two fingers, and he waved them away from the crowd. "That's where you're heading," he said, pointing to a table being bussed in the back corner. "Tell the commissioner we miss him. And before you even ask, he's been following the doc's orders and switched to turkey. I sneak him one little slice of the fatty stuff on the side, though."

As they walked to their table, Frankie leaned toward Laurie and whispered, "That was so cool. Very VIP."

Laurie smiled as they passed the photograph on the restaurant wall of her father posing with the former mayor and police chief. "Being a semi-regular has its perks."

Laurie knew from Frankie's LinkedIn profile that she was in her final semester at Chapman University in Orange, California, with a double major in economics and political science. She was a Dean's Scholar, an editor for the school's undergraduate law review, and a member of the university choir. Once they were seated, Laurie asked Frankie more about what she was doing in New York.

"My school allows you to spend a semester of your senior year in a full-time internship for credit. I'm working at the courthouse, studying the plea-bargaining system and writing my thesis on it. I was leaning toward going to law school, but now that I've seen how the courthouse actually works, I find it pretty depressing. So much fighting."

"Not all lawyers do trial work," Laurie said.

"I know. That's what Walter says, too. I suspect he wants me to follow in his footsteps the way his son did."

"The Wards' son is also a lawyer?" Laurie asked.

"Yeah, his name's Dennis."

"Are the two of you close?"

She appeared to be pondering the question for the first time. "No, not really. He was already in college by the time I went to live with Betsy and Walter. He was nearby at Northeastern and then at BC for law school, but he lived off campus with roommates. I'm a lot closer to Michelle since she's always been with Simon. But we're like one big, blended family now. Dennis and Simon are both at the firm that my father and Walter started together."

Laurie noticed that Frankie didn't say anything about Simon's advice about her next steps. "What does Simon think about whether you should go to law school?"

Her expression briefly fell before she answered. "I haven't had time to talk to him about it."

When the waiter came, Laurie ordered her usual—a half pastrami sandwich with matzo ball soup—and Frankie did the same.

"I hope you don't mind the observation," Laurie said, "but you look so much like your mother."

"I know. I'm her mini me. And what I just said about not having time to talk to Simon wasn't true. I've sort of been avoiding him. Ethan too."

Laurie nodded, sensing that Frankie wanted to explain further.

"All these years, I just accepted what Betsy and Walter told me—that the police had it wrong, and my brothers had nothing to do with the murders. But I'm starting to wonder if they have a blind spot when it comes to me and my brothers."

"Why do you say that?" Laurie asked.

"There were times when they should have been harder on me, like if I broke curfew or played hooky. But they'd find a reason to excuse it because I'd lost my parents. Maybe they never stopped to consider the evidence that points to my brothers."

"But now you are?" Laurie asked.

She chewed at her lip nervously before nodding. "Sometimes. It started after you first called me. I mentioned it to my roommate, and she asked me whether I thought they did it. I immediately said no, but she's a true crime buff and started reading more about the case and telling me what she found. I didn't want to believe any of it, but I began replaying everything from the past. Like, it never made sense that my brothers stopped talking to each other. They both told me that it was too hard to stay close after everyone said they had teamed up for such a horrible crime. When you're a kid, you don't really understand the world and just accept what the grown-ups tell you. But it's so obvious now. If anything, that shared experience of being suspected should have brought them closer, right? When I pressed each of them about it, they finally both admitted that they each think the other one did it. I'm still trying to wrap my head around the possibility."

"But as I understand it," Laurie said, "the police always believed that Simon and Ethan planned that night together."

"And you're right about that. But Simon and Ethan both insist they never left the party, which means they both think it must have been the other one. That's why they're estranged."

"But why accuse each other? Couldn't it have been someone else entirely—just as the Wards always told you?" Laurie had spent the rest of the morning reviewing press clippings about the case and had an idea why the police blamed the twins, but she wanted to hear Frankie's thoughts.

"Well, there's the video showing that the Range Rover my brothers took to the party that night showed up at the house right after my dad's car."

"But your brothers valet parked at the yacht club, and the valets would leave the keys inside the cars, so in theory, anyone at the party could have taken the Range Rover, followed your parents home, and then abandoned the car in the overflow lot."

"Except my dad's law partner says he saw one of my brothers walking away from the overflow lot. He didn't see them directly in the car, but both Simon and Ethan swear they never left the party until the police arrived."

"You mean Walter? I thought he believed your brothers were innocent?"

Frankie shook her head. "Sorry, that was confusing. My dad started the firm with Walter and a third lawyer named Howard Carver. He's the one who told police he saw either Simon or Ethan as he was leaving. He couldn't tell them apart."

Laurie knew that a witness claimed to have spotted one of the twins near the Range Rover, but she had assumed it was one of the valets or someone driving past the club. The fact that the witness knew the Harringtons well made the identification even more incriminating. She slipped a notepad from her purse and jotted down Howard Carver's name. His statement to the police would be critical.

"Plus," Frankie said, "whoever drove the Range Rover knew the passcode for the front gate. And our dog Bacon was practically a witness. The video at the gate had audio, and the police figured out it could pick up the sound of Bacon barking, but not his quieter noises. The tape didn't pick up any sounds of barking that night until the police arrived."

"And you think that's important?" Laurie asked.

"Our dog's ability to know who was at the front door was uncanny. My mom said we should have named him Doorbell. He always knew when someone was on the porch. If it was someone he didn't know or had met only once or twice, he'd bark up a storm. If it was someone he knew, he'd make this hyper, whining noise because he was so excited to have a visitor. And then there was the matter of the gun safe."

Laurie knew that the Harringtons were killed by a handgun they kept at the house for protection, but she had not read anything about a safe. "Tell me more about that," she said, adding vigorously to her notes.

"My parents kept the gun locked away, so either the killer knew the combination or one of my parents took the gun out first—and I can't imagine them pulling a gun on anyone who was friendly enough with Bacon that he didn't bark. When you put it all together—Howard seeing one my brothers in the parking lot, the use of their car, knowing the gate code, knowing Bacon, and knowing the safe combination . . ." She let the thought linger, not wanting to state her conclusion out loud.

"But the house was in complete disarray. Drawers opened. Books pulled down from shelves. As if someone had been searching for valuables."

"Which is what someone would do if they wanted the police to think it was a burglary gone wrong when my parents came home early." Laurie could hear the sadness building in Frankie's voice.

Despite the strength of the evidence, something else was bothering Laurie. "My understanding is that the gate camera's mounting had slipped but the camera was still functioning and able to record the appearance of cars coming and going. Your brothers would have known that. Why use the Range Rover? If the valets were leaving keys in cars, they could have taken another guest's vehicle. Or they could have even walked there on the beach. Your house was only half a mile from the yacht club."

"Because they didn't know the camera was operational," she said. "When the police asked Simon and Ethan if we had any security cameras, they told the police we had the one camera at the gate, but that the camera was broken. It turns out that they'd overheard my father talking to Peter two days earlier about work that needed to be done on the house and Dad mentioned that the camera was broken. They both assumed it wasn't working at all."

Laurie was beginning to think that Frankie would do quite well in law school. "And who is Peter?" she asked.

"Peter Bennett. He was a local guy who'd check on the house in Harbor Bay when we were home in Boston. I guess it's called a caretaker? He'd turn on the heat before we arrived. Do handyman stuff. That kind of thing. A beach house apparently needs a lot of caretaking. I remember my brothers joking that he should have a room in the house because he always seemed to be around."

"So at the end of the day," Laurie asked, "what do you think actually happened?"

She shook her head. "I don't know, and I really want to. That's why I called you. I remember it like it was yesterday. It was Simon and Ethan's graduation party, and everyone was there—family, friends, classmates. It was a perfect night, until it wasn't." She paused, and Laurie could see her reliving the memories.

"I was inside with a small group of other kids my age, playing jacks in the corner of the ballroom. That was the last time I saw my mother. She told me she was leaving to go home, but she'd be right back and to stay at the party. When I play the scene back in my head, there's something in her tone, an urgency I couldn't quite place at the time. I remember wondering why she was in such a rush. But then she never came back. Instead, the police showed up. They found my brothers to bring them to our house. When Ethan and Simon couldn't find our parents, they were going to take me with them, but then the police said they shouldn't. They called Betsy and Walter to come get me instead. All we knew was that something had happened at the house. We thought it was a break-in or something. I vaguely remember Simon mentioning vandalism. We had no idea that our parents were gone. Betsy and Walter told me the next day, and the entire world crashed around me."

"Did you see either of your brothers leave the party before the police came?" she asked.

Frankie's gaze grew distant, as if she were watching a screen on the wall behind Laurie. "I feel as if I saw them both the whole night, but not at the same time. They were usually inseparable unless they were away at school. But that night, they were always separate. My parents made us pose together for some family photographs at the very beginning of the party, and I asked Ethan and Annabeth to dance with me while Simon danced with Michelle, but after that, it was as if they were taking turns where to be."

It was exactly the theory the police had floated. "Did that strike you as odd?" Laurie asked.

Laurie was eager to hear the answer, but Frankie remained silent as a waiter meticulously placed their lunches on the table.

"I didn't notice it at the time—only after I started wondering about what really happened that night, playing it all back in my head. If one was on the dance floor, the other would be at the bar, and vice versa. One of the only other photos showing them both in the same place was when the photographer asked everyone to pose with the ice cream sundae station, but that wasn't until ten o'clock."

Laurie knew that the Harringtons were shot shortly before 9:30 and lived less than a half mile from the boathouse. "So you can't really say that both of your brothers were there the entire time."

She shook her head as she took a tentative taste of her matzo ball soup. “It’s strange, isn’t it? All of us eating ice cream and having fun, having no idea our lives were changed forever.”

“Frankie,” Laurie said gently, “don’t you think you would have noticed if one of your brothers was pretending to be the other? Even with the most look-alike twins, the family can tell them apart.”

She sighed, her brow furrowed. “Most of the time, of course. In pictures, they look the same, but there were always subtle differences, like the way they carried themselves, their expressions, even their laughs. Simon is super focused and serious, and Ethan’s always goofing around, trying to make people laugh. But they were always really good at impersonating each other. They loved trying to fool their friends and their teachers—even our family. Dad and I would sometimes fall for it, but not once did my mother.”

Laurie could see the torment in the young woman’s eyes, a struggle to reconcile the memories of her brothers with the accusations she was clearly beginning to entertain.

“And you think maybe my show could help?”

“I hope so,” Frankie said.

“You realize what that means, don’t you?”

“It means that I might find out that at least one of my brothers killed our parents.”

“In which case, they’ll be prosecuted and punished.”

“Or maybe we’ll find out someone else did it, and we can go back to being a family again.” Laurie could hear the longing in Frankie’s voice. She wanted to trust her brothers again.

“When I talked to Betsy before, she told me that she spoke not only to you about the show, but also your brothers. She says they were both adamant they wouldn’t participate.”

“I think I can persuade them to do it.”

“What makes you think that?”

“Because they both love me and don’t want me to stop loving them back. Trust me. They’ll do it if I tell them to.”

"Who should I talk to first?"

"Simon," she said definitively.

"And why is that?"

"Because I just spoke to his wife this morning. It was actually Michelle's idea for me to call you. She wants to know the truth, too."

# Chapter 7

Laurie was rubbing her eyes to stay awake as she climbed into the passenger seat of the Mercedes convertible waiting outside her building at 6 a.m. the following morning. She landed in the passenger seat to the sound of the song "Lovely Day" by Bill Withers.

Her driver gestured to a Starbucks paper cup awaiting in the console cupholder. A grande skim latte. Her driver was one of her best friends, Charlotte Pierce.

Laurie had met Charlotte during the production of the third *Under Suspicion* special when her show was reinvestigating the disappearance of Charlotte's younger sister immediately before her wedding. *Under Suspicion* eventually determined that Charlotte's sister had been murdered, and even identified the killer, but Laurie and Charlotte's friendship had been a surprising additional consequence of the investigation.

After the trauma her family experienced, Charlotte had stepped into the role of CEO of her family's business, LadyForm. What had begun as an underwear company was now, thanks in large part to Charlotte's vision, a leading manufacturer of high-end women's activewear.

"Hey, chica." Charlotte greeted Laurie as the car hummed to life. Her messy, shoulder-length brown waves framed her round face. She was wearing a white hoodie and black joggers that managed to be both intimidatingly fashionable and absurdly comfortable. "Ready for another whirlwind adventure?"

"This music is so very loud," Laurie said.

"But it's cheery." Charlotte swayed her shoulders to the beat.

Laurie turned up the volume even more, deciding to embrace her friend's good mood. She'd need the extra energy today. "I can't believe a car ride to LaGuardia is our girls meetup," she said. "We can't let it end like Thelma and Louise."

"We need clones," Charlotte said. "One body to do the work, one to have all the fun. Ready for the recirculated oxygen of a commercial flight? I hear it's horrible for your skin." In theory, they were supposed to have had dinner together that night, but suddenly work got in the way for both of them. Frankie had been right. She and Simon's wife, Michelle, had convinced Simon to at least hear Laurie out, and she wanted to strike before he changed his mind. As for Charlotte, an A-list pop star had called LadyForm out of the blue yesterday to say she was interested in launching her own line of athleisure with the company and had asked to meet as soon as possible while her "creative energy was in the right space."

So now Laurie would be kicking off the first day of March in thirty-two-degree Boston while Charlotte would be heading to a luxury high-rise in sunny Miami. It didn't feel like an even swap.

Laurie nestled her backpack between her feet in the passenger footwell of Charlotte's convertible. "You're the one with the jet-setting lifestyle. Meeting celebrities, reinventing fashion—it's like a page out of a glamorous magazine."

Charlotte laughed as she expertly swerved around a double-parked delivery truck to reclaim her place in standstill traffic. "You know we're working too hard when a ride to the airport is our catch-up time together. You really think you can get this Harrington family locked down for your next special? For what it's worth, I personally think they did it."

"I didn't realize you knew so much about the case."

"I didn't, not until you told me you were working on it. By all accounts, their father was super controlling. He used his money as a carrot and stick to try to run those boys' lives for them. That can mess with a kid's head. It can lead to real anger. It's not just about getting the money they inherited. Maybe they just wanted their father's pressure on them to end."

"Honestly?" Laurie said. "In my gut, I think they did it, too. But my show doesn't always have to be an exoneration. Maybe the guilty parties need to be exposed. And the family members who are left to wonder can finally have closure. You should have seen how torn Frankie was, not knowing what to believe."

Charlotte shared Laurie's empathy for victims and their families. "I've been there. After my sister went missing, it was so hard, not knowing what happened, not to mention the speculation that I might have even been involved. It was devastating to find out that she'd been murdered by someone I had trusted. I hope Frankie's prepared emotionally for that."

*Please let it be so,* Laurie thought.

# Chapter 8

When Laurie's Uber driver pulled in front of the Boston address she had entered for Ward & Harrington LLC, she was surprised to find a large Cape style house adapted into a law office. She was used to law firms in Manhattan high-rises.

The small law firm's lobby was mismatched and clumsy, a mix of dark wood antique furniture and a few sleeker, modern pieces, as if two different people had decorated without speaking to each other.

A woman sitting on the leather chesterfield sofa immediately stood as Laurie stepped inside. She wore a sunflower-yellow sheath dress, her blond hair twisted into a braid at the nape of her neck. "Ms. Moran, so nice to meet you in person," she said, extending her hand for a shake. "I'm Michelle."

They had spoken on the phone the previous day to arrange this meeting. "I take it your husband is still willing to speak with me?"

She nodded eagerly. "I'm so nervous I'm almost shaking."

Laurie gave her hand a small squeeze. "It's going to be okay."

As Michelle led the way up the staircase to the second floor, Laurie asked how long the law firm had been located there.

"I was in the tenth grade when they bought the house and converted it, so I guess that makes it sixteen years? It was Richard's idea. He was pretty much the head of the firm. He said it would be cheaper in the long run to own their own building. This floor originally had six bedrooms. After some reconfiguring, it was the perfect size for three offices. One for Richard. One for my father. And one for Howard."

"Howard Carver," Laurie said. "The witness who said he saw one of the twins in the parking lot."

"One and the same," she said, her voice sharp enough to cut glass. "He was the Carver in what used to be Harrington, Ward, and Carver."

"Past tense?" Laurie asked.

"Long ago retired," she said, her voice suddenly brightening. Laurie found herself wondering if there was more to the story of Howard's departure from the firm but sensed that it was too early to pull at that thread. "Now Simon is in his old office. Dennis is in Richard's. And my dad still has his office but he's in once a month, tops." She rapped her knuckles against a partially open door. "Hey, Dennis. You got a second? I wanted to introduce you to Laurie before she sits down with Simon."

Laurie followed her into the office to find bright white walls, a white lacquered desk, and a thoroughly modern seating area. The man behind the desk rose to shake her hand. Unlike his blond sister, he had dark hair. His tortoiseshell glasses reminded her of Alex's. "Dennis Ward. Sorry about the weird decor in the lobby. I finally convinced my dad to let me modernize our look, but some of the furniture is on back order."

She noticed that he didn't mention any role Simon would have played in making that decision. "Ah, the dreaded back order. I'm very familiar with it. My husband and I just finished a remodel last year."

"So Michelle was telling me you might do an entire show about the Harringtons?"

"I'd certainly like to."

"Would I be on it?" he asked with a laugh.

"Do you know anything about where Simon and Ethan were around nine-fifteen to nine-thirty-five that night?"

He shook his head. "I left around eight-thirty with my dad."

"No fun at the party?"

"No fun being the only sober kid. I was too young to drink and the twins' friends were all getting a little wasted."

“Then we probably wouldn’t interview you on screen,” she said.

“Shoot. There goes my shot at stardom. Come to think of it, it’s probably for the best not to mention my firm. I honestly can’t believe Simon’s considering doing this. Stirring up all that attention again when his life’s on a good track. I think he’s making a huge mistake.”

First, the furniture. Now it was *my* firm. Even the firm name was now Ward & Harrington instead of the other way around. The law partners were not equals.

Michelle cleared her throat and looked at her brother sternly. “Dennis, we talked about this.”

“I just worry about you guys. You’re taking a huge risk of upending his entire life again, with very low odds of discovering anything new. And frankly, it could blow back on Dad and me since he’s a part of this law firm.”

“Please, Dennis,” Michelle pleaded, “you promised me you wouldn’t say anything to change his mind.”

He held up his palms. “Promise kept.”

“You’ve never had concerns about working with Simon?” Laurie asked.

“Concerns as in, do I think he’s a murderer? Of course not. He’s my brother-in-law. I’ve known him since I was a kid. Once he started dating Michelle, he was almost like a member of our family. I think our mother and Sarah were secretly planning Michelle and Simon’s wedding for years.”

“And what about Ethan?”

The pause that followed was telling. “He was my parents’ friends’ kid. I don’t know him the way I know Simon.”

“Do you think he could be a killer?” Laurie asked.

Dennis shrugged. “I know my parents don’t think so. But the guy’s own brother thinks he probably is, so . . . talk to Simon.”

Laurie planned to do exactly that.

# Chapter 9

Michelle Harrington hadn't lied when she said she was so nervous she was practically shaking. She knew that this producer Laurie Moran had contacted her mother and Frankie a few years earlier. At the time, the entire conversation had made her so anxious, she felt sick to her stomach.

She had worked so hard on her romance novels. And Simon worked so hard at the law firm, even though it didn't amount to the career he had once dreamed of.

What mattered was that she and Simon had Sophie and Daniel. And they had Michelle's parents, who were convinced Simon was innocent. And until Frankie went to college, they'd had her, too.

But she knew from her mother that Frankie was beginning to delve into the details of her parents' murders. And Frankie had recently turned twenty-two, which meant that she was entitled now to oversee her own trust fund, a third of the estate that the Harringtons had split equally among their children under the terms of their will. As she understood it from her parents, when the Harringtons first wrote the terms of the will, Sarah insisted that Richard not try to "control their children from the grave." They'd appointed Michelle's mother, Betsy, to administer trusts for the children until the age of twenty-two and would simply have to have faith that they had raised them well enough to go it alone from there.

Simon had already lost both his parents and any type of relationship with Ethan. She could see that he was worried he was losing Frankie now, too. And if he could lose his sister because she began to ask questions about their parents' deaths, might Sophie and Daniel someday get curious about their grandparents? If he agreed to do this show, it would be more to clear his name to Frankie, Sophie, and Daniel than to anyone else.

Even if this television show was able to prove that Ethan had killed Richard and Sarah, Michelle knew that Simon would always feel partially responsible. In retrospect, she should have done more to encourage Simon to defend Ethan to their father instead of taking Richard's side.

It was as if Ethan could do no right in his father's eyes. He forced him to go to college immediately after high school, even though Ethan had pleaded for a gap year to see if he could make a living as a musician. And when Ethan's grades faltered because he wasn't committed to his studies, Richard would yell at him and call his own son a failure instead of trying to help him find a way to be happy. When Ethan finally did find happiness—by meeting Annabeth—Richard had declared her to be an "unsuitable" companion. All he knew was that her father owned the local hardware store, her mother was a housekeeper, and Annabeth was working as an au pair because she could not afford college tuition. He tolerated the relationship for a year, but as Simon and Ethan's graduations approached, he threw down the gauntlet: *Drop the girl or I'll cut you off financially.*

If Michelle could build a time machine, she'd crawl inside with Simon and force him to confront his father. For the most part, Simon had managed to meet Richard's impossible expectations, but not without consequences. She remembered the day Simon came to her house over spring break and confessed he had cheated at school. "Why?" she asked. "Why would you have done something so wrong and reckless?"

"Because of my father," he had explained, nearly breaking into tears. "I can't fail, can't you see that? I can't even be average. I have to be perfect. I don't want him to treat me like Ethan."

If she and Simon had defended Ethan and Annabeth, would

Richard have eventually relented? Would he have welcomed Annabeth into the Harrington family, as he so readily had welcomed Michelle? They would never know. But at the time, neither she nor Simon had had that kind of strength. Just as Simon did not want to be treated like Ethan, Michelle had not wanted to be treated like Annabeth. So they had remained silent. No, even worse, they had told Richard whatever it was he wanted to hear so he would continue to view them as "the good ones."

And now her husband, for the first time, was about to tell a television producer why his brother killed their parents. It had all started with Michelle, and there was nothing she could do to take it back.

# Chapter 10

Laurie had studied many photographs of the Harrington twins, but she was nevertheless taken aback when Simon welcomed her into his office. He had thick dark brown hair, the same intense eyes she recognized from decade-old photographs, and an undeniable confidence, despite the fact she knew he was uncertain about meeting with her.

He wasted no time. "Ten years ago, I thought my entire life would be perfect. And after one night, I thought life wasn't worth living. Now? Michelle and I are happy. We have our kids, Sophie and Daniel. Why shouldn't I keep the status quo?"

His wife, Michelle, was sitting beside him on a leather sofa that matched the one downstairs in the lobby. Reaching for his hand, she began to speak but then looked to Laurie instead.

"That's not for me to answer, Simon," Laurie said. "My understanding is that Frankie and Michelle think your entire family might be better off knowing the truth."

Simon's jaw tightened, a flicker of tension in his eyes before his expression softened. "I know I can't hide this from my children forever. My biggest fear is that they might somehow be tarnished by my family name. But what makes you think you can figure out what the police couldn't? I don't want to dredge this up again and put us in the spotlight unless we learn something new."

It was the same concern his brother-in-law, Dennis, had expressed. *You're taking a huge risk of upending his entire life again, with very low odds of discovering anything new.*

Laurie leaned forward in the wingback guest chair and held Simon's gaze. "A fresh perspective can uncover new leads. And our show's role isn't to accuse anyone, Simon. We just want to hear your side of the story and then find the truth. Do you believe that's how the Harbor Bay Police approached the investigation?"

"Absolutely not," he said, a flash of anger revealing itself. "Understand, Harbor Bay isn't a place with a lot of old money. It was a small, sleepy, unknown Cape town until people like my parents realized it was close to Boston with beautiful beaches. The locals would complain about getting run over by outsiders, and our family counted as such. When a double homicide hit their small town, it was easier for the police to blame the victims' spoiled rich kids than do the actual work. They never even bothered to try to tell Ethan and me apart. As far as they were concerned, it's like we were the same person."

"When you first learned that your parents were killed, who did you think was responsible?" she asked.

"It looked like a robbery. Even the police seemed to believe that. Their bedroom, the living room, and the kitchen were ransacked."

"Not the whole house?"

"Not really. Which was weird. You'd think a robber would have tossed my father's home office first, but it was completely untouched."

Laurie removed a legal pad from her backpack and scribbled her first note of the day.

"I also told them about a weird incident when we'd gone to Harbor Bay for a weekend in late April. Someone vandalized the sidewalk in front of the house. They spray-painted something like *This Family is a Lie*."

Laurie had never read anything about the family being targeted this way, and she made another note.

"I thought it could be related," Simon continued, "but the police never looked into it as far as I knew. We told them the camera by the gate was broken, but when they checked with our house manager, Peter, he got them the footage. Once the police saw the Range

Rover, they narrowed in on us. In hindsight, I probably should have lawyered up, but I kept trying to get them to see the truth."

Tunnel vision. Laurie had seen it before in a police investigation. Detectives become convinced a suspect is guilty and then focus on that suspect to the exclusion of other possibilities. It's not as if they intentionally frame an innocent person, but they stop being objective, seeing only what they want to see and hearing what they want to hear. Add in a local population suspicious of newcomers, and she could see all the makings of a flawed investigation.

"Do you remember who the lead detectives were on the case?" Laurie had left a message with the Harbor Bay Police Department the previous day but hadn't heard back from them yet.

"How could I ever forget? Chief Bruce Collins and his deputy, Roberta Hanson."

"Are they still with the department?" she asked, jotting down the names.

"I have no idea," he said. "Harbor Bay used to be my version of heaven. After my parents died? If I never saw either the Cape or the ocean again, I'd be fine."

"When you learned the killer had used the car you and your brother had driven to the party, did you immediately suspect Ethan?"

"No. Of course not. I thought it might be this kid I went to college with named Tom Keenan. The police looked into him, but he had a rock-solid alibi. He and some friends were partying down in Nashville that weekend. He'd been to our beach house a bunch of times. Bacon probably would've remembered him, and he could have seen the gate code when he was in the car with me."

"So he was your friend," Laurie noted.

"Emphasis on *was*."

"I'm sorry. Why would you suspect him of harming your parents?"

He paused, and Laurie saw him exchange a glance with his wife. "She can't help us if she doesn't know the whole story," Michelle said.

"But Tom didn't do it. The whole thing I went through with him is irrelevant. And it makes me look like an idiot."

"Look," Laurie said. "You haven't even agreed to do the show yet. And if it's not relevant, we won't use it. But for all you know, it could end up being helpful information."

He nodded reluctantly. "I paid him to write a paper for me in my history class. I had gotten a C on a midterm and my father was furious. He said he wasn't paying all that tuition for me to goof off. I was terrified it was going to tank my GPA, and I panicked. I was taking too many demanding classes and felt like I couldn't do my best in all of them. I knew Tom wrote papers for other students and always got high marks, so I took the easy way out. But after I got admitted into law school, I suddenly got an anonymous email threatening to report me to the dean if I didn't leave twenty thousand dollars at a designated drop spot on campus. When I tried to talk to Tom in person, he denied sending the email, but it was obviously him. I hadn't told *anyone* what I'd done."

"Except me," Michelle said. "Simon immediately felt guilty about what he'd done and when we were both home from college for spring break, he came over to talk. He felt so guilty but there was no way to undo it."

"Did you pay him?" Laurie asked.

He shook his head. "I was a college student. I didn't have twenty grand lying around. I broke down and went to my father to ask for it. I've never seen my father that angry. He just snapped. He grabbed my arms and was shaking me so hard my teeth rattled, and then he began hitting me. I wanted to fight back, but I froze. I couldn't believe he was physically hurting me. He only stopped when my mother heard him screaming and came into the room. It was like a switch flipped inside of him. He was immediately back to his usual, unflappable self. I was in complete shock."

In Laurie's research of the case, she had never seen any mention that Richard Harrington could be physically abusive. "He had never been physical with you or your siblings before?"

"Angry, definitely—sometimes to the point of cruelty. He believed that pressuring us, insulting us, belittling us, would make us stronger. But he had never been violent before. He would have thought it beneath him, because of the loss of control. Even afterwards, he wouldn't acknowledge what had happened. He tried to make it sound like I was blowing things out of proportion and admonished me never to mention it again."

Simon was describing a very different man than the patriarch of the "perfect family" the media had described in the aftermath of the murders. "After the switch flipped, what happened?"

"He said Tom would own us forever if we paid him and that I'd have to work it out some other way, even if it meant Tom reported me to the school. I thought my mother might find a way to give me the money without him knowing, but she told me she couldn't help. I still remember her crying over the decision. It burns to think about. I had never in my life felt such shame. I kept buying time with Tom, going back and forth by email. The emails suddenly stopped shortly before graduation, but when my parents were killed, I wondered if he had taken matters into his own hands and gone to them directly. He could have known about the party from our mutual friends and taken our car from the yacht club."

"But then it turned out he had an alibi," Laurie said.

"Correct. And then the whole thing backfired on me. When the police found out about the blackmail, they saw it as a motive for me to kill my father—so I could pay off Tom."

"The police seemed convinced that you and your brother planned it together so you could get your inheritances," Laurie said. "You had turned twenty-two six months earlier, the age at which you could retain full control over your trusts under the terms of your parents' will."

"Why in the world would I have done that? I had been admitted to a top law school and had every plan to go. I wanted to join a big law firm, where I would have earned far more than I inherited. If anything, we almost got cut out of the life insurance when the insurance company accused us of committing the murders. And the estate also could have taken us to court."

"But you did eventually inherit?" she asked.

He nodded. "Only because Betsy agreed as the executor of the estate and as Frankie's legal guardian to waive Frankie's claim to our parts of the inheritance. If we had been cut out, it all would have gone to Frankie."

"And if you don't mind my asking, how much money was involved?"

"Slightly less than ten million dollars. Once it was clear Frankie wasn't trying to get it all, the insurer and the probate court divided it all equally among the three of us."

He did have a point. Three-plus million dollars was a lot of money, but it was less than he would have eventually been worth as a successful commercial lawyer at a large firm. A twenty-two-year-old with a controlling father may not have been willing to wait, however.

"How about Ethan?" Laurie asked. "Is it possible he was in a rush to get his inheritance?"

She noticed Simon look again to Michelle for guidance. Michelle gave his hand a quick squeeze. "Tell her," she said. "It's time for the entire truth to come out."

"My father was threatening to cut off Ethan if he didn't break up with his girlfriend, Annabeth. She was from a local working family. He was adamantly opposed. Dad had been riding him for months. He seemed convinced her family was after his money, because a chain hardware store had opened along the highway, and the little store in town owned by Annabeth's father was rumored to be going under. But after my father found out about Tom extorting me, it's like he got angry at both of us at the same time. He was threatening to cut us both off. Ethan told Dad it was none of his business who he dated. But I was so desperate to get back into my father's good graces that I decided that I could be the hero if I could get Ethan and Annabeth to end things."

Laurie could not write quickly enough to keep up with his narration. "And how did you go about playing hero?" she asked.

"Two nights before our graduation party, we went to a local pizza place together—Pizza Palace—me and Michelle, Ethan and Annabeth. Ethan and I picked up the girls in the Range Rover. As we were leaving, I pulled Annabeth aside. I told her that Dad was about to cut Ethan off financially because of her."

Simon was staring at his knees, clearly unproud of his younger self's decision. Michelle placed a comforting hand on his shoulder.

"Simon's taking all the blame, but that was my idea. I told myself at the time that I was only trying to protect Simon's relationship with his father, but I was being selfish. I had seen the way Richard treated Ethan and Annabeth, and I didn't want him to turn on Simon and me, too. I told Simon that Annabeth should know the kind of tension she was creating for Ethan's family."

"And Ethan found out what you did?" Laurie asked.

Simon nodded. "To Ethan's credit, he was willing to take his lumps as far as our father went. But I was afraid dad was going to stop supporting both of us given my situation with Tom. I was extremely unkind, telling her she wasn't suitable for my brother, that he'd never marry her and she was wasting her time. It was like I was taking out my own shame on her. I thought if I was cruel enough, she might walk away voluntarily."

As Simon spoke, Laurie could sense the weight of the past bearing down on him. "But she didn't," Laurie said.

"No. Instead, she told Ethan what I had said to her. He was, to put it lightly, extremely angry. That's why we were fighting that night. He even threatened to boycott the party altogether, but my mother convinced him that he shouldn't miss such an important night. I don't want to speak ill of my parents, but they cared a lot about appearances. Ethan and I were both accustomed to putting on a happy face when necessary. We agreed to ride there together in the Range Rover. We picked up Michelle first, then Annabeth. When we picked up Annabeth, Ethan was the one to go to the door. Even so, her father made a point to come out to the car to say hello to Michelle and me."

Michelle put her hands to her face. "That was so awful."

"He was angry about what you'd said to his daughter?" Laurie asked.

"Honestly," Simon said, "I would have preferred that. He was incredibly nice. So much so that I was certain he knew about it and wanted to make sure we felt ashamed."

"And it worked," Michelle said.

"Ethan was still furious," Simon said. "Once we got to the yacht club, we were definitely trying to steer clear of each other. And then the police assumed it was all part of some ruse." He placed his face in his hands and rubbed his eyes before looking up again. "Sorry. Almost a decade later, and it still feels like an impossible nightmare."

"So whatever happened to that guy, Tom? Did you end up paying him off?"

For the first time since she'd met him, a sly smile broke out slowly across Simon's face. "I did not. I told him I wouldn't press charges against him for blackmail if he promised never to contact me again. Wrote up an agreement and everything."

"You lawyered him," she said.

"Indeed. He never did admit to it, but he signed the papers."

"Simon," she said, "I know your wife and your sister practically forced you to sit down with me today."

He chuckled softly. "There was definitely some emotional arm-twisting involved."

"I don't want you to agree unless it's truly your decision." She reached into her backpack and slipped out copies of the legal agreement for her show's participants, handing one to each of them. "I took the liberty of bringing the standard release we ask people to sign before we go into production."

They accepted the documents from her and began perusing them.

"If I do the show," Simon said, "I'm assuming the risk that all the family secrets come out? The purchased term paper. The horrible way I spoke to Annabeth. The pent-up resentments against my father. All on full display for a national television audience."

Laurie did not want to mislead him. "Yes, those are the kinds of things we'd get into."

"And your host—he'll grill me like a suspect, right? Confront me with all the evidence pointing to me and my brother?"

She nodded. "He's a very skilled cross-examiner, yes."

He was nodding slowly as he scanned the pages. "And he'll grill Ethan just as thoroughly?" he asked.

"Yes," she confirmed. "If we can persuade Ethan to sign on."

He rose from the sofa and went to his desk. "That's all I needed to hear," he said, signing the document and handing the pen to Michelle to do the same. "What time are you going back to New York?"

"I'm booked on the three p.m. flight but there are other options if I need to change. Why?"

"So you have time," he said.

"For what?" she asked.

"To get Ethan's signature, too." Without saying anything else, he picked up the cell phone resting on his desk and pulled up a number.

# Chapter 11

Simon felt blood rushing to his face as he listened to the fourth ring of the unanswered call. When it went to voicemail, what was he going to say? *Hi, it's your brother, the one you haven't spoken to in more than seven years. How's it going?*

He was surprised when the ringing sound suddenly stopped. Silence, followed by a tentative, "Hello?" The voice sounded almost exactly like his own. Ethan.

"It's Simon," he said.

"Yeah, that's what my phone said. I guess we both still have the same numbers."

Simon felt the tension in his fingers as he gripped the phone tightly. He had so many conflicting emotions. All those hours spent with the police in the weeks and months after the murders, undergoing multiple interrogations, Simon had gotten a good sense of the evidence. Whoever killed his parents had used the family car, knew the family dog, knew the family gate code, knew how to access the family gun. There were only five members of the Harrington family. Two of them were dead. One was a little girl. And that left Simon and Ethan.

And what did Ethan go and do when confronted with that same evidence? He had pointed an accusatory finger at Simon. He had told the police that Simon was desperate to please their demanding father but that the psychological pressure of being the Harringtons' favorite son had led Simon to suffer from pent-up resentments against the family. He made Simon sound like a volcano that would inevitably erupt. What Ethan had done to him was unforgivable.

And yet . . . The sound of his voice brought back so many memories. Body surfing at the beach. Basement Ping Pong tournaments. Wondering which one would get to kiss a girl first (it was Ethan). Fooling the teachers at school by impersonating each other.

He swallowed, as if he could literally ingest the intense feelings that had resurfaced. "Where are you right now?" he asked.

"At work."

It dawned on him he had no idea where his own brother worked. He knew from Frankie that he still played lead guitar with a couple of local rock bands and made his living as a sound engineer, but he didn't know where Ethan physically worked.

"But like *where* are you, as in the address? Where will you be in about half an hour?"

"Why?"

"There's a woman here who needs to see you. Laurie Moran. She's the producer—"

"*Under Suspicion*," Ethan said. "Frankie told me. I'm not doing it. Frankie's mad, but that's a final decision."

"No, it's not," Simon said.

Simon could imagine his brother's sarcastic grin in the scoff that followed. "Excuse me?"

"We need to do this," Simon said. "I know you've got a baby on the way. We need to clear our names."

"That's pretty rich coming from you. You told the police about Dad pressuring me to stop seeing Annabeth. You threw me under the bus."

"Only after you pointed the finger at me," he said.

"That's such bull, Simon. You haven't changed at all, have you? The mental gymnastics that you're capable of playing, all so you can convince yourself you're the good guy in every story. Sometimes I think you've convinced yourself of your own lies."

"Give me the address," Simon said.

"I'm not talking to her," Ethan said.

"You think I threw you under the bus all those years ago? If you don't do this show, you're going to feel like you're under the entire Greyhound station when I'm done talking about you on national television. What's the address?"

A long silence followed and then the call ended. Ethan had hung up on him.

Seconds later, a new text message arrived. It was an address in Back Bay, followed by a note: *You pulled the trigger. Don't forget that.*

# Chapter 12

Laurie didn't know the Boston area well, but her Uber driver had explained to her that she was going to Back Bay, which he said was modeled after Paris's urban design plan. It was supposed to be home to some of the city's finest shops and restaurants, but the address Simon had given her for Ethan had popped up online as belonging to a recording studio called UltraSound. She was confused when she stepped out of the car to find a high-end chain furniture store, until she noticed a neighboring door bearing the UltraSound name.

Laurie was entering a five-star rating and a generous tip into her Uber app when the phone buzzed in her hand. A new FaceTime call from Alex.

"Hey you," she said. She could see that he was at his desk in his chambers, his judicial robe draped on the back of his office chair.

"I felt bad you had to wake up so early this morning for a hard day of work in Boston, and it turns out you're furniture shopping."

"I wish," she said. "We could buy a small country for the price of a sofa in that place," gesturing to the store behind her. "How's the courtroom drama unfolding for Judge Buckley today?" She knew he had a complex cryptocurrency fraud trial beginning that day with jury selection.

"Well, it's not every day that you have a potential juror declare during voir dire that he can tell the defendant's guilty just by looking at him."

"Was the juror right?"

"No comment," he said, "but I did thank him for his honesty

and excused him from jury service, which I suspect was his goal all along. I also granted the defense attorney's request for a moment to confer with her client about his courtroom demeanor, which is why I now have time to confer with my very busy wife."

When she first met Alex, he was a well-known criminal defense attorney. He had made headlines by defending a mogul accused of murdering his business partner. Against tremendous odds, he secured a shocking verdict of acquittal, which the press played up as a horrible injustice. But both the mogul and Alex were vindicated after the murder victim's wife committed suicide, confessing in the note she left behind that she was the one who murdered her husband.

Laurie knew how much Alex loved the courtroom, and she had assumed he'd be one of those lawyers trying cases until they were no longer capable of the work. But a year ago, the President nominated him to serve as a federal judge in the Southern District of New York, and Alex had accepted.

"I'm not the only person in our household who's busy, Your Honor. How did the morning shuffle go after I left at the crack of dawn?"

Alex grinned again and she could tell there was a story. "Let's just say Tim may have been testing my boundaries while Mom was gone."

"Let me guess: He wouldn't get out of bed?"

"Oh, he was up. But he wouldn't put down the Joy-Cons."

She chuckled softly. "I'm sorry, but why is it so funny to hear a federal judge say such a silly word? I refuse to call them that." She usually referred to her son's video game controllers as *the hand grip things*.

"In any event, he was deeply immersed in Mario Kart and pretended not to hear me tell him to turn it off."

Her son was a truly sweet child. His teachers all remarked on his thoughtfulness and consideration toward others. But in the years

Tim had known Alex, Alex had always been the "fun" friend. The guy who had the "most awesome" courtside season tickets to the Knicks. The cool dude who got him a meet and greet with Wynton Marsalis at Lincoln Center through a charitable auction.

Now the fun friend lived in his apartment 24/7 and did things like make him stop playing video games.

"I'm sorry. I'll talk to him about it when I get home."

"Already handled," he said. "I told him I could never be his father but that I had made a promise to you that I would help you make sure he'd become a man his father would be proud of. And part of that meant making sure he did things like go to school on time and listen to his elders."

"*Listen to his elders*, huh?"

"I know," he said, sharing her smile on the screen. "I felt like I was a hundred and twelve years old. But it worked. He apologized and told me that when he blew out the candles on his ninth birthday cake, he had wished for us to get married."

She shook her head. That kid was her heart. "Now, why are my eyes suddenly wet?"

"Same response I had this morning," he said. "I knew you'd want to know."

"Most definitely. Now I have to hope my talk with Ethan Harrington goes just as well."

"Ethan? I thought you were meeting Simon at his law firm?"

Alex had been worried about Laurie going by herself to meet with a man who might or might not be a murderer, but he had taken comfort in the fact that she was meeting him at his law office during business hours with his wife also present.

"It's a long story but Simon talked Ethan into hearing me out, too. But it's at a sound studio in a crowded neighborhood. Even if he had a reason to try to hurt me, he wouldn't do it here."

"Text me as soon as you leave, just so I know you're safe. I'll have my phone on the bench with me."

She promised she would and then hung up and opened the door marked *UltraSound*. The door opened with a creak, revealing a steep, narrow staircase. She held the railing tightly as she made her way upstairs, trying not to think about the possibility of someone meeting her at the top and pushing her down.

# Chapter 13

When Laurie reached the second floor, another door at the top of the landing opened into a small office decorated with vintage music posters. The television mounted on the wall was playing the movie *This Is Spinal Tap* with the sound on mute. The man sitting behind the desk had a shaved head and wore a padded set of headphones, his attention focused on the laptop in front of him.

"I'm looking for someone named Ethan Harrington," she said. She stepped closer to the desk and bent forward to get within his line of vision. The man flinched in surprise and slipped the headphones around his neck.

"I didn't mean to scare you," she said.

"You got me pretty good. Sorry, I wasn't expecting anyone to walk in. I've got all three studios booked for the day."

She repeated her request to see Ethan.

"Got it. He's in Studio B," he said, gesturing to a hallway past the lobby. He flipped a switch on the wall behind him. "He's recording now but I just let him know he's got someone here. Wait for that red light to go off above the door before you enter. It's a whole sound production thing."

She nodded. If he only knew.

The red light dimmed and she walked inside.

* * *

Ethan Harrington glanced up from the soundboard as Laurie entered the control room, and she was immediately awed by the physical resemblance to his twin brother.

"Eerie, right?" he asked.

"It's like you read my mind," she said, slipping off her backpack and placing it on a small end table in the corner.

"It's been a long time since I've met anyone new who's also seen my brother, but I remember that look." He offered her a quick handshake. "I'm Ethan, obviously. The younger brother by two minutes. Funnier too." He laughed. She had a feeling that had been a joke between the two of them before the estrangement.

The woman who walked out of the recording room was statuesque, her long brown hair piled on top of her head in a loose bun. She looked vaguely familiar. "Perfect timing, Ethan. I could use a break. I'm going to walk down to Starbucks. Can I get you guys anything? I'm Donna, by the way," she said, nodding in Laurie's direction.

The name was enough for Laurie to place her. A recurring secondary role on a sitcom she watched before it was canceled. "If you don't mind my asking, what are you recording? I'm a television producer."

"Have a role for me?" Donna asked.

"It's a news program, so no roles." She had already said too much and hoped the woman didn't ask her the name of her show, which could lead to her asking why she was meeting with Ethan.

"That's too bad. My agent tells me I've reached an age where I have to start playing the main character's mother, and I'm still in my forties. Anyway, that's why Ethan's helping me record an audiobook demo. It's a huge market, and no one will care if I get old so long as I can sound like any character they can imagine."

Laurie noticed a stack of three novels left on the bar stool near the microphone in the live room. Angie Kim, Janelle Brown, and Wendy Corsi Staub. She made a mental note to check them out.

Once Donna left the studio, Ethan immediately got to the point. "I didn't appreciate my brother threatening to blame everything on me unless I agreed to do your show."

"I get it," she said, holding up her palms. "I had no idea he was going to do that, and that's not my style."

He held her gaze and then his expression softened. He gestured toward the only other chair in the sound room, and she took a seat.

"I understand your past has been painful, Ethan, but sometimes it's necessary to reopen old wounds. Your sister and your sister-in-law both think it's time for the family to know the truth."

"I couldn't care less about Michelle's opinion of me, but it really did hurt to find out that Frankie was having her doubts. She and I have always been close, even after I stopped talking to Simon. I assume he told you that he thinks I did it."

She nodded. "But you think *he* did?" she asked.

"I mean it had to be, right? My dad's own law partner told the police the next day that he saw one of us out by the Range Rover right after it happened, and I know it wasn't me. Maybe it would be different if Simon said he was over there for some other reason, but he insists he never left. Plus the fact that it was our car and our security code, plus Bacon never let out one of his stranger-warning barks? It all adds up."

Now that Ethan was opening up to her, she could see the subtle differences between the twins. Simon had exuded an air of confidence that bordered on assertiveness. His eye contact held a certain intensity, hinting at a determined mind constantly at work. Ethan, on the other hand, had a quieter demeanor, and his eyes, while equally intelligent, carried a softer glint. She sensed an underlying calmness to Ethan that his brother did not possess.

"But why would Simon do something like that?"

"You don't understand the kind of pressure my father tried to put on us. He was an extremely controlling man. For whatever reason, I was the one who'd push back. He'd threaten to kick me out of the house or cut me off, but I wouldn't let it get to me. I did finish college even though I didn't want to, but that didn't seem like an unreasonable request. I was *not* going to let him tell me who to fall in love with though. Did Simon already tell you about that?"

She nodded. "For what it's worth, he admitted he was very unkind to Annabeth."

"Too little, too late," he said sadly. "Anyway, Simon was never willing to stand up to my father. It was a point of pride for him that he was the better kid but he also carried a lot of pent-up resentment. I'm convinced the whole reason he wanted to go to a highbrow law school and a big fancy firm was to one-up my father. When it came out that he'd cheated on a term paper and my dad wouldn't help him buy his way out of trouble, I think he had some kind of psychotic break where he just wanted my dad to be gone."

"Frankie told me that when your mother left the party that night, she said she'd be coming back. She also remembers thinking that your mother seemed to be in a rush. Does any of that ring a bell? Do you know why your parents left?"

He shook his head. "I don't know what Frankie might be recalling, and my mother didn't even tell me when she was leaving the party. But when I saw my father leave, he looked almost angry. I thought at the time it was because I was there with Annabeth. But afterward, I wondered if he and Simon had gotten into it again about the term paper. He could have stormed off to go home, and then Simon followed him in the other car to confront him again about not giving him the money and then he went for the gun. If Mom knew about the argument and saw Simon walk out, she might have gone home to calm them both down."

Laurie could begin to see the scene falling into place in her mind.

"So you think your mother left separately from your father?"

"I can't be sure, but I am certain my father was alone when I saw him heading for the exit. It was only a ten-minute walk on the beach back to our house. If I had to guess, Simon didn't mean to shoot my mother. I think he either hit her by accident or panicked when she walked in and saw what he'd done. Did Frankie tell you about the flowers?"

Laurie shook her head.

"She and I went to visit our parents' graves one weekend. It was probably three years after they were killed. There was a beautiful flower arrangement at my mother's headstone. Nothing for my dad. We asked Betsy and Walter about it, but it wasn't them. I was sure it was Simon. That's when I realized he probably didn't mean to hurt Mom. Then Frankie told me it was the same a few years later when she went there with Betsy. Flowers had been left only for my mother."

Laurie had noticed that Simon's criticism of his parents had been limited to Richard. "Your brother said his father physically assaulted him when he found out about the term paper."

Ethan's eyes darkened, a flash of anger crossing his face. "My father wasn't perfect, but he never laid a hand on Simon. He was always pressuring him, yes, but that's not the same as abuse."

"Your brother said your father could even be cruel at times."

Ethan winced at the word. "I try to focus on the good times."

"And yet—"

"Let's say his parenting style was more drill sergeant than anything. He could be very cold."

"Why would Simon make up the assault? If nothing else, it gives him another motive for wanting to hurt your father back."

Ethan shook his head, frustration evident in his voice. "I don't know. Maybe he's trying to set the stage, create a narrative that justifies what he did. I don't trust anything he says anymore."

"You've already told me more than I knew about the case. Did the police ever check to see if anyone saw your mother walking on the beach, for example?"

He shrugged. "I seriously doubt it. Those cops wouldn't listen to a word I said. They saw two rich guys from Boston they wanted to put away."

"Well, you and your brother agree on one thing," she said, evoking a sad smile. "If there's new information, don't you want to pursue that?"

"Honestly? I don't think so. I've spent a lot of years and a lot of hours in the therapy chair trying to move forward. I like my work, my music. I'm married to the love of my life. We've got a kid on the way. We're all good and I don't want to mess that up."

"But what about Frankie? And what are you going to tell your children when they ask about your family?"

He folded his arms. "You know how to make it hurt, don't you?" he said with a squint.

"I promise I'm not trying to force you into anything. I don't know the pain you've experienced, but I did have my own. My first husband was murdered in front of our son eight years ago, and it went unsolved for five." His eyes widened and his lips parted in shock as he held her gaze. "I could feel the trauma in my son at a cellular level, as if it was in his blood. No one could bring his father back or undo the pain of that loss, but when the police finally figured out who did it, I could feel a change in him—in both of us. Like a heaviness had lifted. It was easier to find happiness."

He looked down at his lap and then pressed his hands together, thinking. "What makes you think you can find something the police missed?"

"Because I've done it before and I'm good at my job," she said confidently.

Ethan's eyes searched hers, a complex mix of emotions playing across his face. "I need something more. I need to know that this isn't just another futile attempt to rehash the past. If you can prove to me that there's something new, something worth digging into, I'll do your show."

"I can't promise you that," she said.

"But I thought you've done it before and are good at your job," he said with a grin. He wasn't lying when he said he was the funnier Harrington twin.

She nodded. "Fair enough." She reached into her backpack and pulled out a blank production agreement. "Read that over with your wife. Because you're going to want to sign it."

Now she just had to find something the police had missed.

# Chapter 14

Annabeth had an episode of her guilty pleasure—a cheesy reality dating show—playing quietly on the television as she perused nursery ideas on a home decorating website from the living room sofa. She added two crib possibilities to her online inspiration board.

Ethan was in his favorite swivel chair, his laptop and earphones in place. Edits for a podcast were due back to the host for review the following morning, but he had insisted on working beside her while she watched her show.

The two of them had always been as inseparable as feasible, but she sensed that proximity had become an even bigger priority since she'd become pregnant. Once, when she asked him whether she was right about that, he had explained that he believed in the power of auditory memory. He wanted their child to know the sound of his voice as early as possible.

He pulled off his headphones and set his laptop on the coffee table just as a potential couple on the reality show was finishing their date.

"Done," he announced with a sense of satisfaction. "Did I miss the rose ceremony?"

He swore he only watched this show to make her happy, but Annabeth could tell he enjoyed it, too, even though he would never admit it.

"No, they're dragging it out as long as possible." When the program broke to a commercial, she hit the mute button on the remote.

"After all the cribs we've looked at, I think I managed to find two that are perfect."

"Guess we need a second baby."

"Someday, as we've always planned." She handed him her iPad. "Until then, see what you think."

Ethan, usually eager to discuss anything related to the baby, seemed distracted as he scrolled between the choices. "They both look good," he replied absentmindedly, returning her tablet to her.

Annabeth raised an eyebrow. "Okay, spill it," she said, even though she already suspected where his mind had wandered. "You're usually even more excited about shopping for the baby than I am. What are you thinking?"

"Ah," he said wistfully, "the four words every man wants his wife to ask at the end of the day: *What are you thinking?* I was thinking there's no way for me to focus on cribs when my beautiful wife is sitting next to me looking like that." He moved over to the sofa, sat beside her, and gave her a quick kiss.

She was wearing one of his old concert T-shirts and yoga pants. Her long hair was in a messy pile secured with a giant claw clip. Red carpet ready, she was not.

"Nice try, but I'm in sweats and one of your ratty shirts. Now, seriously, what's going on in that head of yours?"

He sighed, the humor fading. "I'm just wondering if I made the right decision today with Laurie. It feels like a big step."

Annabeth put down her iPad, focusing on him. "First of all, you didn't make any promises so there's nothing to regret. And you gave her an incentive to dig up something new, which is far more than the police have done in almost a decade."

He met her eyes, gratitude flickering in his expression. "I just don't want this to blow up in our faces. I don't trust my brother."

"And for good reason. That goes for Michelle, too. They had no right to corner you like that today, basically threatening you. They haven't changed at all, still manipulating other people to get what they want. But you handled it perfectly."

He was nodding along, as if still trying to convince himself he was doing the right thing. "I can't let them give a one-sided story to that show. If we stay in contact with Laurie, we at least have a chance to counter unsupported claims."

"Does Laurie know yet that Simon initially tried to hold up the distribution of your parents' estate?" Annabeth asked.

He shrugged and sighed. "I have no idea. She didn't mention it, but that might be the kind of thing the show could spring on us once we agree to appear on camera."

Or, Annabeth thought, a dramatic stunt Simon and Michelle might pull in the middle of an interview to make Ethan and her look bad. She began to wonder what else might become public if the television production went forward. "What about my father? Did she mention him?"

"Not a word." He reached over and held her hand. "No matter what happens, I would never do anything to hurt your father. He treated me like a son after I lost my entire family—everyone but Frankie."

It was further confirmation that Frankie was the real reason he was entertaining the idea of cooperating with the show right now. Their child wouldn't be in a position to ask questions for years, thank goodness.

She avoided his gaze. "I've seen *Under Suspicion*, Ethan. They question everyone. Then they begin pointing fingers, asking whether someone other than the original suspects could have done it."

"Isn't that what we want?" he asked.

When Ethan had come home and told her about Laurie Moran's visit to the recording studio, she had promised herself that the decision belonged entirely to Ethan. He was the one who lost his parents. He was the one whose name would always be under a shadow of doubt. She vowed not to interfere.

Yet here they were.

"What if they point the finger at my father?" she asked. "The whole situation makes my family look like—"

She tried to block the words from her thoughts as she replayed the conversation Simon had had with her two days before the murders. *My dad sees you and your family as money-hungry gold diggers from the wrong side of the tracks, and it's only a matter of time until Ethan comes around.*

She felt tears forming, rekindling the fears she'd had when Michelle initially called about *Under Suspicion*.

"It's going to be okay, Annabeth," Ethan said.

"But the money—"

He shushed her. "We promised a long time ago not to talk about that anymore. Your father and the two of us are the only people who know about it, and nothing's going to change that, okay?"

She was wiping the tears from her eyes before she realized they had already stopped. She took his hand. "You always know how to calm me down."

"Another superpower. Now, back to the nursery. I think the second crib is perfect."

# Chapter 15

Laurie was checking missed messages on her phone as she stepped off the plane at LaGuardia. She was in the middle of a text from Alex explaining that he would be staying late at the courthouse when she did a double take at one of the passengers waiting near the gate.

She almost didn't recognize Frankie Harrington. When they'd met at Katz's, Frankie had come directly from her internship and was dressed accordingly. Now her tiny frame was swallowed by an oversized flannel shirt and baggy faded jeans with a hole in one knee, a beanie pulled over her dark, wavy hair, and a backpack and parka bundled on her lap. She looked like a regular college student.

"Frankie?"

Startled, Frankie looked up, removing her AirPods from her ears. "Oh my gosh, Laurie. Did you just get off the plane from Boston?"

"I did."

"That's so funny. It sounds like the trip went well. I already talked to Simon and Ethan."

Laurie had been on the plane for less than an hour and yet her time in Boston felt like an eternity away. "Simon and Michelle are officially on board for the show. I still need to convince Ethan."

"He told me," Frankie said. "That's why I'm at the airport. I'm going up to Boston. My judge said it was fine to take a long weekend."

A woman sitting nearby removed her coat and purse from the seat next to Frankie to make room for Laurie.

"Don't push Ethan," Laurie said, nodding thank-you to the

woman and settling in beside Frankie. "Give me a little time to work the case. I'm confident I can find a new angle, and that will be enough to convince him."

"But I might be able to help in that regard." Frankie's dark eyes widened with optimism. "Most of my parents' belongings have been in storage all these years. Maybe I'll find something relevant to the investigation."

Laurie's curiosity piqued. "Have you ever gone through their things before?"

"No, it's kind of a long story. As I understand it, by the time anyone started talking about my parents' estate, the police already suspected my brothers. They notified the probate court and the life insurance company, trying to keep my brothers from inheriting."

"Simon mentioned that," Laurie said.

"The thing is, I always thought my parents' personal belongings were in storage because my brothers were too upset to sort through it. As I got older and had the option, I felt the same way. But Betsy only recently told me that as part of the probate process Simon and Ethan agreed not to take anything and to leave it all for me."

Laurie was about to ask why when she answered her own question. "Neither of them wanted the other to have it."

Frankie nodded sadly. "I can't believe I went all these years without realizing they suspected each other. Betsy convinced them not to hold up the entire estate over it. They eventually took their trust accounts and their part of the life insurance, but the personal effects still belong to me. I'm ready to go through it all. Maybe I'll find something new, and we can use that to convince Ethan."

"I appreciate the help, Frankie. But I assume the police already searched the house before everything went into storage?"

She shook her head. "No, that's the thing. They had posted crime scene tape at the beach house for days. When they were done, we didn't want to be in the place where . . . you know, it all happened. We went back to Boston. I stayed with the Wards, and my brothers stayed at our house in the city until the estate sold it, but there was a lot of back-and-forth. Point is, I don't remember the police ever showing up at our house in Boston."

Laurie made a mental note. It was yet another item on her list of things to discuss with the Harbor Bay police. If true, their failure to search the house was consistent with the twins' claims of a shoddy investigation.

"Ethan also mentioned that someone left flowers at your mother's grave, but not your father's. Do you remember that?"

"Oh that's right. That was a while ago, but it happened a couple of times. I always assumed it was one of her friends from church or something."

Laurie didn't mention Ethan's suspicions that it had been Simon. An announcement at the gate advised passengers on the next flight to Boston that they were beginning pre-boarding.

"Frankie, before you go, did you know anything about the argument your brothers had the night of the graduation party? They both say that's why they were keeping a distance."

Frankie sighed. "I know that now, but it's yet another thing they kept from me until I started asking questions. I've always sensed that Annabeth didn't like to talk about Simon or even Michelle, but I never knew the source of her grudge. Apparently, my father didn't approve."

It was becoming clear to Laurie that, despite their differences, both of Frankie's brothers had tried to protect their younger sister from getting pulled into their feud.

"Do you think it's possible my show could have access to the items you have in storage? If we go forward, we'll be filming in Harbor Bay. We'll try to get permission to film at your family's old house and the yacht club. But having a sense of what your life in Boston was like would be helpful," Laurie explained.

"Of course. Anything at all."

Laurie reached into her bag for a blank copy of the Fisher Blake production agreement. "I should give you a copy of this while we're here. It's our studio's standard—"

With one glance at the agreement, Frankie asked Laurie if she had a pen. "Simon, Dennis, and Walter all read it for me after you gave copies to Simon and Michelle."

"Helps to have three lawyers in the family, I guess." Laurie pulled a pen from her bag.

"Trust me," Frankie said as she signed, "I could practically recite every clause by now."

Frankie popped up from her seat just as the gate attendant was making the final boarding call. She gave Laurie a quick hug before rushing toward the gate.

Laurie watched her until she disappeared into the jetway, then turned and slowly walked away.

She'd initially been desperate to land this case to appease Brett and keep Ryan from homing in on the production of her show, but now she was truly invested. She could see how much Frankie loved her brothers and wanted to trust them again. And having met Simon and Ethan, she sensed they both wanted to remain close to their little sister. She found herself hoping she could somehow bring the Harrington family back together again.

*Was it possible they didn't do it?*

# Chapter 16

Laurie's father was a true New Yorker, which meant if his destination was five minutes away, he walked. If it was fifteen minutes away, he walked. Same thing for thirty. Unless police work or a family emergency was involved, Leo Farley walked.

And tonight, their destination was J. G. Melon, which was only eleven short blocks from Laurie's apartment. Alex was working late at the courthouse, hearing motions from the parties in his cryptocurrency trial. In his absence, Leo and Tim had decided the rest of the family should grab dinner at a nearby neighborhood joint once Laurie got home, so Ramon would not need to cook for them before his own night off.

Naturally, Leo had walked first to Laurie's apartment, assuming they would head to the restaurant on foot together from there. But when the rain began to pour, Ramon insisted on driving them to dinner. He was taking the car out anyway, he explained, on his way to a bimonthly mahjong tournament in Chinatown that he had joined in October.

As a result, they had been in the car longer than it would have taken them to walk eleven blocks. Seeing her father clenching his jaw beside her, Laurie tilted her head toward Tim, who was in the front passenger seat, blissfully unaware of the Second Avenue gridlock. He was explaining to Ramon how Chet Baker's trumpet "melded" with Paul Desmond's alto sax on the version of "Autumn Leaves" he was streaming over the car speakers.

Even if they weren't at home or walking down the street together, they were having family time, New York City style.

"Thanks again, Dad, for staying with Tim after school until I got home. You didn't have other dinner plans tonight?"

Her father had met Chief Judge Maureen Russell at Alex's induction nine months earlier. Leo wasn't one to share details about his personal life, but she knew the two of them had kept in touch.

"Alex isn't the only federal judge who had to work late," he said coyly.

When they finally came to a stop at 74th Street and Third Avenue, Laurie's father unfolded himself from the backseat of the car. As he opened the door to J. G. Melon for her, he had a message. "You deprived me of about twelve hundred steps, but I'm still getting a hamburger. With cheese. And don't sass me about it."

"No bacon," Laurie said.

"Fair enough."

The waiter had taken their order by the time Laurie asked about the science fair that afternoon. She'd had it on her calendar for weeks but had to miss it for her trip to Boston.

As it turned out, the teacher's list of potential scientific projects consisted of fairly standard experiments for Tim's grade. Tim's project had been to construct a bridge made from drinking straws.

"It held more than an entire cup of pennies before it collapsed," he declared gleefully. "Mrs. McKennan said it was because of the way I used triangles to support the total weight. She said I should redesign the Verrazzano when I grow up."

"Add that to your ever-growing bucket list," Laurie said.

"I think she was only being nice," Tim said. "I Googled it later and found out people have made straw bridges that held more than fifteen pounds. But they used a lot more straws, and that's bad for the planet."

"I'm sure your bridge was great," Laurie said. "What about the other projects?"

"Pretty fun. But between the Mentos and Diet Coke experiments and the baking soda volcanos, you would have been calling 911 about the school exploding, Mom."

"You love to tease your mother," she said, nudging him with her knee beneath the table.

"Sometimes." He flashed her a toothy grin.

Her father was well into the third bite of his cheeseburger, looking satisfied, when Laurie brought up the subject of the Harbor Bay Police Department. "I'm told the department was small and insular. Both Ethan and Simon think the police jumped to conclusions but never bothered to nail down the details."

Leo wore a grimace as he ate a sweet potato fry. "I hate to break it to you, Laurie, but all criminals say that."

"I called the police department while I was waiting for my flight in Boston," Laurie said. "Chief Bruce Collins passed away four years ago. His deputy, Roberta Hanson, left the department two years before that. No one seems to know how to reach her. Someone must have contact information for her, right?"

Leo looked at her with an arched brow. "Of course they do. But they're not going to send a reporter to her door."

"You know I hate to ask favors—"

"Consider it done. I'll call first thing in the morning. Professional courtesy, etcetera."

"I really need this case to come through." She gave them an abbreviated summary of her fear that Ryan Nichols was undermining her again with Brett.

"He shouldn't do that," Tim said. "It's like Mrs. McKennan told us today: You can be happy for another person without feeling bad about yourself."

"Sage advice," Laurie said.

"While I'm helping out my daughter, I'd be happy to pay them both a visit, too." Leo sat up straight in his chair, crossed his arms, and donned his sternest expression. “What do you think, Tim? Intimidating enough?”

Tim feigned a shudder. “Downright scary, Grandpa.”

“Are Abbott and Costello almost done?” Laurie asked, laughing. “I am an adult woman who can take care of her own workplace, thank you very much.”

“You have what they call boss moves, Mom.”

Yeah, she did. Now she needed to remind Ryan of exactly that.

# Chapter 17

Annabeth retreated to the sanctuary of her bedroom, quietly closing the door behind her. The glow of the bedside lamp cast a warm light across the room. Ethan was answering late night emails before bed, giving her a few moments of solitude. She pulled up the number of her childhood home in Harbor Bay on her cell phone and hit enter.

Her father, Jimmy Connolly, picked up on the second ring. "Annabeth, is everything all right? Is the baby okay?" His voice, weathered by the years, sounded panicked. It was unusual for her to call so late.

"The baby's fine, lots of kicking today. And I'm fine, too." She took a deep breath, steadying herself. "I do need to talk to you about something. Are you alone?"

"Your mom's taking one of her sleepy-time baths with her herbal tea and whatnot. But you've got me worried now."

"I don't think you need to be, but I felt like I should keep you in the loop." As Annabeth delved into the details of Ethan's communications with the *Under Suspicion* producer, she could feel her own anxieties about the renewed attention to the case growing. "I'm fairly certain Simon will point the finger at Ethan, saying he did it because his father was threatening to disown him if he continued seeing me."

"Not to speak ill of the dead, but if anything, those people were never good enough for you. Treating you like that."

Her father's voice rumbled with a simmering anger, but it was nothing compared to the rage she had seen when she had come home after Simon and Michelle had pulled her aside at the Pizza Palace, trying to scare her away from dating Ethan.

Her mother had been at the grocery store, so it was Annabeth's father who found her sobbing alone in her bedroom. When she told him what had happened, he was so angry she honestly feared that he would drive to the Harringtons' house to give them a piece of his mind. Even when he learned about their deaths, she had overheard him telling her mother that Ethan would be better off in the long run without such a horrible father in his life.

"Here's the thing, Dad. This show digs deep into every detail. If it comes out that Ethan dipped into his inheritance to help you pay off your loans, they're going to make it look like another reason for him to hurt his parents. Or they might even insinuate that you were in on it, too, since you ended up getting money from their estate."

"So why is Ethan doing this? Especially when you're about to have a child."

She did her best to explain her husband's fears that his sister and eventually his child would doubt his innocence.

"What are you asking me, Annabeth?"

Good question, she thought. "You, Ethan, and I are the only ones who know that he gave you that money."

"*Loaned*," he emphasized.

Her father had insisted on paying them back and still sent periodic checks to Ethan and her.

"Ethan promises me he's not going to tell the producers about the money, even if he agrees to do the show. And neither will I."

"That's not like you to lie, Annabeth."

"I know, but it's not really a lie. It's just keeping family business private—as it should be."

"And you don't want your old man messing things up by letting something slip. Not to worry. Taking money from your daughter and son-in-law isn't something a man boasts about."

"Please don't talk that way about yourself, Dad."

Her father was a proud man. She remembered the pain in his eyes when he had asked to speak to her in private, making her promise that she would not reveal their conversation to her mother. Annabeth had recently mentioned that Ethan's parents' estate was about to be distributed, and her father wondered if Ethan might be willing to lend him money to prop up the hardware store. She had been so afraid to ask Ethan, but the desperation in her father's voice had nearly broken her heart.

Ethan hadn't even hesitated. By then, he had grown suspicious of Simon and viewed their inheritance as "blood money." If he could use it to help Annabeth's family, that was what he wanted to do.

She was worried he would regret the decision and resent her later for asking. *Are you sure?* she had asked. *That money is for you and your siblings—for your security, for your future.*

*You are my security*, Ethan had said. *You are my future.*

She had known at that moment that she would spend the rest of her life with him.

"Look, Annabeth. There's something you should know if Ethan does this show." Her father's tone turned somber. "Things I thought were long behind me. You know my father was tied up with some bad people in Boston. He considered it the family business and assumed I'd be continuing the tradition. When I started dating your mother, he disapproved. Thought she wasn't the right fit for me."

"You've told me this. That's why you were so angry when the Harringtons were trying to drive a wedge between Ethan and me." She also knew that "bad people" was her father's way of referring to the Boston Mafia, and that "not the right fit" was code for her mother having moved to the United States from Mexico as a child with her parents.

"Hear me out. I went my own way with your mother. Opened up the hardware store. Vowed to run it as a legitimate business. I struggled sometimes, but it was working. Then came the chain store off the highway, threatening to shut me down."

She knew all of this as well. It was the reason he had so many loans and was on the verge of bankruptcy before asking if Ethan could help him out. She was afraid that Ethan might be pouring good money after bad, but her father had a plan to make the store work. Today, Jimmy's was more a home goods boutique than a hardware store. The tourists kept him in the black with overpriced candles and fancy serving platters, while the locals still shopped there for batteries and extension cords. By no measure were her parents wealthy people, but to her knowledge, the crisis had passed.

"The loans, Annabeth. They weren't only through the banks."

She sat down on the bed, absorbing the impact of his words. "Oh."

"Yeah, *oh*. I was desperate. I went to my father's old buddies. I should have known that my connection to him would only take me so far. I would have let the store close before turning to you and Ethan, except they were threatening me, including you and your mother."

Annabeth felt a chill run down her spine. "But the bad people are out of the picture now?" she asked.

"Very much so," he said to her relief. "But it really would not be good if these TV people started asking questions about my old financial problems."

"I understand."

As Annabeth hung up, she vowed to herself once again not to let her family—Ethan, her parents, their baby—get hurt. She found herself praying that Laurie Moran would be able to prove that Simon was a murderer, once and for all.

After the conversation ended, Jimmy Connolly tried to focus on the Robert Parker novel he was reading, but found his thoughts drifting into the past. His wife, Maria, emerged from the shower in a fluffy bathrobe, hair wrapped in a towel. "Were you on the phone? I thought I heard your voice."

He hesitated for a moment before replying. "Annabeth. Just catching up."

"Shoot, I would have liked to talk to her."

"Remember when we had to buy a new phone after you dropped the last one in the tub?" he said.

Her eyes sparkled as she smiled at the memory. "It was only once, and I've never used that bath oil again. I'll give her a call tomorrow to see what I missed."

He had met Maria when they were only seventeen years old. They'd been married thirty-five years, but had been together for nearly half a century. If it was possible, he loved her more with every passing year. Everything he had ever done—even his worst mistakes—had been to make a good life for her and Annabeth.

As Maria crawled into bed next to him and turned off the lamp on her nightstand, he tried to tell himself that the dangers he had feared all those years ago would remain in the past where they belonged. The show would not find out about the threats he had faced from his so-called "lenders."

And, pray God, do not let them find the video. It was a secret that his good friend Chief Bruce Collins had taken to the grave.

# Chapter 18

The next morning, Grace and Jerry joined Laurie in her office to hear about her trip to Boston.

Grace had photocopied and filed the signed agreements Laurie had gotten from Simon, Michelle, and Frankie. Laurie had also emailed copies to Betsy and Walter Ward. According to Frankie, they were happy to go on camera if it was important to her and Michelle.

"What if Ethan doesn't agree to it?" Jerry asked.

Grace shot him a sideways glance with her heavily made-up eyes. "Way to be a Debbie Downer. Laurie's got this."

"No, Jerry's got a good point," Laurie conceded. "Of course I want both brothers on camera. It's the only way to ensure it's not a one-sided hatchet job." But in her heart, Laurie knew that Brett would never let her pull the plug now that she had two of the three Harrington children on board, along with Sarah's best friend and Richard's law partner. Her stomach hurt at the thought of being forced to do the show without Ethan and Annabeth.

"For now," Jerry said brightly, "let's assume we get them too. Who else do we need?"

"The cops," Grace said immediately.

"You always say that," Jerry said, "and they *never* go on camera."

"It's a tiny department," Laurie said. "The Chief was the lead investigator, but he passed away. The other lead was his deputy, Roberta Hanson, who left the department a few years after the Harrington murder. That could work to our advantage. She might agree to at least speak off the record since she's no longer part of the department."

"Plus she's a *she*," Grace said. "Women are more likely to do the right thing."

"Sexist," Jerry muttered. "Need I remind you how many female killers we've covered on this show?"

"You two are on fire today," Laurie said.

"You know our fights are shtick," Grace said.

She did. "My father's pulling some strings to see if he can locate Deputy Hanson for us. Fingers crossed. The Harringtons also had a caretaker named Peter Bennett. He'll be key, because he's the one who knew that the camera at the front gate was still operational. But I also got the impression he was around the house on a regular basis, so he may have picked up on the Harringtons' interfamily dynamics. Same with the dog walker who found Sarah and Richard's bodies."

In Laurie's experience, many people had no idea how much their housekeepers, handymen, nannies, and other household helpers noticed about their personal lives. Ramon had worked for Alex for more than a decade and arguably knew him better than Laurie did.

"And her name is . . ." Grace was keeping a running list.

"Jenna Merrick," Jerry said. "I already looked her up online. She still lives in Harbor Bay. She has a website for dog walking, dog sitting, dog grooming, all the dog things."

"What about the caretaker, Peter Bennett?" Laurie asked.

"No website," Jerry said, "but I did find an address and phone number for a Peter Bennett in Harbor Bay. I assume it's the same guy."

Laurie was beginning to see the sketched edges of a production schedule. "The person I really want to talk to is Howard Carver."

"That's the other law partner?" Jerry asked.

"Yes, the one who told police he saw one of the twins near the Range Rover in the overflow parking lot at the yacht club. Ethan and Simon have been convinced all these years that the other brother was the killer, and Howard's statement to the police is a major reason why."

Jerry raised a tentative hand. "If I can offer a correction: They've *claimed* to believe that. The police have suggested it's all part of the act. If they planned the killings together, pointing fingers at each other could be just a way to keep prosecutors from ever having proof beyond a reasonable doubt against either one of them."

"That's correct," Laurie said. "My point is there's too much evidence suggesting that it was at least *one* of them, and that's what has put them at odds—at least publicly."

She, Jerry, and Grace had already made a list of the evidence implicating the twins. The killer drove their Range Rover, knew the gate code, apparently knew the family dog, and had access to the family gun that had been locked in a safe. They both had a motive—resentment toward their overbearing father, combined with the promise of an inheritance.

"But without Howard's statement about seeing one of them near the Range Rover," Laurie noted, "it could be someone else close to the family, someone who used the car the twins had driven to the party so their own wouldn't be spotted at the gate."

"Now I get it," Jerry said. "So, yes, let's add Howard Carver to the list."

"Sooner rather than later," Grace said, adding a star next to his name on the list she was keeping.

Laurie realized she had not told them yet about the iciness in Michelle's voice when Howard's name came up at the law firm. "When I was in Boston, Simon's wife mentioned him during a tour of the offices. She did not sound like a fan. She said he was long retired, but I sensed there was more to the story."

"The man threw her husband and his brother under the bus to the cops," Grace said. "Of course she's mad."

"But she could have simply said that. Instead, she seemed to be putting up a false front. I want to make sure we're not missing something. If there's a reason to doubt his version of events that night, it would change everything."

She felt herself hoping once again that she might be able to offer

Frankie an alternative explanation for her parents' deaths—one that didn't involve sending one or both of her brothers to prison.

"Anyone else?" Grace asked.

"I think that's it—for now," Laurie said.

"The fun begins when these people start pointing us to witnesses we may never have heard of," Jerry said. "I can't wait to start."

"Start what?" a male voice asked.

Laurie turned to find Brett Young nearly filling the threshold to her office, Ryan Nichols looming behind him. They hadn't even bothered to knock on what had been her closed door.

# Chapter 19

Frankie skipped down the familiar staircase of the Wards' Beacon Hill home, which had become her home nearly ten years ago. The scent of freshly brewed coffee wafted through the air.

She found Betsy and Walter in the kitchen. Betsy was clad in workout gear, ready for her twice-weekly Pilates appointment. She was sipping from an insulated travel mug personalized with her name, a birthday gift from Frankie the previous year. Walter sat at the kitchen table with a stack of papers and an open laptop.

"Looks like I'm the late riser this morning," Frankie said.

"As is a college student's right," Walter muttered, his eyes not leaving the computer screen. "Enjoy it while you can."

Frankie gave Betsy a puzzled look. It had been years since she'd seen Walter hard at work so early in the morning.

"Bernie Linton is buying a new building," Betsy explained.

Frankie didn't know much about the details of Walter's legal work, but she knew about Bernie. One of Walter's earliest clients, he refused to let Dennis or Simon work on his projects, insisting that no one born after the advent of disco had "a sense of the world."

Frankie was pouring herself a mug of coffee when she felt Betsy's eyes on her. "A candy for your thoughts," Frankie said.

The phrase that had once belonged to Betsy and her mother was now part of her lexicon, too.

Betsy's brow was furrowed with concern. "Are you absolutely sure about going to the storage unit today?"

Walter looked up from his work for the first time since Frankie came downstairs.

"It's the whole reason I came up from New York."

"And we thought you missed us," Walter said with a chuckle.

"Seriously," Betsy said, "we trust your judgment, but it's a lot to take on at once. Between this and your meetings with that journalist, I just want to make sure you're not overwhelming yourself."

Despite the comfort and support she had found in the Wards' home, Frankie had never called Betsy and Walter "Mom" and "Dad," and they had never tried to step into those roles. They were more like very close family friends, bound to her by a shared love of her parents and brothers. It wasn't a lack of appreciation, but seeing them as parental figures would have felt like a betrayal to the mother and father she had lost.

"You know how much I appreciate everything you've done for me," Frankie said, giving Betsy a quick hug. "But this feels like the right time. I'm about to turn twenty-two. You've told me that's the age my parents thought we could be trusted to make our own decisions. And I'm ready to learn more about what happened that night."

"Putting on my lawyer hat," Walter said, "twenty-two's the age when you'll have responsibility over your trust fund, but that doesn't mean you have to rush into everything all at once. You still need to finish college, including that internship. Not to mention some big decisions about what to do after that."

"I feel like you're trying to talk me out of this," she said.

They both denied any attempt to interfere with her decision.

"Good, because I'm going to the storage unit today. I'm actually looking forward to it. Even if I don't find anything relevant to the investigation, I like the idea of seeing my mother's dresses and my father's collection of baseball memorabilia. Oh, and the books my mother used to read to me when I was little. I hope they're still there."

"Everything should be there, sweetie. A mover came and stored it all away for you." Betsy's voice had softened. Frankie hoped she could see how important this was to her. "What if I go with you? I can cancel Pilates. Just in case the emotions are too much."

"Please. I really want to do this alone. It's important to me."

They both nodded their acceptance.

"Just take care of yourself," Walter said. "And promise you'll call if you need anything. Betsy will be contorting herself on those torture devices at the Pilates studio, but I might need an excuse to get away from Bernie and his incessant emails."

"I promise," Frankie said.

Betsy was grabbing her car keys from a bowl by the kitchen phone when they heard the sound of the front door open. A voice rang out from the foyer. "Your favorite son is here!"

Dennis entered the kitchen, a paper coffee cup in one hand, a box of Union Square doughnuts in the other. "Morning, one and all."

"To what do we owe this pleasure?" Betsy said, pulling her son into a tight hug.

"Everything okay at the office?" Walter asked.

"Michelle told me Frankie was coming to town. Thought I'd drop by and say hello."

Frankie was genuinely surprised. "Just to see me?"

"I haven't seen you since Christmas. I assume every college student could use some doughnuts."

In truth, Dennis had never taken much interest in Frankie over the years. The younger of the two Ward children, he had always been the baby of the family until Frankie suddenly appeared to demand his parents' attention just as he was about to leave the nest.

"Dad told me you were thinking about applying to law school," Dennis said. "Any interest in shadowing me at my office today?"

She thanked him for the invitation and explained she was going to spend the day at the storage unit.

Dennis raised an eyebrow. "Storage unit? What's that about? I didn't know we had one."

Frankie looked to Betsy and Walter, but they said nothing. "It was for my family's things," she said. "From all those years ago."

It took Dennis a moment to clue in. "I had no idea. Oh . . . wow. You're doing that now? When you're finishing college? And also talking to that TV show? That must be tough."

Frankie could not bring herself to explain her feelings again. "It's what I want," she said firmly.

Dennis suddenly shifted topics. "Dad, you look busy over there. What's up?"

"Bernie."

It was becoming clear that Bernie was a one-word explanation for many things.

"Love seeing you," Betsy said, giving Dennis a kiss on the cheek. "Running off to my workout now. Will put back the calories times two with those doughnuts when I get home. Love you!"

Walter's attention was back to his laptop and whatever work Bernie was dropping on him.

It was only Frankie and Dennis now.

"Need a ride?" Dennis asked.

"I was going to take an Uber."

After asking Frankie the address for the storage facility, Dennis announced that it was not very far out of the way, so Frankie grabbed a rainbow sprinkle doughnut to go and followed him to the Audi sedan he had parked at the curb in front of the house.

They arrived at the address Dennis had entered into his GPS to find a sprawling complex of freestanding garage-like units. It looked abandoned.

"Creepy place," he said. "Do you know where you're going?"

She pulled the paperwork for the original rental contract from her purse and unfolded it. "Here it is," she said, reading the number of the assigned unit. "I'm sure I can find it from here."

As Frankie stepped from the car, she sensed that Dennis had something else to say.

"That was nice of you to come by to see me," she said before closing the door.

"To be honest, it was also for my parents," he said. "They thought they were done raising their children, and then they had you. It's important to them that we're close, and I know I've often been too busy to make the effort."

She realized this was probably the first time she had been alone with him since Betsy and Walter had asked him once or twice to babysit her when she was young.

"It's okay," she said. "I'm so grateful to your family."

"Then you should know that my parents don't want you to do this show," he said. She had never heard him speak so bluntly.

"They said it was my decision," Frankie said.

"Two things can be true at one time."

"What are you trying to tell me?" she asked.

He pulled the passenger door shut and drove away without another word.

# Chapter 20

"Sorry to interrupt, team," Brett announced. Even though his tone was polite, his impatience was evident.

Where Laurie's office had felt alive seconds earlier amid the buzz of a busy brainstorming session, an awkward silence had fallen over the room with the sudden appearance of Brett and Ryan.

"No problem," Laurie said. She managed to maintain her composure as she tucked a strand of her honey-colored bob behind one ear. "Did we have a meeting scheduled?"

"I didn't know I needed to schedule a meeting to find out what happened in Boston. Given the circumstances, I expected you to brief me by now. When Ryan was in my office, I asked him what he knew, but he was in the dark as well. So here we are."

By *the circumstances*, Laurie assumed he meant the fact that Ryan Nichols had somehow convinced Brett that he needed to breathe down Laurie's neck about the next *Under Suspicion* production.

"You know I don't like to draw on your valuable time until we have a game plan in place," she said diplomatically, "and we're not quite there yet with the details. I was just discussing next steps with Jerry and Grace."

Brett glanced at Jerry and Grace as if he were only now realizing that other people were in the room.

"Of course. Always nice to see two of the best dressed employees of Fisher Blake," Brett said, one of his unsettling smiles spreading across his face. "Jerry, Grace, if you could give us a moment."

"Of course," Jerry replied, his affable tone belying the mischief in his eyes.

As they walked toward her office door, Laurie caught the exchange of a knowing glance between Jerry and Grace. Approximately once a year, a Photoshopped image at Brett's expense would mysteriously appear on the office copy machines. Brett's face pasted onto the body of a swaddled baby grasping his rattle. Brett holding the hand of a smaller version of himself, on which someone had pasted Ryan's face. The caption: "I love my mini-me."

Laurie had long suspected that sweet, innocent, earnest-appearing Jerry was the culprit behind the high jinx, but she had taken a don't-ask-don't-tell approach to the situation. In the shared amusement she witnessed between Jerry and Grace as they left her office, she believed she had found confirmation. If she was right, Brett should expect to have another photocopy forthcoming soon.

"Now, Laurie, why are you stalling?" Brett asked, his tone a mix of frustration and anticipation. "Did you convince the twins or not?"

Laurie took a deep breath, choosing her words carefully. "We're making progress, Brett, but there's a roadblock. Ethan Harrington won't agree to participate until we have something new to bring to the table."

"We *are* the something new," he said, plopping himself down behind her desk. His fingers tapped rhythmically on the desktop as he looked to Ryan for answers.

Ryan sat in one of the chairs across from her desk, making her feel like she was an outsider on the sofa, observing a meeting in her own office that she wasn't invited to.

"We can just tell him he's going to look guilty if he doesn't speak up," Ryan said, his back now turned to her.

She rose from the sofa and took the seat next to Ryan. "I suggested as much, but he doesn't care. I need a breakthrough or Ethan won't budge," Laurie explained.

"*We* need a breakthrough," Ryan emphasized.

At that moment, her phone buzzed with a text. Glancing at the screen, she felt a sudden spark of hope. It was from her father. He had found a New York cop friend who knew someone in the Salem, Massachusetts, police department who knew someone in the Harbor Bay department. Long story short: he had contact information for Roberta Hanson.

"Good news," she said. "I located the deputy police chief who handled the original Harrington investigation." She explained that the lead investigators were the Chief and his deputy, but that the Chief had since passed away and his deputy had left the department. "Apparently she traded in one beach town for another. She opened a bookstore in the Hamptons."

"From a cop to a bookstore?" Ryan said derisively. "Clearly not a woman who cares about money."

Laurie suppressed an eye roll. Is that why Ryan wanted to steal her show? For money? She wanted to tell him that Alex had earned far more as a hardworking lawyer than she had ever made as a producer, but she decided to take the high ground.

"The important thing is that I know where she is now. If she'll talk to me, even on background, that should be enough to prove to Ethan that I—" She quickly corrected herself. "That *the show* is worth his time."

"Now *that* sounds like a plan," Brett said, holding up an enthusiastic index finger. "Get out there as soon as you can." Now the index finger was wagging between Laurie and Ryan.

"I'm happy to do the initial screening," she offered, even as Brett was already shaking his head. "Ryan usually gets involved when we're closer to filming."

"You said this deputy chief person is a she, right?" Brett asked.

Laurie had a bad feeling she knew where his thoughts were leading. "Yes. Her name's Roberta Hanson."

"So take Ryan. Women can't resist this guy."

Laurie was quite certain there was at least one woman who would disagree.

"Go out there today," Brett said, as if he hadn't already made the urgency clear. "Use the studio car service. Lock this down, you two. I want this show. Otherwise, we're going to need to talk about some major changes."

# Chapter 21

Laurie recognized the driver who held open the back door of the black Lincoln Navigator parked outside the 50th Street exit of 15 Rockefeller Center. "Nice to see you, Joey," she said as she climbed into the backseat.

"Always a pleasure, Ms. Moran."

Once Ryan stepped into the SUV after her, Joey closed the door and took his place behind the wheel. "Says here you're going to Main Street in Southampton?"

She confirmed the address.

"When I saw Mr. Nichols with you, I thought you might be going to Chelsea Piers to work on your tee shot." His blue eyes gleamed as he caught her gaze in the rearview mirror.

Apparently Ryan used the company car service to go to the driving range.

Ryan forced an awkward laugh. "That's only when the boss is in tow."

Between their various emails, texts, and phone calls, she and Ryan managed to work silently from the backseat of the SUV until they were exiting the Long Island Expressway at Manorville. She closed her laptop to rest her eyes. Ryan stared blankly out of the window as they passed one strip mall after another.

They rode along in an awkward silence that Ryan finally broke as the driver turned onto Highway 27.

"I hope you know I'm only trying to help," he said.

Laurie glanced at him, trying to maintain a guarded expression. "I never suggested otherwise."

He sighed. "Not directly, but I can tell you're resentful of my involvement. I thought we were finally working as a team."

"Or perhaps you're reading something into my feelings because part of *you* feels bad for undermining me with our boss. Insinuating that a married woman can't handle the job? What decade are you from, Ryan? Frankly, it's embarrassing."

"Hey, Joe," Ryan said, leaning toward the driver's seat. "Mind putting the glass up?"

A privacy partition rose to wall them off from the driver.

"I never meant to imply—"

"Of course you did," she said, cutting him off. "How else would Brett have known about that card on my office desk if you hadn't told him? You took a small, sweet thing that my son did for me and used it against me at work. How low can you be?"

He sat in stunned silence. They had had their problems when he first took over as the host of *Under Suspicion*, but she had never attacked his character this way.

"I wouldn't blame you if you wanted more time with Alex and your son—"

"Save it. I managed to do this job while mourning a husband and raising a terrified child without his father. I don't need your assumptions or your pity. What I need is to be able to trust you not to try to go after my job."

Ryan paused, studying her. "You think I want your job?"

She met his question head on. "Don't you?"

Ryan ran a hand through his well-groomed hair. "Honestly? I don't know what I want. I gave up being a real lawyer to come to Fisher Blake. Brett and my uncle made it sound like I'd have more influence in media than I could as a practicing attorney. But it hasn't turned out as I wanted. Most of the time, I feel like an empty suit reading lines off a teleprompter. And when I'm supposed to be a legal consultant to our scripted shows, the writers ignore my advice because they'd rather it be entertaining than realistic. Sometimes I think I made a huge mistake."

She was caught off guard by his seeming honesty. "So why are you taking it out on me?"

"I didn't realize I was until now. I guess your show is the only one where I feel like I can make a difference. You have to admit, I'm a good cross-examiner. And the times I've encouraged you not to use kid gloves with witnesses? I've been right."

"Not always, but . . . yes."

"I know you see me as a spoiled nepotism baby, but I'm smart, Laurie. And an excellent lawyer."

"I've never doubted that," she said.

"But you don't like me. Or trust me. You want me to stay in my lane until the cameras turn on, and then say exactly what you tell me to say."

Now she was the one who didn't know what to say. "I'm the producer, Ryan."

"But when Alex was host, he was your main brainstorming partner. You shared the investigation with him."

"Alex is my husband."

"Well, he wasn't then. And, no, I'm not suggesting anything like that. You should be so lucky," he added with a smirk.

She couldn't help but let out a small laugh.

"You didn't hire Alex, one of the best criminal lawyers in the country, only for his good looks. You wanted his insight. And I'm telling you, Laurie, I have insight. And I enjoy working on your show, both on camera and behind the scenes. Let me help. Let me be valuable."

As Laurie listened, she felt her anger begin to subside. She didn't like the way Ryan kissed up to Brett at her expense, but she at least had a sense now of where he was coming from.

As the SUV rolled into Southampton, Laurie tapped on the privacy partition, signaling to Joey that he could lower the glass.

"Good timing, Ms. Moran. We've arrived in the land of the rich and famous."

"Everywhere Ryan goes is the land of the rich and famous," she said slyly, giving Ryan a knowing smile. "Ryan, do you know that old tale about the scorpion and the frog?"

"Of course. The scorpion couldn't swim and so asked the frog to carry him across the river. The frog was afraid of being stung, but finally agreed after the scorpion argued that stinging the frog would cause them both to drown. Sure enough, midway across the river, the scorpion stung the frog, dooming them both."

"I'm not going to be the frog in this situation."

"And I'll try not to be the scorpion," he said.

"Unless it's just in your nature," she said with a wink.

She hoped her message to Ryan was clear. They might be entering another period of détente, but she'd be keeping one eye open.

# Chapter 22

The bookstore had a charming wooden sign above the entrance reading *The Book Nook*.

Laurie had called ahead from her office, inquiring about the store's hours. Fortunately, the woman who picked up the call had answered, "Book Nook, this is Roberta." They just had to hope that Roberta hadn't left for the day, making their two-hour drive a waste of time.

A bell hanging inside the front door announced their entrance. Inside, Laurie spotted a few customers browsing the various genre sections. One child sat criss-cross-applesauce on a brightly colored rug in the back corner, a picture book open in her lap, as a woman Laurie presumed was her mother lingered nearby in the travel section.

A young woman with several tattoos and a pierced nose was arranging books on a bestseller table at the front of the store. A second employee, a young man with a handlebar mustache, was restocking a round rack of novelty socks. That left the woman behind the cash register. She appeared to be in her late forties. She wore blue jeans and a pink oxford cloth shirt, and her salt-and-pepper hair was pulled into a braid that reached halfway down her back.

Laurie and Ryan exchanged a look. She had to be Roberta.

Approaching the counter, Laurie asked, "We're looking for Roberta Hanson?"

The woman nodded. "That's me. Can I help you with something?"

Laurie introduced herself and gestured toward Ryan. "And this is Ryan Nichols, who's also with the show. We were hoping to talk to you about Sarah and Richard Harrington."

Roberta turned her back to them and began rearranging stacks of books held behind the counter. "I left that part of my life behind. I don't usually talk about it."

"Please, Deputy—"

The woman spun toward them. "Don't call me that. I'm just Roberta now."

"Roberta," Laurie said, "please. Just a few minutes of your time. We're working with the family to try to get renewed attention to the case."

"You mean you're in the tank for Simon and Ethan?" The tone of her voice was cutting.

"Not at all," Ryan said, flashing his most charming smile. Roberta did not return the gesture. If anything, she seemed annoyed by it, glancing quickly at Ryan and then immediately returning her attention to Laurie.

"It was actually Frankie who first came to me," Laurie said. "She's ready to know the truth about what happened to her parents—even if it means her brothers face the consequences."

Roberta's stony expression softened at the mention of Frankie's role in the inquiry. "That poor girl. When I finally got a few hours to try to sleep after working the case all night, all I could think about was her, learning that both of her parents were gone."

"She's asking for your help, too," Laurie said. "I've been a journalist for twenty years. Ryan's a lawyer—a former prosecutor. We understand how to keep sources confidential. We're not asking you to go on record. Just background information, so we know if we're on the right track."

Roberta glanced between them, contemplating, then scanned the bookstore floor. "Yeah, okay. Just for a little while."

She led them to the back of the store, through a narrow corridor, and into a storage room. It was a small space, stacked high with boxes and shelves. A cart filled with signed Harlan Coben novels caught Laurie's eye. That was her father's favorite author.

As they settled into the cramped room, Roberta let out a sigh. "Honestly, I should have left that police department as soon as I joined."

# Chapter 23

Laurie cleared her throat, unsure how to follow up on Roberta Hanson's remark about her departure from the Harbor Bay Police Department.

She noticed Ryan open his mouth to speak, but then he looked to her for guidance instead.

"You don't look back on your time there fondly?" Laurie asked.

Roberta shifted in her seat. "Harbor Bay's a beautiful place. A rural feel but with fantastic beaches and dramatic sandy cliffs. It's the kind of town where everyone knows everyone, and the community is tight-knit."

"Sounds nice," Ryan said.

"Well, it can be a blessing and a curse. When something as heinous as a double murder goes down, it can be hard to fathom that someone from the community could be responsible. The wagons circle quickly."

Laurie's gaze remained fixed on Roberta. "So the community goes looking for an outside explanation of the danger?"

Roberta nodded. "Chief Collins was adamant from the start. Initially, he assumed it would be connected to shady business dealings in Boston. But once he saw the video recording from the front gate, he was certain it was one of the sons—who, let's face it, were also outsiders as far as Harbor Bay was concerned. Once Simon and Ethan started blaming each other, Collins became convinced it was all part of their plan. The brothers were in on it together."

"But as we understand it," Laurie said, "there was no blood found on either of the twins' white outfits they wore that night."

"Of course not," Roberta said. "If there'd been blood, at least one of them would have been arrested and charged. There was also no blood in the Range Rover. The Chief was convinced they had a third matching outfit to change into after the shooting, dumping the bloodied clothes before returning to the party. We never found them, but they could have been thrown anywhere."

"You keep saying the Chief was convinced. You weren't?"

Roberta paused, pondering the question. "Do I think they did it? Yeah. But am I *convinced*, as in *beyond a reasonable doubt*? No. There's a reason they were never charged. To have a convincing case, you'd have to have a thorough investigation."

Laurie noticed that Ryan had slipped a legal pad from his briefcase and was taking notes. Maybe he really did want to help with the work.

"And it wasn't thorough?" she asked Roberta.

"Not in my opinion. On the one hand, the Chief was sure the twins did it. On the other, he seemed more concerned about getting them out of town and assuring the locals they were safe than actually building a case against them."

Everything she was saying was consistent with Simon and Ethan's description of the investigation. "Did the department look into alternative explanations? Make a list of other suspects?"

Roberta shook her head. "Not once we saw that Range Rover tail the parents onto the property. And then the dad's law partner saying he saw one of the boys near the Range Rover at the yacht club was the nail in the coffin. A lot of the evidence against them made it around town by word of mouth. I can tell you one thing that wasn't public, but if you're trying to prove those boys are innocent, you're not going to like it."

"Why not?" Laurie asked.

"It's another piece of evidence against the twins. The camera at the front gate wasn't the only camera at the house. There was a hidden one disguised to look like a wall clock hanging in the hallway outside the home office at the back of the house. We found it in the search. It was functional, but someone had removed the memory card."

"And you think it was one of the sons?"

"It had to be. Who else? Even the caretaker didn't know about it, and he seemed to run everything in that house. When the Chief asked Simon and Ethan about cameras on the property, they said there was only the one at the gate, and it was broken—which it turned out not to be. Our theory was that they planned the murders for that night thinking the gate camera was broken, and then tried to make it look like a robbery gone bad. Before leaving, whichever one was the shooter removed the memory card from the hidden camera. Then they told us there was only the one camera outside, hoping we wouldn't notice the clock was actually a video recorder."

Laurie could see that Ryan was furiously jotting down notes, leaving the questioning to her.

"Simon mentioned that someone had vandalized the Harringtons' property about a month before the murders," Laurie said. "Someone spray-painted something like *This Family is a Lie* onto the sidewalk outside their house in Harbor Bay. Did you ever look into that?"

"There wasn't much to look into," she said. "There was no police report or photographs to back up the incident."

"You thought he was making it up?"

"Could be. Alternatively, the brothers might have done the spray-painting themselves so they could claim later that someone had a grudge against the family."

"Or," Laurie said, "someone actually did hold a grudge."

"Like I said, we didn't look into it. There's a reason I left law enforcement. It got to the point where I realized I wasn't proud of the work I was doing."

Laurie thought she noticed Ryan wince slightly at the observation.

"What about the family's primary residence in Boston? The Harrington kids seems to think it was never searched for evidence."

"It wasn't," Roberta said. "Because that would have required the Chief to work with the Boston PD, and he liked to be the big man in charge of a small department. He was convinced the answers he needed were in Harbor Bay and left it at that."

"Can you think of concrete investigatory steps you would have taken if the Chief hadn't been so focused on the twins?" Ryan asked.

Laurie nodded to Ryan in appreciation. It was a good question.

"Well, you pointed to two already. Search the Boston house. Figure out whether the vandalism incident actually occurred by talking to neighbors." She looked up at the ceiling, searching for other items to add to the list. "Oh, I know. I had suggested going through the available footage from that camera at the gate. See if we could identify any other vehicles that came and went in the days before the murders. The Chief shot me down, saying it was a waste of time. We didn't even ask the neighbors whether they might have surveillance camera footage that could be helpful. We also didn't do a deep dive into the victims' work lives."

"Richard was a lawyer," Laurie said, reminding her of the facts. "And Sarah was an artist but didn't officially work outside the home."

"I recall," Roberta said. "It's possible Richard could have had a disgruntled client or some other conflict related to his law firm, but we never even asked the right questions."

Laurie thought again about Howard Carver, Richard's second law partner. "What was your impression of Howard Carver?" she asked.

"It's been so long—"

"The law partner who said he saw one of the twins near the Range Rover," she prompted.

"That's right. I remember that his affect was surprisingly flat. He must have realized he was implicating one of the sons of his murdered friend, but he seemed almost matter-of-fact about it. When I commented on his demeanor to the Chief, he said the guy was probably in shock."

"Howard Carver retired from the law practice some time ago. Do you know anything about that?"

Roberta shook her head. It was another indication that no one had ever pressed Howard Carver about his identification of one of the twins. She could feel in her bones that this was a topic where her show might be able to change the narrative.

"What about alternative suspects?" Laurie asked.

"There honestly weren't any. There was no evidence either of the parents was wrapped up in anything dangerous. They appeared to be the picture-perfect family. A few people told us Richard could be pretty hard on the kids—"

"Abusive?" Laurie asked.

"No," she said. "Again, the Chief was sure Simon was lying about that one incident. Both the dogwalker and the caretaker told us that Richard could be demanding of the children. Controlling. But again, if anything, that gave the sons a motive for removing their father from the picture."

"But why kill their mother?" Ryan asked.

"To get their inheritance. Or, in my opinion, if they did it—and I *do* think they did it—they didn't expect their mother to be home. Shooting her may have been an accident, or the shooter panicked when she walked in on the murder of the father."

It was the exact scenario Ethan had floated when he was implicating Simon.

"Part of what we do on our show," Laurie said, "is cast a wide net and ask whether there might be someone out there the police never looked at."

"Like I said, we had no alternative suspects."

"With the benefit of hindsight, Roberta, if you absolutely *had* to name someone you're curious about, who would it be?"

Her expression was blank, but then she closed her eyes tightly, trying to remember.

"Perhaps someone else with a motive other than Simon and Ethan?" Laurie prompted.

When Roberta opened her eyes again, she seemed to have found clarity. "The girlfriend's father," she said.

"Simon's girlfriend, Michelle Ward? Her father, Walter, was Richard's law partner. He and Betsy took Frankie in after the murders. They were practically family—so close they had keys to each other's houses. That kind of thing."

Roberta was shaking her head. "No, the other girlfriend. The local girl."

"Annabeth? Her maiden name was Connolly."

"That's the one," Roberta said, snapping her fingers. "Her father owned the hardware store in town. It was called Jimmy's. Rumor was, he was going into foreclosure. A chain store down the road was too much competition. But a couple years after the murders, the store got a big makeover. A lot of high-end inventory. The new rumor was that Annabeth had moved to Boston and was engaged to Ethan. Everyone assumed he'd bailed her father out. I suppose it's possible he saw Ethan as his daughter's gravy train and didn't want Richard Harrington standing in the way."

"Did you raise that possibility with the Chief at the time?"

"I didn't. It seemed too far-fetched."

"You didn't even mention it?" Laurie asked.

"No, because here's the thing: Jimmy Connolly was one of Chief Collins's closest friends."

# Chapter 24

Ryan spoke first once they were in the backseat of the SUV. "If you wanted a new piece of information to prove yourself to Ethan, I'd say you found it."

"Except the new information points to his father-in-law. I don't think he or Annabeth is going to be pleased by that."

"So don't tell them."

She chewed her lip, saying nothing.

"Laurie," he said, "you can't. You're the one who was telling me how special your show is. You search for the truth, no matter what. Your job isn't to please the family."

She nodded, knowing he was right. "Can I admit how annoying it is that you of all people are reminding me of this?"

"You might find this shocking," he said dryly, "but you're not the first person I've annoyed in my lifetime."

She shared a small laugh with him. "We did get more than just the information about Annabeth's father," she said.

"*We?*" he said, arching a brow.

"Take what you can while you can, Nichols. Roberta admitted the department had tunnel vision. That the Chief was rushing the investigation to appease the locals. They never dug into Richard's work at his law firm. And importantly, it's clear they took Howard Carver at his word about spotting one of the twins in the parking lot. Eyewitness identifications can be very unreliable."

"What about the hidden camera?" Ryan asked.

"I don't think we can tell Ethan or Simon about that yet. Wait until production to see how they respond." She would never promise a participant in her show to share all the evidence with them or it would undermine the entire purpose of the re-investigation. "Do you think we have enough to convince him?"

"There's only one way to find out," Ryan said, glancing at the phone in her hand.

By the time Joey was crossing the canal that connected the Great Peconic and Shinnecock Bays, she had the answer. Ethan Harrington was on board.

# Chapter 25

Frankie realized her shoulders were hunched nearly to her ears as she leaned forward to stabilize her balance against the freezing headwinds. She forced herself to lower them and to "let the cold in," as her mother used to coach her when Frankie would complain about the winter weather as a child. For reasons she would never understand, it worked. Frankie felt a few degrees warmer already.

For lunch she had walked from the storage facility to the closest restaurant she could find online, a diner half a mile down the road. She had a grilled cheese sandwich and tomato soup and was ready to get back to work.

Opening the storage unit door, the sight of the cramped space struck her anew—towers of stacked boxes, each one unmarked, creating a maze that barely allowed room to navigate. Even though she was on her second day of work at the storage unit, she felt as if she had barely made a dent. She had seriously underestimated the task she'd taken on. She had been so determined to sort through her parents' belongings on her own, but now that she was doing it, a deep sense of loneliness was settling over her.

*It shouldn't be this way*, she thought. *My parents should still be here. My brothers should be speaking to each other. I shouldn't have to face this alone.*

The previous night over dinner, she had asked Betsy and Walter once again if they had reservations about *Under Suspicion*. It wasn't until she revealed that Dennis had told her as much that Betsy finally admitted they'd prefer if she "left well enough alone."

She could still hear Betsy's voice. *You already lost your parents. Do you really want to lose your brothers, too?* So, in short, despite Betsy's insistence all these years that her brothers must be innocent, part of her clearly feared they were not.

Determined to press on, Frankie continued her meticulous search, one box at a time. She had created enough open space to form three piles: keep, trash, and donate. So far, almost everything was in the third pile, but her "keep" collection had been worth the work already. A small box filled with photographs, including her parents' wedding album, had captured her attention for nearly an hour before she realized how much time had passed and forced herself to set it aside to study further at home. Her mother's perfectly intact English tea set with a beautiful butterfly motif. Her grandfather's antique pipe, which her father had displayed proudly on the desk of his home office, even though he never smoked.

Frankie inhaled audibly as she opened a new box to discover a collection of familiar books. She immediately recognized them as the ones that used to live on the lowest shelf of the huge bookcase that had lined one full wall of their den. Her mother had called it the Frankie Section of their home library.

She leafed through the titles, stopping when she came to the one she'd been hoping to find, *From the Mixed-Up Files of Mrs. Basil E. Frankweiler* by E. L. Konigsburg. Her mother had given this to her in the third grade, after it had become clear that Frankie would be the other avid reader in the family. The title alone had captured her attention. Who was this woman with the funny name and why did she have mixed up files? She became obsessed with the book, re-reading it between other stories, dreaming of a world where she, like Claudia Kincaid, could live in plain sight at the Metropolitan Museum of Art and eventually untangle an age-old mystery. She eventually moved on to other books and authors, but she would always treasure this gift from her mother and the memories of them reading it together.

As she flipped through the pages, something slipped out and

tumbled onto her lap. A small black disk—square, marked with the letters *MicroSD*.

She reached for her phone on the top of an adjacent box before remembering she couldn't get a signal inside the storage unit. Pulling on her coat to step outside, her mind raced with possibilities as she typed *MicroSD* into Google.

It was a memory card.

According to the web, they were typically used for storage in smartphones, cameras, gaming consoles, and other devices. Why in the world was a memory card tucked inside one of her old books?

She had no idea how to take a black plastic disk and figure out what was stored on it. She began to call home, but Walter and Betsy were complete Luddites when it came to technology.

Ethan. He would know. He was an expert about all things digital.

Disappointment was settling in as the fourth ring ended and the call went to voicemail. She was leaving a message when a new call came into her phone.

"Ethan—" she said, not giving him a chance to say hello before telling him where she was and what she had found. He was in the middle of a job but told her to meet him at his house right away.

As Frankie was ordering an Uber, she wondered if she had made a mistake turning to Ethan. What if there was something on the card that incriminated him? She shook the thought from her head. She hadn't even hesitated to call him, and that had to mean something. In her heart, she could not bring herself to believe that either one of her brothers was a murderer.

*Please, God, let this be the evidence we need to be a family again.*

# Chapter 26

Any regrets Laurie had about leaving the office for an impromptu lunch date with Charlotte were immediately squelched when she stepped inside Oceana. Graceful and elegant, the white-and-blue dining room was designed to resemble a luxury ocean liner, complete with floor-to-ceiling windows, custom brass chandeliers, and gleaming walnut accents. She had tried to tell her friend that she had far too much work to meet her for lunch, but then Charlotte countered with the offer of one of Laurie's favorite midtown restaurants and the promise that she had good news to share.

The hostess escorted her to a banquette in the back corner, where she found Charlotte waiting, a martini in hand and a raw bar tower centered on the table. "I took the liberty of getting us something to start with since I know you're on the clock," Charlotte said, standing to give Laurie a hug.

"Didn't I tell you? My doctor says I have a major seafood allergy."

Charlotte's face fell as she pondered the generous display of oysters, clams, shrimp, and lobster.

"Oh no," Laurie said, giving her friend a nudge. "I'm just kidding, Charlotte!"

Charlotte lifted an oyster with two fingers and handed it to Laurie. "That was mean, Moran."

Laurie took a sip of the iced tea that had already been waiting for her. "I'd rather have one of those," she said, eyeing Charlotte's martini.

"You're the one with the busy day at work. I should be running on fumes after that trip, but I'm completely amped."

"You said you had good news." Laurie asked if that meant that Charlotte's meeting with the big pop star had gone well, whispering the celebrity's name in case other diners could overhear.

"The meeting turned into two full days at her house in South Beach. She sleeps until two in the afternoon and stays up until four in the morning, which means I slept on the plane ride home. But I left with a signed licensing agreement contingent on design approval. Her line should be out in time for this year's Black Friday. It's going to be huge."

Laurie held up her glass for a quick toast. "My best friend the mogul. You're not going to replace me with A-list celebrities, are you?"

"Nobody replaces Laurie Moran."

"Not yet. Ryan might be trying, though." She gave Charlotte the latest news about Ryan's moves at work and the previous day's confession that he felt stalled at Fisher Blake.

Charlotte's eyes narrowed with suspicion. "I'd be careful with that one," she said. "He's pulled this stunt with you before. Wasn't he suddenly playing nice in the sandbox with you last year after an ex-girlfriend dressed him down? She said he was born on third base and went through life believing he'd hit a triple."

"I almost forgot about that." Charlotte's memory for detail was always impressive.

"And he's back to his old ways already. You called him out on it, so he backed off for half a minute. It won't last."

Laurie made a mental note of her friend's advice but then decided to pick Charlotte's brain about something else instead. "How common was it ten years ago to have a hidden camera in the house?"

"Like a nanny cam? I don't have kids so I would never have one, but don't parents get them for peace of mind?"

"I never did." She told Charlotte about the hidden camera the Harbor Bay police had found inside a wall clock in the Harringtons' hallway, with the memory card removed.

"It sounds like whichever brother pulled the trigger also pulled the memory card," Charlotte said.

"That's what the police assumed, too. But it's possible the Harringtons bought it when the kids were younger, and they just weren't using it anymore. I'd like to ask Frankie if she remembers anything about it, but I don't want Simon and Ethan to know that I know about the camera yet."

"You think she'd tell them?"

Laurie nodded. "I can tell she really loves them and wants to believe they're innocent."

"I get the sense you want to believe that, too."

"Maybe." It wasn't the first time that Laurie had wondered if her desire for a happy ending might be interfering with her judgment.

Her gut was telling her that the hidden camera wasn't simply an overlooked detail. It was an important piece of the puzzle. She just needed to figure out where it fit.

The waiter was delivering their entrées when Laurie's cell phone buzzed on the banquette. Recognizing the Boston area code, she told Charlotte she had to take the call and then found a quiet spot away from the table before answering. "This is Laurie."

"Laurie, this is Dennis Ward, Michelle's brother. We met in Boston at my firm."

Laurie said that of course she remembered.

"Frankie told me she signed her participation agreement. Her brothers did, too."

"Yes, she said you reviewed it for her, so thank you for that."

"I really don't want to interfere," Dennis said, "but my parents are getting older, and I worry this is stressful for them. And Frankie is dead set on plowing ahead, but she's still a kid. This is really about Ethan and Simon, but it's affecting my family, too. I feel stuck in the middle."

"Why would this be hard on your parents?"

"Sarah and my mother were like sisters. Mom was devastated after the murders. And as much as she would want the killer to be punished, she can't bring herself to suspect Ethan or Simon. She has managed to convince herself all these years that they're innocent."

"If they aren't, I would think she'd want to know the truth." Something about Dennis's explanation didn't add up. She remembered him saying in Boston that he didn't want to attract negative attention to his law firm. "Is this perhaps about your law practice?"

"Of course not." His denial seemed overly adamant.

"Whatever became of Howard Carver, your father's other former partner? When Michelle mentioned him at your office, I got the impression there was some awkwardness there."

"See? This is the kind of thing I'm worried about. I watched a couple episodes of your show. You raise a bunch of red herrings to point fingers at other people. My parents don't need that kind of stress in their lives."

"And neither do you?" she asked.

"I told you, this is about my parents. I feel like I'm the only one looking out for their interests."

"If I'm not mistaken, it was actually your sister who initially suggested this, so are you saying Michelle's not looking out for them? I don't know why any of this should bother you—unless, as I mentioned, it has something to do with the law firm."

"Wow, you're back on that again? Howard retired. It's not complicated. Maybe my father and I just don't want the case in the news again. The Harrington name is still on our practice."

So where he began with supposed concerns about his mother, Dennis was now conceding he was worried about the firm's reputation.

"I appreciate the call, Dennis, and I'll be mindful of your misgivings, but your sister, Frankie, and her brothers have made their decision."

The line fell silent for a moment as he must have realized that Laurie was not going to back down.

"I have this horrible feeling that opening the door to the past is going to lead somewhere really bad. I hope you know what you're doing."

As soon as the call ended, she pulled up Ryan's number. He answered almost immediately.

"You still interested in getting more involved behind the scenes?" she asked.

"Yes, indeedy."

"See what you can find on what a retired Boston lawyer named Howard Carver was up to about ten years ago."

# Chapter 27

"Is it crazy that I'm afraid to watch this?" Frankie clasped her hands together to keep them from trembling.

She had been right about Ethan. He immediately identified the memory card and had whatever doodad was required to play it. Frankie and Annabeth watched as Ethan, seated between them at the kitchen table, inserted the thin black square into a memory card reader connected to his laptop.

"Don't think like that," Annabeth said. "It's probably filled with old baby pictures your mother didn't want to lose."

The room fell into a hush as Ethan clicked on the screen to begin viewing. A person's torso initially blocked the lens's view of the room. Within seconds, her mother's face appeared. She was bending forward to look directly into the camera. Frankie recognized their old Boston living room in the background. Given the vantage point, the camera must have been located somewhere on the fireplace mantel.

"This is memory card two of two in the Boston house," her mother said. "Once again, this is a motion-activated camera hidden inside a picture frame."

Frankie forced herself to shift her attention from the video to Ethan, who was staring intently at the screen. When he turned to catch her gaze, his eyes were filled with fear and confusion.

From what Frankie could remember of their childhood, they rarely spent time in the living room. They usually used a side door from the garage into a mudroom to go in and out, and typically spent their time in either the family room or the kitchen. She thought of the living room as the formal seating area they used for company or when her parents wanted to read quietly or have an aperitif alone while the kids were being noisy.

They watched as younger versions of themselves and their family walked through the living room at various moments, a time-and-date stamp at the bottom of the video tracking their movements, beginning in April—nearly a decade ago, about seven weeks before her parents were killed.

"Why would Mom do this?" she asked.

Ethan shook his head as he pressed a double arrow on his computer screen to play the video at a faster speed. He suddenly paused when they reached a scene of their mother entering the living room, their father trailing close behind. This time, her parents didn't walk out the front door or head up the stairs. They stayed in the living room.

It was as if her mother had intentionally positioned them directly in front of the camera.

Ethan turned up the volume on his laptop.

"The more you try to drive him away from her, the more dead set he'll be. Keep it up, and they'll end up married before graduation."

It happened so quickly. Frankie had turned her head for just one second—to confirm that Ethan and Annabeth realized that her parents were talking about them. Annabeth suddenly gasped, her hand moving to cover her mouth.

When Frankie looked again at the screen, her father's hands were gripped tightly around her mother's arms. Her mother let out a stunned scream, but her father yelled over her. "How dare you speak to me that way?!"

Frankie closed her eyes and then forced herself to open them again. Her father's anger escalated from there. So did his physical violence. His face was red, his expression twisted with rage.

The words he was speaking to Frankie's mother—to his own wife—were hateful. Her mother tried to raise her hands to protect herself, but her attempts only seemed to incense him further.

The assault ended only once her mother was curled into a ball on the floor. Her father walked away, clearly unaware of the camera that had captured every second of his ire. Frankie felt a pain in her chest as she watched her mother cry alone, the sound of her father's angry footsteps receding up the stairs.

After a minute, the video briefly fell to black. The camera had stopped detecting motion. When the video began again, the timeline had jumped six minutes. Her mother rose unsteadily from the floor and moved to the sofa, looking directly into the camera until her gaze shifted at the sound of footsteps getting closer.

Her father was back. Her mother flinched slightly as he sat beside her, reaching gently for her hand.

"I'm sorry, Sarah." Her mother allowed him to hold her hand but said nothing as she stared down at her lap. "You know how much pressure I've been under at work. We could lose everything. We could even be disbarred. I just need the family to be on my side for once. Even Simon—pulling this stunt at school? Asking for money to buy his way out of the problem? It's not like him. And I swear, Ethan's only seeing this girl to cement his place as the family rebel. I'm sorry, what did you say?"

Frankie had seen her mother's lips move, but, like her father, she hadn't been able to make out the words. When her mother spoke again, her voice was low but audible. "That was the point I was trying to make. The best way to find out how Ethan actually feels about Annabeth is to stop telling him what to do."

"But it's the way you said it, Sarah. You know how I get when you undermine me with the kids. I'm sorry, but you have to admit you were pushing my buttons."

Frankie's heart was pounding against her chest. She had never seen her father act like this. Tears formed in her eyes as she listened to her mother mutter an apology. She noticed that Ethan's fists were clenched on either side of his laptop, his knuckles turning white.

"You forgive me?" her father asked, wrapping an arm around her mother's shoulder.

Her mother nodded.

"I just need to get through this crisis at work, and everything will be better. You understand, right? You can't leave."

"Of course not," Frankie's mother said. "Until death do us part."

She looked directly into the camera before following their father from the room.

# Chapter 28

Laurie stepped back, marker in hand, admiring her handiwork on the sprawling whiteboard in her office. Jerry and Grace were gathered at the nearby conference table.

Jerry began a round of applause, which Grace quickly joined, declaring, "Your plans are looking good, Coach." They had begun referring to these whiteboard sessions as their "locker room meetings," with Laurie serving as the team's head coach.

"I can't remember a special where we've moved so quickly," Laurie said.

"Am I crazy to think we're actually ready to start filming?" Jerry asked.

He was right. Jerry, always the meticulous researcher, had successfully located both Jenna Merrick, the dog walker who had stumbled into the tragic scene at the Harringtons' house the night of the party, and Peter Bennett, the property's caretaker. According to Jerry, they both spoke fondly of the Harrington family, especially Sarah, and said they'd be happy to sign the production agreements Jerry forwarded to them.

And Jerry wasn't the only one showing an impressive display of initiative in their planning. "I took the liberty of contacting the Harbor Yacht Club to check their policies on allowing access for filming," Grace said. "There's a fee—of course—and some paperwork and insurance requirements involved. I sent it all to in-house counsel for review. They're also in the process of reviewing our agreement to film at the Harringtons' house. The owners actually live in New York and only use the house in the summer, so their timing is flexible."

Laurie couldn't help but marvel at how valuable these two had become to *Under Suspicion.* Jerry had started at Fisher Blake as an intern after majoring in media arts, back when he used to hide his long, lanky body beneath turtlenecks, cardigan sweaters, and baggy pants. It took only three years for him to work his way up to assistant producer, and he now had the confidence to wear outfits almost as flashy as Grace's.

As for Grace, she had always had tenacity and good instincts, but she had made it clear to Laurie the previous year that she was more ambitious about her career than Laurie had initially understood. After that conversation, Laurie had given her a well-deserved raise, and she noticed since then that Grace was finding ways to dig into their work above and beyond as Laurie's assistant.

It turned out that Grace was not finished. "I also found the perfect place for us to stay while we're filming at the Cape." She slid her phone across the conference table toward Jerry. "It's a big house right by the water. And since it's offseason, it's a lot cheaper than getting us all rooms at a hotel. It will be like a big slumber party."

Jerry was scrolling though the listing. "Nice house, but, Grace, don't you remember the last time we rented a house to film? I ended up in a coma." When Jerry had been badly assaulted, Laurie had wondered if the entire production was cursed.

Grace covered her mouth with one hand. "Oh my gosh, I didn't mean to traumatize you—"

"Grace, I'm only kidding. The house wasn't the one who beat me up. But just in case, I expect you to be my bodyguard during this prolonged slumber party."

They were interrupted by a tap on the open door. "We're having a slumber party?" Ryan asked, making his way to the conference table with a flirtatious grin. At least this time he had knocked.

Grace smiled broadly and batted her eyes. "In your dreams, Nichols."

He dropped a thin stack of documents onto the table and pressed his palms against his heart. "You crush me on a daily basis, Miss Garcia."

"Do I have to call HR on you two?" Laurie said. "We were just going over production plans. We've contacted all the obvious subjects except for Howard Carver. Did you find anything on him?"

"I think so, and I'm pretty sure you were right about there being something hinky with his departure from the law firm. He's not just retired. He's no longer a member of the bar."

"Is that unusual?" Jerry asked.

"In my opinion it is," Ryan said. "You never know when you'll need that word 'esquire' after your name. It's a lot easier to keep paying the bar renewal dues than trying to get your bar membership back after giving it up—unless of course, the lawyer didn't have a choice."

Laurie continued the thought. "You think he was disbarred?"

"I called the state bar association and asked to speak to one of the administrators. Gave her the full Ryan Nichols charm offensive," he added, giving Grace an amused glance.

"And she served you with a restraining order?"

"No," he chuckled. "But she didn't fall in love either. Said she's a fan of our show but couldn't tell me much. Just that there was no record that Howard was ever formally disciplined."

"Any complaints?" Laurie asked.

"Apparently complaints are confidential unless it leads to formal action. But there's something else. I looked up his litigation history—the online legal research sites have databases for that. Most settlements are sealed, but certain kinds of lawsuits come with reporting requirements—ones against governmental entities or class actions, for example. He had a two-year window where he filed an awful lot of lawsuits—almost all of them leading to pretty quick settlements. It's an unusual amount of litigation activity for such a small firm, and the lawsuits had only his name signed to them, not Richard Harrington or Walter Ward. By contrast, those two were barely in the database."

"I got the impression they don't do a lot of trials," Laurie said. "Frankie mentioned they mostly did transactional work."

"Well, not Howard. He was filing lawsuits left and right. But here's the thing. It was only for that two-year period." He flipped to a page in the stack of papers that showed the list of lawsuit settlements. "Two final settlements in March, then a sudden stop. He resigned from the bar on June 20th."

Laurie contemplated the implications. "Only three weeks after the Harringtons were killed."

"I noticed that, too," Ryan said. "But is it connected or are we down a rabbit hole?"

"Funny you should say that." She used her marker to point to the spot on the whiteboard that read *Rabbit Holes?* She added the words "Howard's retirement" beneath "Harbor Bay nanny cam" and "*This Family is a Lie* vandalism."

"Anything else?" she asked.

"I tracked down his last known address and phone number," Ryan said, handing her a different sheet of paper. "Obviously I didn't call him. Don't want to overstep my boundaries."

She couldn't tell if the comment was sincere or a veiled barb, but her phone buzzed against the conference table before she could explore the thought any further. It was Frankie.

When Laurie answered, Frankie's words were tumbling out so quickly, Laurie barely had time to say hello. Something about a camera and a terrible fight.

"Can you slow down, Frankie? Are you saying you found camera footage?" Roberta had said that the police department never revealed that a hidden camera had been found inside a wall clock at the Harringtons' beach house.

"Yes. A memory card tucked inside a book in the storage unit.

My mother had some kind of nanny cam on the mantel in our living room in Boston. It's horrible, Laurie. My father was abusing her, and it wasn't the first time. Ethan's emailing you the video clip right now. I'm going to put you on speaker. We're here with Annabeth."

Without hanging up, Laurie opened the new message on her laptop and hit play.

# Chapter 29

They sat in stunned silence in Laurie's office as the video ended, the dark reality of the situation settling over them. Frankie was right. It obviously wasn't the first time that Richard Harrington had abused his wife. *You know how I get. You pushed my buttons. Everything will be better. You can't leave.* It had happened before, and yet he found ways to blame her and excuse himself.

"I'm sorry," Laurie said. "That was hard even for me to watch. I can't imagine how the two of you must feel."

"I'm just so confused," Frankie said. "I never saw him act that way."

Once Laurie had asked whether it was okay to put the call on speaker phone at her end, she briefly introduced Jerry, Grace, and Ryan, then said, "Your mother seemed to know that the camera was there."

Ethan spoke for the first time. "She definitely did. I only sent you that one clip. She introduced the video by stating where the camera was hidden and that it was the second memory card at the Boston house."

Laurie nodded, taking in the information. So it had to also have been Sarah who installed the wall clock camera at the beach house. She was about to tell them about that camera too and then stopped, reminding herself they weren't partners or clients. They were witnesses in her investigation.

"Your father says at the end that she can't leave him. Did your parents ever talk about getting divorced?"

"Never," Ethan replied. "You have to understand: Appearances were everything to my parents, especially my father. You can't hold yourself out as the perfect family if you get divorced."

She could hear the bitterness in his voice.

"Ethan, you told me before you didn't believe Simon's account of your father getting physical with him when he found out that he paid his friend Tom to write his term paper. Does this change anything?" she asked.

"Maybe? Or maybe Simon knew about the abuse and that was part of the reason he snapped. I've always thought that he didn't expect Mom to be at the house that night."

"Have you shown this to anyone else?" Laurie asked.

"We watched it first," Frankie said. "Then I sent it to Simon and to the Wards to see if they knew anything about it. We're all in complete shock. I gave it to you because it feels important, but we can't figure out whether it's even connected to our parents' murders. Maybe we're too close to it."

Laurie couldn't see an obvious nexus either, and so far no one else around the table had any suggestions.

"Is that the only memory card you found?" Laurie asked.

"So far, but I've barely made a dent in the storage unit. Mom said it was the second one, so that means there's at least one more."

"And to your knowledge, she didn't have a hidden camera at the beach house?" Laurie asked, still not revealing the information she'd obtained from the former deputy chief.

Frankie and Ethan both said they knew nothing about hidden cameras at either property until today.

"Okay, keep looking," Laurie said. "And thanks for keeping me in the loop. I know it must be hard."

"Really hard," Frankie said, her voice cracking. "I was actually thinking that maybe the Wards were right about leaving things be. This is so much, so fast. It's a little overwhelming."

A worried expression crossed Ryan's face.

"Are you changing your mind?" she asked as Ryan began to shake his head frantically.

"No. In fact, it was Ethan who said this video convinced him even more that we need to stop avoiding whatever other secrets may have been hiding behind the image of our supposedly perfect family. Warts and all, maybe we'll finally get the truth."

"And I hope we can get that for you too."

As she ended the call, Laurie noticed Brett lingering at the entrance to her office. "You asked the girl whether she was *changing her mind*? What were you thinking?"

Sometimes she wondered if he had the offices bugged so he could show up at the worst possible moment.

"I tried to stop her," Ryan said.

Grace and Jerry both glared across the table at Ryan. So much for teamwork.

"She's a kid, Brett. And a vulnerable one at that."

"I'm sorry," he said sarcastically. "I was under the impression she was about to be a very wealthy twenty-two-year-old. That's an adult as far as I'm concerned. I stopped by to see if you had an ETA on production."

She remembered Jerry's earlier question during the locker room meeting. *Am I crazy to think we're actually ready to start filming?*

She took another look at her whiteboard, where she would need to add Richard Harrington's violent streak to the list of rabbit holes that might or might not be related to the murders. If it were up to her, she'd spend weeks nailing down every loose end before turning on cameras, but Brett had made it clear that very little remained up to her.

"We're all set to go," she announced. "Let's start packing."

Brett clasped his hands together in satisfaction. "Good to hear it. Start filming before the family gets cold feet. We need a blockbuster."

# Chapter 30

Jerry was inspecting the Harbor Bay rental house as if he were a buyer on the verge of making a multimillion-dollar offer. "I could live here for the rest of my life," he exclaimed. "Grace, I didn't think this place could possibly live up to the photos online, but it's even better."

Laurie decided Jerry and Grace deserved a few more minutes to marvel over the luxury coastal real estate before pulling them back into work mode. They had been grinding away nonstop for the last three days to make it possible to begin filming in record time. And their housing for the shoot was admittedly glorious, perched high on a bluff, with a wraparound porch and panoramic views of the bay.

Bathed in the glow of the late afternoon sun, Grace was gazing out the window toward the stairs behind the house leading to the beach below. "Why couldn't we have filmed this episode four months from now? We could do our brainstorming sessions while we sunbathed on the sand."

Laurie could only imagine the elaborate beach apparel Grace and Jerry would have packed for the occasion. "If we waited four months, the two of you would be working an entirely different investigation: my murder at the hands of Brett Young."

While Grace and Jerry moved on to admiring the gourmet kitchen, Laurie was distracted by a new message on the group thread among her, Tim, and her father. She had texted them first thing after landing at the airport to make sure the walk from school had gone smoothly.

*All good here*, her father replied. *Tim's doing his homework. Planning on TV night once Alex gets home. And, yes, it's that show you don't like.*

They had fallen into a rhythm of bingeing shows as a family, promising not to watch new episodes unless they did so together. *Bosch* was their longstanding favorite. Tim shared his grandfather's fascination with the procedural ins and outs of policing, and sometimes Laurie wondered if he might follow his footsteps into law enforcement. But Tim's most recent addiction had been for a distressing dystopian saga that was too dark even for Laurie. She happily gave them her blessing to binge without her.

The next message was from Tim. *Send photos of your new beach mansion.*

Oh, how she wished he were here with her and his Auntie Grace and Uncle Jerry. Ramon had offered to make the trip to Harbor Bay so Laurie could bring Tim with her. The house was large enough to accommodate all of them, and Ramon had even volunteered to serve as the home chef for the entire crew. Laurie had been tempted, but Tim was getting too old to pull from school for days at a time, and now that he also had Alex and Ramon in his life, she didn't need to lean so hard on her father when she traveled for work. She could trust three of the best men she had ever known to hold down the fort in her absence.

But she still missed her son like crazy. She was determined to keep this shoot on schedule. Tim's birthday was in seven days.

A smile lingered on her face as she typed her reply. *Turn your phone off per the rules. I'll trade you fancy house photos for your finished homework.*

Jerry and Grace, still enamored with the elaborate kitchen, were dreaming of all the meals that Ramon could have cooked had he joined them.

"I never should have told you two about his offer," Laurie said.

"We could totally cook dinner ourselves, though," Grace said, looking to Jerry for confirmation.

"Us?" Jerry said incredulously. "Cooking? Calling Lucy and Ethel at the chocolate factory."

"Who are Lucy and Ethel?" Grace asked.

Even though Jerry was only one year older, Grace loved to tease him for being such an old soul.

Ryan suddenly appeared in the kitchen. "I happen to be an amazing chef," he said nonchalantly.

"Do you mean that?" Grace asked. "Or is this part of the whole I'm-Ryan-Nichols-so-I'm-amazing-at-everything act?"

Laurie admired the way Grace never let Ryan get under her skin, and she could see that Ryan did, too.

"Scout's honor," he said, holding up three fingers. "Northern Italian is my go-to, but I'm getting there with French cuisine. I'm almost done working my way through the entire Julia Child cookbook."

Laurie noticed Grace give Jerry a worried look. How many times had Grace said she'd love to date a man who could cook? That was enough banter for now.

"I hate to be the buzzkill," Laurie said, "but we're more likely to be eating takeout pizza than whipping up any Michelin star meals. Finish unpacking and then meet in the living room in twenty minutes?"

Grace and Jerry headed up to their rooms, but Ryan lingered behind with Laurie.

"Mission already accomplished. I don't do anything on a trip until I unpack," he explained.

She had the same compulsive habit. "Great. You can help me with these whiteboards."

She had asked Grace to have two mobile whiteboards delivered to the house from an office supply store. As they each began to tackle one box, Ryan said, "You know you can storyboard on a computer, don't you? Then cast it onto the screen of your choice when you want to share it with other people."

Laurie would be turning forty soon and did not need another

reminder that she was already viewed as past her prime by some people. "What you *can* do isn't necessarily what you *should* do. I read books made of paper, and I write on whiteboards. Call me old school."

"It wasn't a criticism," he said, avoiding her gaze as he scanned the assembly instructions. "Just a suggestion."

Laurie was already popping one of her board's casters into place. "It's honestly hard to tell the difference with you sometimes."

He nodded but said nothing.

She was almost done with her handiwork but wanted to say one more thing while she had Ryan to herself. "Grace is tough as nails but she's also hopelessly romantic. Leave her out of whatever games you're playing."

The Allen wrench in his hand suddenly stopped turning. "I'm not playing games. I like her. But she thinks I'm a jerk, because . . . well, maybe I am. Maybe I was raised to be the scorpion."

For the second time this week, Ryan was admitting his own faults. She hadn't yet formed a reply when he tilted his whiteboard upright.

"Ha, I win!" he declared. "Caught you off guard."

She could tell from his facial expression that he was looking for a change in subject matter. "You got me," she said, handing him a marker. "Now let's see how fast we can transfer our notes, old school style."

# Chapter 31

By the time Jerry and Grace joined them downstairs, Laurie and Ryan had transformed the new whiteboards into an exact replica of the plans they'd been working from in New York.

"We have local contact information for everyone, right?" Laurie asked.

Jerry and Grace both nodded. After the murders, the Harringtons' closest friends, Betsy and Walter Ward, had found themselves spending less and less time on the Cape, until a local real estate agent convinced them to treat the property as an investment rental. Their house was vacant during the offseason, so they would be staying there during the shoot, along with Simon, Michelle, and Frankie. Meanwhile, Ethan and Annabeth were staying with Annabeth's parents.

"Did the storage unit move go okay?" Jerry asked.

Given Frankie's discovery of the hidden camera footage, Laurie had not wanted to halt her progress of sorting through her family's belongings in Boston. Frankie had taken Laurie up on her offer to pay to have everything moved temporarily to a storage facility off Route 6 so it would be available while they worked on the production. She had sounded especially relieved when Laurie said that she and her team could provide extra hands for the work if it was not too intrusive.

"All good. The movers met Frankie there this morning. She's already back at work on it and said she'd call if she found anything interesting."

It did not take Laurie's team long to review the flow of the scenes they had mapped out. Usually, by the time they filmed, Laurie had a gut feeling about where the evidence was likely to lead. But because Brett had rushed them into production, she now had more unanswered questions than when Frankie first called her only a week earlier.

It was impossible to know what, if any, fresh information they might glean from the new interviews, but they at least had the physical locations and production agreements in place.

"I want to make sure we have a clear list of suspects," Laurie said. "First up, of course, is the predominant theory: the twins planned this together. One was the shooter while one remained at the party."

Jerry chimed in next. "Or, it's like the twins say. Either Simon or Ethan acted alone, but we don't know which."

Laurie had assumed when she first got involved in the case that those would be the only theories worth exploring, but she was no longer willing to confine the list of suspects to Simon and Ethan. She added two other names to the board: Richard Harrington's other law partner, Howard Carver, and Annabeth's father, Jimmy Connolly.

"Have you tried calling Howard again?" Jerry asked.

"Too many times to count," Laurie said. "Straight to voicemail, on repeat. I'm pretty sure he blocked me."

Of everyone she had contacted about the case, Howard Carver had been the only person to refuse to speak to her. Without even mentioning the law firm, Laurie had told Howard that *Under Suspicion* was reinvestigating the Harringtons' murders and wanted to discuss what he had seen at the yacht club the night of the graduation party. He declared that he "wasn't interested," abruptly hung up, and had not answered any of Laurie's calls since.

The violence Richard Harrington unleashed upon Sarah in the video Frankie had found in the storage unit had been a landmine, and they still did not know how the abuse related to the couple's murder. But the video had also provided concrete proof that Richard had been deeply disturbed by something going on at work.

Laurie spelled out the evidence suggesting that the *something* had to do with Howard Carver. "When Richard was so furious with Sarah in that video, he said they could lose everything. That *we*—plural—could even be disbarred, meaning the problem involved at least one other lawyer. Michelle and Dennis were both uncomfortable when I asked about Howard, and that was before Ryan found the flurry of settlements Howard handled before the Harringtons were killed and he suddenly retired from the bar. We definitely need to lock this down, especially since Howard is the witness who supposedly saw one of the twins by the Range Rover."

If Laurie had read Michelle and Dennis correctly, they both knew the circumstances surrounding Howard's retirement, which meant Simon and Walter probably did, too.

It had been Ryan who persuaded Laurie to wait until cameras were rolling to press any of them further on the subject. If Richard had really been worried about the risk of being disbarred, the matter had been serious. She didn't want to risk losing their participation if they realized the questions would be moving in that direction.

Grace was tapping her pen against a notepad. "What about that kid who bribed Simon about writing his term paper? Should he be on the list of possible suspects?"

"Tom Keenan," Laurie said. She realized she had not told them that she'd eliminated Keenan from consideration shortly after Simon first told her about the blackmail attempt. Keenan had been easy to locate. He was a history teacher now at a private boarding school in New Hampshire, and Laurie had confirmed for herself that he was in Nashville when the Harringtons were killed. "He still had the travel receipts and everything."

Jerry squinted skeptically. "After a decade? Maybe I'm getting jaded, but that almost seems suspicious."

"He said he was so freaked out when the police contacted him," Laurie said, "he vowed to retain the evidence forever in case the subject ever came up again. He also swore up and down that he never blackmailed Simon, which we can't confirm one way or the other without tracing anonymous emails from ten years ago. Regardless, he's definitely not our shooter."

Laurie was about to move on to the subject of Annabeth's father but realized that something about Tom Keenan was still nagging at her.

"I know that look," Grace said. "Her wheels are turning."

Laurie held up a finger, buying time while she tried to put her thoughts together. "When I spoke with Tom, I promised to keep it completely off the record if he'd admit he was the one who sent those emails to Simon, but he insisted he knew nothing about it. At the time, I assumed that a reputable teacher at an elite school didn't want to admit he'd done something so underhanded as a student."

"And now?" Jerry asked.

"We know a lot more about the Harrington family than we used to. Everyone said they were so perfect. Both brothers have said it repeatedly—Richard and Sarah cared about appearances. But no family is perfect. Simon was under so much pressure that he cheated at school, and then his father assaulted him when he found out. We also know that Richard was violent toward his wife—so much so that Sarah hid cameras in both houses, probably so she could prove that this picture-perfect father was abusing her and keeping her from leaving the marriage."

"But what does that have to do with Tom Keenan and the blackmail?" Grace asked.

Laurie looked again at the whiteboards and found the list of subjects they were calling "rabbit holes." She circled five words as she read them aloud. *This Family is a Lie.*

"After the murders, Simon told the police about this spray-paint incident. The former deputy chief admitted to Ryan and me that the police never bothered to ask whether there might be a connection."

She began checking off other topics on the board. Howard Carver's retirement. The hidden nanny cams. Richard's violence.

"Secrets," she said. "The image of the perfect family was actually a perfect facade for a mountain of secrets."

Ryan, who had been silent until now, was staring at her, expressionless.

"Do you see it?" she asked.

He nodded. "The family *was* a lie. And whoever left that graffiti knew it."

"Exactly. This whole time, we've had a list of all these loose ends, not knowing which might lead to a breakthrough. But what if all the ends meet in the same place? What if one person knew about all the secrets and all the lies? An anger that began with blackmail messages to Simon and a spray-painted insult may have eventually boiled over into a double homicide with the beloved twin sons as the lead suspects."

Jerry and Grace were both writing notes furiously. "Our suspects stay the same, right?" Jerry asked.

Laurie quickly ran through the list. "That seems right. Simon wouldn't blackmail himself but I suppose it's possible he made the whole thing up to try to get money from his father. If the killer was behind the spray-paint incident and the blackmail messages, it gives us a better sense of the motive. This resentment was building for some time, and it was personal."

Ryan looked determined. "I'll go over my notes for interviewing Simon and Ethan. The bones are already there, but we'll lean more into long-term resentments. And once we get someone to come clean about what happened with Howard Carver, he might change his mind about offering his side of the story."

She nodded. "That leaves Annabeth's dad. If it weren't for the fact that Jimmy Connolly was close friends with the police chief, I would probably let it go. I'm still working to get someone from the police department or DA's Office to give us access to the evidence. Maybe that would allow us to check him off our list. I don't want to approach him directly yet because that might scare off Ethan and Annabeth."

"At the very least," Ryan said, "once we get everything we need from them, I can start asking how much Jimmy knew about the pressure Richard was placing on Ethan to end the relationship."

"And ask about the money," Jerry added. "Whether Ethan bailed out his business."

"Oh, I know," Ryan said, confidently tapping his temple with an index finger. He looked to Laurie expectantly. "Coach Old School, what do you think? Are we ready?"

She snapped the cap onto her marker with satisfaction. "So who's calling for the pizza?"

# Chapter 32

Laurie could barely hear the other side of her FaceTime call over the sounds of a black Lab and beagle wrestling each other on the floor behind her in Jenna Merrick's living room.

She had called Alex's phone, but Tim was the one to answer. "Hi Mom!" His cheeks were impossibly pink, his expressive brown eyes peeking out from beneath a wool New York Giants beanie.

"How are my two favorite fellas?" she asked. "I'm waiting for one of our witnesses to go through hair and makeup and figured I'd check in." She thought she recognized the background as Rockefeller Center. "Are you at my office?"

"That would be silly," Tim said. He held out the phone so she could get a broader view on her screen. "We're going ice skating. I'm with Alex."

Alex appeared beside her son, smiling at her, bundled up in the down Marmot coat she had given him for Christmas. "I told Tim it might be a good idea to practice his skating in a more genteel environment than his hockey practices."

"I wish I were there." Laurie was a notorious wobbler on a pair of skates, but winter was her favorite time of year and the rink at Rock Center was a quintessential New York City winter experience.

"I asked Grandpa to come," Tim said, his eyes widening.

"And then I made the mistake of adding that perhaps Chief Judge Russell might want to join us," Alex said.

"And how'd that go over?" Laurie asked.

Tim was already giggling at the punchline that was sure to come. "He told me to have fun," Tim said, "and told Alex to find someone else to call when he falls down and breaks a hip."

"Do I hear . . . dogs?" Alex asked.

She tilted her screen so they could see the pandemonium unfolding around her. "The witness we're about to interview has a doggy daycare business. I'm surrounded by piles of pooches."

Tim's eyes sparkled at the sight of it. "They're so cute! Are any of them rescues? Can you bring one home?"

"Sorry, buddy, these cuties all have parents. But do you want to say hi to my new friend?" Laurie bent down and a black-and-white French Bulldog puppy immediately rushed to her for attention. "This is Double, and I think he likes me. Apparently his human dad is a golfer and named him Double Bogey after his usual score, but the dog sitter says it's because he's Double Trouble. What do you think?"

"I think you should put him in your suitcase and bring him home," Tim said.

Laurie exchanged a glance with Alex through the screen. Getting a dog wouldn't be the worst idea. Laurie hadn't told Tim or her father yet because she didn't want to get their hopes up, but she and Alex had been trying to add another member to the family. Having a dog first might be a good way to ease Tim into being a big brother.

Grace suddenly appeared in the living room and announced that Jenna was done with hair and makeup and they were ready to begin filming. Laurie blew a kiss and before signing off told Tim and Alex to be careful on the ice.

She found Jenna Merrick taking a final look at herself in the mirrored armoire in her bedroom. She appeared to be in her mid-forties, about five years older than Laurie, with close-cropped blond hair and wide-set hazel eyes. "Wow, I had no idea I could look like this! It only took an hour and a pound of makeup. I can't believe some people do this every day."

"Yet another reason I stay behind the cameras," Laurie said. "Ready to do this?"

"A little nervous to relive that night, but, yes, I want to help."

Even though Laurie had seen photographs of the Harringtons' beach house, she inhaled sharply at the sight of the property when Jerry pulled their SUV to a stop as directed by the GPS. Jenna's station wagon came to a halt immediately behind them.

"Wow," Grace exclaimed from the backseat, where, once again, Ryan had chosen the seat next to her. "This makes our Airbnb look like a dive."

The homeowners had explained that, along with other efforts to rid the house of its tragic history, they had removed the security gate. Laurie was pleased to see a stocky young man climbing out of the large white van that was already parked at the curb in front of the house, a sound blanket tucked under one arm. The media company she'd subcontracted with had set up in advance as instructed. The lights and cameras were already in place.

Despite her expressed nervousness, Jenna was a natural on screen, leading Ryan from the spot where she had parked in the driveway on the night of the graduation party to the Harringtons' front porch.

"Did anything strike you as unusual when you got here?" he asked.

"Well, the gate camera was knocked over. It used to be next to the keypad, right by the driver's side window. But it was also down two days earlier when I came by for a walk. What did give me a bad feeling, though, was that I didn't hear Bacon when I got to the door."

She explained that Bacon would either bark at strangers or make excited, playful noises if he could tell that the latest visitor was one of his friends.

"And you were a friend?" he asked.

She smiled at the memory. "I loved that dog and, yes, it seemed mutual. When I didn't hear him at the door, I got nervous, wondering if he might be sick or even worse. Bacon was an older dog by then. But I never could have imagined the horror I was walking into."

Laurie was still trying to work out an agreement with the Harbor Bay Police Department and the Cape Cod District Attorney's Office to view the underlying evidence in the case, including photographs of the crime scene. If they could not gain access, they would have to rely on their witnesses' descriptions, and Ryan did a good job of getting Jenna to recall that night without getting into gory details. Their bodies. Blood. A gun cast aside on the carpet.

"Were there signs of a struggle?" Ryan asked.

"There were books pulled from shelves, and drawers and cabinets left open, so the first thing I thought of was a robbery—like someone had been searching the house. But an end table was knocked over, a couple of picture frames shattered on the floor. I suppose that could have happened in a struggle."

Ryan folded his arms. "What did you do first when you realized you had walked into a crime scene?"

"Honestly?" She shook her head slightly as if she were reliving those moments in real time. "I froze. Then I started to run to the sound of Bacon barking at the back of the house, but then realized he shouldn't see the Harringtons that way. And then I started picking up the pearls—as if that mattered at all."

"Pearls?"

"Yes, Sarah must have been wearing a pearl bracelet that broke—so I guess that would be a sign of a struggle, right? And there I was on the floor, helplessly trying to gather these little pearls. I think I was in shock. Then I realized I shouldn't touch anything. And only then did it dawn on me that the killer could still be in the house. I ran to my car and called 911 from there."

Ryan looked to Laurie for guidance and she called "Cut." They had what they needed from Jenna as far as the footage was concerned.

Laurie made her way from behind the camera. "That was great, Jenna. We have pros who can't do it all in one take."

"I guess I missed my calling," Jenna said. "Any interest in a reality show about a middle-aged dogsitter on the Cape? I can be very charming."

"You never know. I'm wondering if you could tell us more about the Harrington family generally—how well you knew them, their dynamics, that sort of thing."

She shrugged. "They were nice. A lot of the city people don't bother to say please or thank you to the locals, let alone get to know us. But I'd frequently talk with them at the diner where I used to work. Often it was just Sarah and the kids—I got the impression Richard worked pretty hard, so the rest of the family would be out here on their own or come eat lunch with me to give him some quiet time. Then I saw them a few times on the beach and our dogs got to playing. She asked if I knew a dog walker and I volunteered to do it. She insisted on paying me, and before I knew it, I was the town dog sitter."

"Would you say they were generally liked?" Laurie asked.

Jenna looked up, as if searching for the right words. "The out-of-towners aren't really liked or not liked in Harbor Bay. They're just . . . the city people, the mainlanders, the outsiders."

"So you don't know anyone who *disliked* them?" Ryan asked.

She shook her head.

Laurie asked Jenna if she remembered seeing graffiti on the Harringtons' sidewalk.

Jenna squinted, recalling a distant memory. "I didn't actually see it. I came to the house to take Bacon for a beach walk and their handyman was out front with a pressure washer."

"The handyman?" Laurie asked. "Is this Peter Bennett, the caretaker?"

"That's right. The bulk of the cleaning was done by the time I got there, but he said someone had spray-painted the sidewalk. He looked upset, so I said something like *As if you needed more work.*

But then he made clear he wasn't mad about the cleanup. He said the person who did it should be punished."

Laurie and Ryan asked a few follow-up questions, but Jenna did not know anything else about the graffiti.

"Did you sense any conflict in the family?" Ryan asked. "Between the kids and their parents, or between Sarah and Richard?"

She shook her head. "But I really didn't see them much. If I was at their house, it was because the dog was home alone. But there was one time. I let myself in on the assumption the house was empty. I heard Richard's voice booming from the kitchen. He was angry, and I thought I heard Sarah crying. I yelled out hello, and they immediately went quiet. Richard came into the living room like nothing was wrong and helped me leash up Bacon."

"Did you see Sarah afterward?" Laurie asked.

"Not that day. When I came back with the dog, the house was silent, so I just left. And neither of them ever mentioned it to me. I assumed it was just an argument."

"Would Peter Bennett have known more about the family?" Laurie asked.

Jenna's shoulders shook slightly as she chuckled. "I think he would have liked to know *far more* about the family."

Laurie exchanged a confused glance with Ryan, waiting for the explanation.

"Pete's a nice man. A little simple and sort of socially awkward, but a good guy at heart. It was kind of a joke around town that he'd take two weeks to stop by a house to check out a leaky pipe but would drop everything for the Harringtons."

"He favored their family?" Ryan asked.

"More like an unrequited crush on Sarah. If she was in the diner with the kids, he'd nurse a cup of coffee at the next table for two hours, pretending to read the newspaper."

This was the first Laurie had heard of the rumored crush. "Is there any chance he and Sarah—"

Jenna laughed so hard she started to cough. "No. You'll see

when you meet him. Let's just say Pete has no game. Why all these questions about the Harringtons' marriage? If you're thinking it was a murder-suicide, I know for a fact the DA's Office concluded it wasn't. Someone drove away from that house in the Range Rover."

Laurie was surprised at the certainty in Jenna's tone. "How do you know that?"

"Oh, within weeks, the town gossip mill was on fire, but my brother-in-law is the first assistant at the District Attorney's Office. He brushed me up on the basic facts yesterday."

"You told him we were interviewing you today?" Laurie asked.

She nodded. "He's a huge fan of your show and thinks their office should give you access to at least some of the evidence. His boss is resisting."

Ryan was smiling in Laurie's direction. "Do you think your brother-in-law would be willing to meet with us off the record?"

"One way to find out," she said, pulling her phone from her coat pocket.

# Chapter 33

The Green Apple Diner on Harbor Bay's Main Street was filled with old-fashioned charm, its weathered sign creaking slightly in the bay breeze as Ryan and Laurie stepped inside. It was well past lunch hour. A few locals sat solo, scattered across the soda-fountain-style stools, one waitress holding court on the opposite side of the counter.

A temporary hush fell across the front of the diner as they entered. After a quick look at the newcomers, the other customers returned their attention to their meals. The waitress wore cat-eye glasses, her red hair piled high in a bun, a pen tucked behind one ear. She gestured toward a single customer seated alone at a table in the back. Like Ryan and Laurie, he stood out from his surroundings in business attire. "I suspect you're meeting that gentleman. Start you with two coffees?"

Ryan requested a side of skim milk, and Laurie asked for black tea instead.

"Coming up." The waitress donned a smile, but Laurie noticed a couple of the locals exchange an amused glance.

By the time they arrived at the table, the man who was waiting for them was already on his feet, adjusting his suit jacket. "ADA Randy Macintosh," he said, offering a handshake. "Ms. Moran, it's a pleasure. I've been trying to convince my office to give you our fullest cooperation. And Ryan Nichols—well, your reputation precedes you. You've got every trial lawyer's dream job."

Ryan's barely audible groan almost made her feel sorry for him. He had clearly found a fan in ADA Macintosh.

"Mr. Nichols has been dying to pick your brain," Laurie said with a grin.

After a quick sideways glance at her, Ryan spelled out all the advantages that *Under Suspicion* had over official law enforcement once a criminal investigation went cold. They didn't have to comply with the formal rules that governed the police. The witnesses tended to let their guard down once they knew they were in the public eye. And then Ryan added another advantage, which she knew was aimed especially at Macintosh: "It's national television. It's stardom. Who can resist the spotlight?"

Instead of following up with information about the Harrington murders, Macintosh asked Ryan how he went from working as a federal prosecutor to hosting a television show. "I could definitely do trial commentary for the cable news stations," he offered. "How do you get your name on those lists?"

"I'd be happy to help spread the word," Ryan said. Laurie had to hand it to him. The man did know his audience. "I'm pleased you see the value of our work. Ideally, we'd like to assure our viewers that your office hasn't forgotten about the victims in this case. But if we went to air right now, I'm afraid local law enforcement would not come across favorably. From what we've heard, Chief Collins never made much of an effort."

"In that case," Macintosh said, "we wouldn't be able to help you much."

The waitress returned with their drinks plus a pot to refill Macintosh's coffee.

"You could give us access to the footage from the camera at the front gate."

Macintosh was shaking his head adamantly before Ryan could finish the suggestion. "Already ran it by the boss. No can do."

"What about the hidden camera in the hallway?" Ryan asked.

Macintosh pursed his lips. "If you know about that, you should also know why I can't help you there either."

Ryan poured a tip of milk into his coffee mug. "Because the memory card was missing."

"Seriously, how do you know about that?"

Laurie had been surprised that Ryan went directly to their one piece of inside information, but it had clearly captured Macintosh's attention.

"Like we promised when your sister-in-law called you—we don't reveal sources."

"The device seemed new. I'd bet good money the shooter knew about the camera and pulled the memory card. You ask me, that's another strike against the Deadly Duo."

"What about the camera at the entrance gate?" Ryan asked. "Our understanding is that the police never took a long-term view of the footage to see if someone may have been stalking the Harringtons. There was even a report of disturbing graffiti left on their sidewalk: *This Family is a Lie*."

Macintosh's eyes widened. "Wow, you guys really do your homework."

Laurie was about to jump in, but Ryan was not going to allow the change of subject. "So did the police department check out all the footage or not?"

Macintosh's eyes darted around the diner. "Look, I can't cross the police. But after we heard from your show, I jumped back into the evidence, hoping to find something new. The only security gate footage we have starts when the parents show up at the house that night. I think the police department saved that excerpt and didn't preserve the entire file."

Laurie immediately thought about Chief Collins's friendship with Annabeth's father. "I assume that means the police department never tried to track down the graffiti or anyone else who may have been bothering the Harringtons."

"That sounds right," he said.

"Did they ever investigate Jimmy Connolly?" Ryan spelled out Connolly's connection to Ethan's future wife and the pressure Richard Harrington had placed on Ethan and Annabeth's relationship. "Our understanding is the man was close friends with the Chief."

Macintosh shook his head. "Never heard of the guy."

"I thought everyone in Harbor Bay knew everyone," Laurie said.

"Maybe, but my wife's the one from here. I grew up in P-town and work in Barnstable now. Every town on the Cape's its own little community."

"What about Howard Carver?" Ryan asked.

"The witness who saw one of the twins by the Range Rover?"

Ryan nodded. "We think he was having problems with Richard Harrington at work."

"That's the first I've ever heard of it," he said. "I thought you were going to ask about the DUI. Seems like you already know everything else."

Laurie looked to Ryan, encouraging him to follow up.

"Howard Carver drove under the influence?" Ryan asked.

"He got pulled over at the edge of town for a bad taillight a few months before the murders. The officer noticed he had bloodshot eyes and asked if he'd been drinking. According to Carver, he only had one glass of wine, but the officer said he didn't seem fit to drive. The officer was close to the end of his shift and decided to cut him a break. Told Carver he'd let him go with a warning if he could find a ride home. He called a friend, and that was that."

"Who was the friend?" Laurie asked.

"The report didn't say."

She looked again to Ryan. The police didn't interview Howard Carver until the afternoon after the Harringtons were killed.

Ryan was ready with the next question. "Did the police investigate whether Carver was drunk when he supposedly saw Ethan or Simon in the parking lot?"

Macintosh had a knowing gleam in his eye and pointed an index finger at his new best friend. "I knew you were good, Ryan. Is this enough to get me on the show?"

# Chapter 34

Laurie was regretting her decision to let Grace drive to their scheduled appointment to meet Peter Bennett. She was juggling the steering wheel with a Diet Coke in one hand while DJ-ing on her phone with the other, barely slowing as she sailed through a tight curve.

"Grace, did we rob a bank when I wasn't paying attention?"

"Huh?" she yelled over the Beyoncé song streaming over the speakers.

"You're like a getaway driver right now. Are we on the lam?"

Grace slowed slightly and turned down the volume. "Don't worry. My grandmother taught me how to drive when I was twelve years old, and this is how Garcia women drive." She swerved quickly to avoid a pothole. "See? Better than any New York City cabdriver."

"I'm not questioning your skills, but I've got a kid waiting back home."

Laurie had tried to conduct an initial screening interview with Bennett from New York, but the Harrington family's former caretaker was too reserved on the telephone to convey the kind of information she'd been hoping for. Even though he said repeatedly he was trying to help, it had been difficult to obtain more than one- or two-word answers from him.

She hoped that meeting him face-to-face in his own home might make him more comfortable. And there was a reason she had brought Grace, who had a gift when it came to putting people at ease, as if the comfort she felt in her own skin were immediately infectious.

Grace finally eased to a reasonable speed as she navigated the GPS's final turn—a narrow dirt road toward the end of a long block of what seemed to be new, opulent homes built as part of the same development.

As they neared the end of the road, they spotted a quaint cottage tucked away in a wooded area. The gravel driveway was lined on either side by a mix of lush decorative grasses. Beyond a vibrant garden worthy of a five-star resort, an ornate mahogany railing led to the front porch.

The door opened before they had a chance to knock. The man who stepped outside appeared to be about sixty years old, with a small frame, thinning blond hair, and weathered skin. He was not much taller than Laurie, who was five-seven, meaning that Grace towered over both of them in her high-heeled boots.

"Mr. Bennett?"

"Just Peter," he said quietly, nodding awkwardly.

"I'm Laurie," she said, offering him a quick handshake.

"And hi," Grace said, waving enthusiastically. "I'm her girl Friday, Grace Garcia. This yard is so beautiful. It's full-on winter with this gray sky, and somehow I feel like I've been transported to Hawaii."

Peter's face suddenly brightened. "Well, I'm glad you like it."

Grace ran her fingertips along the sculpted porch railing. "And this is a work of art. Did you carve this yourself?"

He was still nodding, but now he was beaming with pride. "I'm a bit of a woodworker. Here, come inside. Sit in the rocking chair. It's my latest little project."

Grace let out a satisfied sigh as she lowered herself into the chair. "Little project? More like a masterpiece. I can barely put together a piece of furniture from IKEA, so I am truly in awe. Anyway, I could bend your ear about this amazing place for hours, but I know Laurie's been dying to talk to you about the Harringtons."

Sadness flashed in Peter's eyes at the mention of their name. "I'm so glad they haven't been completely forgotten about. I was trying to help before, but I'm no use on the telephone. This is better."

Grace had worked her magic. Peter had already offered up longer sentences than Laurie had previously managed to get from him.

"My understanding is that you worked for them for some time," Laurie said.

"Sarah used to joke that I came with the house." He smiled at the memory. "I was admiring the house when it was being built, so as soon as I saw signs of a move-in, I dropped by, explaining how I could help out as needed. Most of my income's from taking care of other people's homes the way I'd take care of my own—if I had a mansion," he added with a chuckle.

"How would you describe them as a family?" Laurie asked.

"Sarah Harrington was nothing short of an angel. Pure kindness. Proud of her children. Never a harsh word, always asking about my family."

"You have family here?" Laurie asked. Jenna had mentioned that the town joked about Peter's crush on Sarah Harrington.

"My wife passed a long time ago. But my son and his wife have their own restaurant up in Provincetown. My grandson Petey's turning ten in May. Anyway, Sarah was always asking about my son. He's not much older than the twins. Those boys were good kids, by the way. I'll never believe they were the ones to do this. Not for one second."

He was the first person other than Betsy Ward who had told Laurie with such confidence that the twins must be innocent. "Do any other suspects come to mind?"

He shook his head sadly. "I wish I knew. I've always thought it had something to do with him."

"You mean Richard?"

"That's right." His mouth was in a stiff frown. "He put on a nice show, but if you work for someone long enough, you can tell when they're not a good person. He didn't appreciate Sarah. Treated her and the kids like trophies."

"Did you ever see him get violent with his wife?"

He looked to Laurie in disbelief, pain registering in his eyes. "Why would you ask that? Was he . . . Do you know that for certain?"

Laurie's poker face must have failed her, because his face fell at the realization. "I never saw anything, never suspected." His voice shook with emotion. "Oh my goodness, that just breaks my heart. Poor Sarah."

"Were you aware of any cameras installed inside the Harringtons' house?"

"No, just the one camera at the front gate."

"A woman who is being subjected to that kind of abuse will often show signs," Laurie said. "Unexplained injuries. A black eye from when she claims to have walked into a door."

Peter's gaze was distant, and if he had heard Laurie's question, it didn't seem to register. "Her long sleeves," he said, touching his own forearms absentmindedly. "Even outside in her own backyard on the hottest summer days, she always wore long sleeves. I'd ask her, *Sarah, aren't you roasting?* She insisted she was always chilly, but it seemed impossible."

Laurie would have to double-check with Frankie, but as she imagined the photographs she had seen of the Harringtons, Sarah's arms were always covered. "Abuse survivors learn how to hide the injuries."

He shook his head sadly. "You said something about cameras? They kept the system simple. Just the one camera at the front gate so they could see who was coming and going. Nowadays people have doorbell cameras for that."

"So if there was something like a nanny cam inside the house, you weren't aware of it?"

"That's right."

Laurie pivoted to the subject of the sidewalk graffiti. "Their former dog walker told us that you were the one who cleaned it up. That perhaps you were pretty upset with whoever did it?"

"You're darned right I was. A practical joke is one thing, but I still remember the exact words. *This Family is a Lie*? Who does something like that? When I got there, she was a wreck, crying and shaking. I assured her it would wash off, but it was clear the words couldn't be erased from her memory. I pulled the footage from the gate camera, and there was a quick glimpse of the person's foot and one hand on the spray can at the very beginning of the paint job. I showed it to Sarah and wanted to give it to the police, but she said no. She was adamant. She said it could be some local kid who resented outsiders who had more than them. She didn't want to get anyone in trouble. Like I said, pure kindness."

The depths of Peter's admiration for Sarah and distaste for Richard were becoming clear. "You sound like you cared for her very much," Laurie said.

His expression suddenly changed, his eyes narrowing with suspicion. "The way you said that—it sounds tawdry. She was just a nice lady. A customer."

"Some people around town seem to think you may have had other feelings for her," Laurie said. "Showing special favor compared to your other clients, finding reasons to sit near her at the diner."

"It's okay to care about someone," Grace offered, clearly trying to ease Peter's apparent anxiety.

Peter was the caretaker. He would have known in advance that the camera was off-kilter. And even though he supposedly jumped whenever Sarah needed him, he left it broken for days. Despite his denials, he could also have known about the hidden camera inside the house. Richard may have been the original target, with Sarah walking into the scene accidentally.

"Do you ever go to Boston?" Laurie asked.

"Sometimes," he muttered. His gaze had moved to the floor.

"The family has found flowers on Sarah's grave a couple times. None for Richard, only for Sarah. That was you, wasn't it?"

He pressed his palms to his face and rubbed his eyes. "You're twisting everything around. I'm not some kind of pathetic stalker. She was a nice woman. That's all. I would have never hurt her."

"We think it's possible someone may have meant to confront

only Richard. Ethan saw Richard leave the party abruptly by himself. Maybe someone who cared very much about Sarah went to the house to protect her—to convince Richard to stop hurting her. If Sarah walked into a struggle—"

"If I had known she was being abused? Yes, maybe I would have tried to help. But I didn't. After the murders, I spent what felt like days watching the video, wondering if there were any signs of trouble other than the one vandalism incident. Nothing. I had no idea she was in danger."

"What do you mean, you watched for days?" Laurie asked.

He shook his head. "Just replaying things in my head."

"That's not what you said, Peter. You said *watching the video*. You had video footage of the Harrington family?"

"You're twisting everything around again."

"So explain it to us," Laurie said. "It's important."

"I made a copy of the video from the front gate when I pulled it for the police," he said. "You think that's weird, don't you?" His eyes darted to Grace nervously. "I promise, I just thought it might be useful one day."

"Peter," Laurie asked pointedly, "where were you when you found out about the murders?"

"At the Cape Cod Hospital. I mentioned Little Petey who's turning ten? He was born that night at 8:32 p.m. Next thing I know, I'm getting a call from the police department asking how long the gate camera had been broken. You know how many times I've kicked myself for not fixing it before going to the hospital?"

She couldn't think of a better alibi. She'd have to confirm it, but she believed him. She had seen his grief-stricken response when she first asked about any signs of domestic violence. He didn't know until today that Richard had been harming Sarah.

"It's not weird to have made a copy," Laurie said gently. She understood. He had wanted a way to remember Sarah. "And you were right: It *is* useful."

"Do you still have it?" Grace asked, clasping her hands in anticipation.

He nodded eagerly. "I can make a copy for you if it might help you find who killed her. I kept the graffiti footage, too."

"Peter," Grace said. "I think Sarah would be very grateful that you did this for her."

He looked away, blinking back a tear. "I'll be right back."

He returned with a tablet computer. "Never thought I'd be so high-tech, but my son taught me all the tricks once people started installing their own security equipment." He handed the tablet to Laurie. "Just hit play there."

Grace rose from her rocking chair to peer over Laurie's shoulder.

The footage gave a sideways view of the front yard where they had filmed Jenna earlier that day. "Coming up in a few seconds," Peter said. "It's real quick. See?" He tapped the pause button to freeze the screen. "That's the little punk's left foot and right arm at the bottom of the screen when he starts the job. If he'd been one foot closer, we might have gotten his face."

The shoe was a light gray sneaker. The brand was unclear. The shirt was black and loose fitting, long-sleeved with broad white and red stripes near the elbow. It would be another detail for her to search for in the Harrington family photographs. If the twins had truly been angry at their parents, either or both might have vandalized the property in an early display of their resentment.

"Did you happen to notice anything else on the footage that might have been helpful? Apparently the police only kept the part showing the Harringtons coming home from the party and then everything after."

He sighed. "No warning signs other than the graffiti. The camera was motion activated so it was just the family members coming and going. Sometimes me or the dogwalker. A van pulled into the driveway the day before the murders and then backed out, but it was from one of the local businesses. I even went so far as to ask the owner about it, just in case I was missing something. He said he overshot an address for a delivery and had to turn around. I couldn't believe it when he said the police hadn't come to talk to him. That's when I realized the police were just blaming those boys—evidence or not. Anyway, I put the footage on here for you," he said, handing her a thumb drive. "Hopefully it's handy."

Laurie thanked him again before asking whether he had ever overheard Richard mention any problems at his law firm.

He shook his head. "No, when it came to me, it was always about whatever work needed to be done on the property. He wasn't the type to become friends with the handyman. Why don't you ask Walter or Howard?"

Laurie was caught off guard at the mention of Richard's law partners. "You know them?" she asked.

"Sure. When I was looking for extra work, Sarah recommended me to both of them. Walter and Betsy built a house around the same time as the Harringtons—not nearly as fancy, but a nice place. Then Howard came out a few years later, back when he was still married. The Wards started renting their house out years ago, but they had me get it ready for them to use this week. Howard's pretty much around full-time though. Ditched city life for the Cape years ago. If Richard was facing trouble at the firm, the two of them could tell you."

Laurie gave Grace a knowing glance. When Ryan had tracked down Howard's contact information, he had only looked in Boston.

"That's a good idea, Peter. Maybe we'll swing by and see what they remember. Do you have the addresses?"

Laurie was so pleased she didn't even mind when Grace drove like a bank robber to their next destination.

# Chapter 35

By Frankie's count, she hadn't been to the Wards' beach house for nearly six years. In the years immediately following the murders, the home had provided a way to extend her memories of long summers on the Cape. Her own family was shattered by then, but Simon, by virtue of his relationship with Michelle, was a frequent houseguest. And when Ethan and Annabeth visited her parents, they were only a bicycle ride away. Sometimes she'd take the ten-minute walk back to their old house, just to remember it. Frankie would close her eyes at night—Bacon curled beside her on the bed—and pretend she was falling asleep with her own family under one roof like the old days.

But as time passed, the trips to the Cape became shorter and less frequent. Simon said it brought back too many sad memories. Ethan's work involved late nights in the city. And Frankie suspected they were both avoiding the Cape because the odds were high they'd eventually run into each other. Then, after Daniel was born, Michelle and Simon said it was simply too much work to make the trip down to the Cape with the baby.

Oh, how Frankie had cried after the Wards told her they'd be closing up the house at the end of the summer so a local broker could run it as a vacation rental. She was sixteen years old, and another chapter of the life she had once known with her own family would be coming to an end. And she couldn't even complain—not after everything the Wards had done for her. She wasn't, after all, their real family. They didn't owe her anything.

Frankie had been excited to return to Harbor Bay again after all these years, hoping to feel the familiar satisfaction of nostalgia. But she was immediately disappointed when she stepped inside. The broker had stripped the home of all the quirks and personal touches that had reminded her of early nights there, playing hide-and-seek with the older kids while the grown-ups chatted on the back deck.

But now that they were settled in, the house was beginning to take on more of its own character, despite the sterile decor. Michelle and Simon had taken the lead in menu planning and were busy in the kitchen preparing fresh vegetables from the roadside farmers' stand and a mix of seafood for the grill. Betsy and Walter were in the den, poring over the box of photographs Frankie had brought home from the storage unit, narrating the images with detailed descriptions of memories made with the Harringtons.

Frankie had already shown Daniel and Sophie all her favorite hiding places and had landed on a "summer BBQ" playlist that managed to satisfy all of them. Even Dennis had decided to join them, making his way now from Boston after an afternoon real estate closing.

"A candy for your thoughts." Betsy was on the sofa, looking at her across the coffee table, an old photo album balanced on her knees.

Betsy had been telling the story of Sarah's first New York City gallery opening, where Betsy's date tried to impress everyone by explaining that the circles in an abstract painting represented femininity being drowned out by the more angular shapes. "Your mother, without skipping a beat, said, *Bravo. I just thought it looked really cool.* Frankie, is everything okay?"

"Sorry," Frankie said. "I spaced out for a second. That's a funny story."

"But your thoughts were somewhere else," she said. Giving Walter a subtle glance, she suggested that his glass of iced tea appeared ready for a refill.

Walter took that as his cue to give the two of them some privacy for girl talk.

"Is everything okay?" Betsy asked once they were alone.

"I was thinking how nice it would be if Ethan and Annabeth were here."

Betsy looked toward the kitchen to make sure no one else was listening. "For what it's worth, I did my best with Simon and Michelle. I thought the video you found might somehow create an opening with them."

"Same with Ethan and Annabeth," Frankie said. "They said it doesn't change the way they feel. I still can't believe my poor mother was living that way in her own home. She never told you?"

Betsy's eyes began to water, as they had every time Frankie had raised the subject of the physical abuse her mother had been enduring at her father's hands. She looked away and shook her head. "I'm so sorry, Frankie."

"It must have been terribly lonely for her to suffer with that and not be able to tell anyone," Frankie said.

Betsy placed the photo album on the coffee table and reached over to pat Frankie gently on the knee. "There's something I want to give you."

After a trip upstairs, Betsy returned with a small velvet box. "I've been waiting for the right time. I was worried it might upset you if you weren't ready. I was going to wait until your birthday, but I think you should have it tonight."

Frankie searched Betsy's eyes for a clue, but Betsy simply said, "Open it."

She lifted the top of the box to find a bracelet. A thin strand of delicate pearls glowed with a slight shimmer of pink. On instinct, she ran the tip of her index finger across the unusual sterling silver link clasp. "I remember this. I would play with these metal links when I sat on my mother's lap."

"Your mother and I fell in love with this bracelet on a trip to New York City when we were in high school. We walked around Tiffany dreaming of all the jewels we'd drape ourselves with someday, but this little pearl bracelet became your mother's obsession. The pearls are classic and demure, as we were both raised to be. But that chunky piece of sterling silver, your mother said, was a dash of rock-and-roll rebellion—a subversive little secret right at your pulse point."

Frankie felt a lump forming in her throat as she continued to touch the cool metal of the clasp. "So she could see the symbolism in art, after all."

"Of course she could. Go ahead, put it on."

The clasp slid easily into place. She centered the metal on her pulse point. It was a perfect fit around her wrist. "Why were you afraid I'd be upset?"

"So let me finish the story. We did a pinky swear that day in Tiffany that we would save our pennies to buy matching bracelets. Other girls were starting to date boys who would buy them baubles and trinkets, but we decided to buy our first pieces of real jewelry for ourselves. Or more accurately—for each other. Your mother bought me that bracelet for high school graduation. And I, in turn, bought her the same."

"This is yours? Betsy, I can't take it."

She began to fumble with the clasp to remove the jewelry, but Betsy stopped her.

"I'll never wear it again," Betsy said. "You see, that night, at the graduation party, your mother was wearing hers, and I was wearing mine. We even ended up with matching pantsuits—not that we had planned it. Your mother's bracelet broke during the—well, it broke later that night. The police found the pearls scattered on the living room floor. I tried to get them back from the police so I could have it repaired for you, but they wouldn't release it. Or maybe they lost it. Who knows. But I never felt right wearing mine again. But you should have it—this little piece of her. That's what Sarah would want."

Frankie wrapped her arms around Betsy and gave her a long hug.

"You're like Sarah, you know," Betsy said when Frankie finally let go.

"Everyone always says how much I look like her."

"That's true, but I meant in another way—demure and well behaved on the outside, with more than a little spunk in the places that really matter."

Frankie sniffed back a tear. "Thank you, Betsy."

Betsy darted a glance toward the front window. Following it, Frankie saw headlights in the driveway.

"Walter, I think that's Dennis," Betsy called into the kitchen.

Frankie suspected it was code to let Walter know it was also safe to return to the den. "My goodness, that was fast," Walter said. "I may need to have a talk with that son of mine about minding the speed limit."

As Walter padded from the kitchen toward the front door, a refreshed glass of tea in hand, four-year-old Sophie popped out from the bottom cabinet of an armoire. "Boo!" she yelled before breaking out into a gleeful fit of giggles. "Is Uncle Dennis here? Should I scare him, too?"

Betsy returned her attention to the photo album, but Frankie noticed her brow furrow at the sound of voices from the foyer. Female. Not Dennis.

Sophie pattered into the den, dragging her stuffed rabbit, CoCoBunny, by a timeworn ear. "There's two ladies here. They're really pretty!"

When Walter appeared, Laurie Moran was at his side, her assistant, Grace Garcia, one step behind.

# Chapter 36

Laurie had been hoping that Frankie would be the one to answer the front door, or at least Michelle or Simon, whom she'd met in Boston. Even Betsy Ward was not a total stranger. They had spoken on the phone several times.

Instead, she and Grace were greeted by a man who appeared to be in his late sixties. He had dark gray hair and bushy eyebrows. He was not quite six feet tall, but Laurie suspected he had once been taller, before the slouching began. The little girl next to him reached for his hand on instinct at the arrival of two strangers. Laurie recognized her as one of two children featured in photographs in Simon's law office.

"Can I help you with something?" His voice was gentle, and he smiled as if he genuinely wanted to help. She noticed his gaze move to the SUV she had parked in the driveway, as if he was wondering if they were having car trouble.

"Are you Mr. Ward, by any chance?" she asked. "I'm Laurie Moran, from *Under Suspicion*. We haven't met yet, but I've been in touch with the rest of your family. This is my assistant, Grace Garcia."

"I've heard so much about you." He stepped aside to welcome them in.

"And you must be"—she searched her memory for the name—"Sophia."

The little girl tucked her chin down and shook her head with a giggle. "Sophie!"

"Oh, so close! I'm friends with your Aunt Frankie."

Her eyes lit up. "Except she's Auntie Frankie." She pronounced the first syllable as *ahh*. "Ant sounds like a bug!" She held her fists over her eyes and tried to make her face look like a bug's, and Laurie could tell it was a running joke between Frankie and her niece.

"Was Frankie expecting you?" Walter said, leading the way into the house.

"No, actually, we were hoping to speak with you."

Sophie was three steps ahead of them in a different room. "There's two ladies here. They're really pretty!"

They found Frankie in the den, sitting across from a woman who had to be Betsy Ward.

"Laurie! Grace!" Frankie hopped up from her chair and greeted them each with a quick hug. "We were just going over all these old photos I found in the storage unit. I figured you'd want to use some of them for the show."

"Absolutely," Laurie said.

"I'm sorry." The older woman set down a photo album. "Laurie, I'm Betsy. And Grace, very nice to meet you."

Sophie, lingering beside her grandfather, pointed to a pearl bracelet on Frankie's wrist. "Is that new, Auntie?"

"It certainly is. You don't miss a thing, do you?" The little girl beamed with pride.

Frankie asked how everything had been going since they'd landed on the Cape.

"It's been great," Laurie said. "We filmed at your old house with Jenna this morning. It turns out her brother-in-law is an assistant district attorney. He's been trying to convince his boss to cooperate with our production, so fingers crossed."

Betsy boosted herself from the sofa. "Frankie didn't tell me you were coming. Are you staying for dinner?"

"I was just telling your husband that I was hoping to bend his ear about something that has come up in our research."

Laurie was about to ask Walter if they could talk to him about

Howard Carver when three new faces appeared—Simon and Michelle, plus a little boy who had to be Sophie's brother, prompting Laurie to explain again why she was here. "We have a question about the state of Richard's law practice around the time of . . ." She was about to say *the murders* when she spotted little Daniel and Sophie. "Back then," she said instead.

"Come on, you two," Betsy said, leading the children from the room. "Let's find a good spot for you to hide when Uncle Dennis gets here."

After the kids had traipsed away behind their grandmother, Simon said he didn't understand why his father's work problems mattered. "Ethan didn't kill our father because of anything at his law firm. It was all because of Annabeth."

"But what if it was someone other than you or Ethan?" Laurie asked. "Howard Carver was the one who said he saw one of you in the field by the Range Rover that night. If he had a reason to make that up, the killer could be anyone—including Howard. Your father said in that video—"

"That *horrible* video," Simon said with disgust. "That's what he did to me when I told him about Tom and the term paper. I had no idea he was abusing my mother."

"Yes, that horrible video," Laurie said. "And obviously there are no excuses for your father's violence, but he explicitly mentioned a problem at work. One that could cost him everything or even get him disbarred. We think it had something to do with Howard Carver. Michelle, when I asked about him in Boston, it seemed to catch you off guard. Do you know what was going on between him and Richard? It's important."

"Are you kidding? If I knew anything at all that could prove Simon was innocent, of course I would tell you. The only thing I know is that there was a falling out. Dad, if you know something, you need to help."

Walter was holding up both of his palms. "Hold on now. You're talking a mile a minute here. Ms. Moran, whatever problems we had at the firm were before Simon and Dennis were even in law school. They don't know anything about it, so just leave them out of it."

Laurie could see from Michelle and Simon's confused expressions that they honestly did not know about any problems at the firm in its earlier years.

"But you're going to tell her, Daddy, right? If it helps Simon, you absolutely must."

"Of course I'm going to help if I can, but please don't get your hopes up. I guarantee you Howard Carver is not some kind of murderer. You two, keep enjoying your night. I'd like to talk to Ms. Moran alone if that's all right with her."

"May Grace sit in, too? Her memory's better than mine."

Walter nodded and gestured toward the sofa for them to have a seat. "And nice try, but I'm no dummy," he said, tapping an index finger to his temple. "You want a witness. Trust me, you don't need to worry. I'll tell you everything—but it's got nothing to do with Richard and Sarah's murders. What are you looking for?"

# Chapter 37

Once Laurie and Grace were alone with Walter, Laurie began to outline the frenetic pattern of Howard Carver's lawsuit settlements. Laurie had called Ryan from the car so he could e-mail her the records. She could tell that Ryan was annoyed that she was conducting another interview without him, but she thought she was more likely to get the Wards to open up to her if she and Grace went alone.

Laurie was only halfway through her outline of the busy pattern of trial settlements in Howard Carver's final two years of practice when Walter told her that she could stop.

"I know about all that," he said. "Let's test my memory. There were a couple last settlements in . . . I think March of that year? Then Howard resigned from the bar on June . . . I'm going to say the 20th."

"Spot on," she confirmed, replicating his own temple tap only moments earlier. "Richard mentioned a problem at work in that video. He was using it as his excuse for abusing Sarah. Was it related to Howard?"

Walter nodded. "I'm sure that's what he was referring to, but, my god, I had no idea he was taking it out on Sarah that way. If I had . . . well, I get sick when I think about it. I thought what Howard did was a travesty. Richard would have had more than disbarment to worry about if I had known what he was up to at home."

"And what was the travesty with Howard?" Laurie asked.

"He was working with a shady network of chiropractors. Finding people with injuries that could be blamed on other people. Taking the cases on contingency and then shaking down insurance companies for quickie settlements."

"Maybe not the most prestigious way to practice law," Laurie said, "but there's nothing unethical about that, is there?" She knew that in a contingency case, the lawyer covered the up-front costs of litigation, but then kept a substantial percentage of whatever damage award resulted from the claim.

He held up an index finger. "Oh, but Howard didn't stop there. He'd tell a guy with a broken leg that the case might be worth a few thousand dollars, but then demand a hundred times that amount. He'd settle for whatever he could get without doing a lot of work, but then tell the client the offer was significantly less than the real award. The client ended up with some paltry amount, while Howard pocketed the difference."

Grace was frowning and shaking her head in disapproval.

"That's fraud," Laurie said. "Was Richard involved, too?"

"Oh no. He was actually the one who busted Howard. We were both furious. Howard went to great pains to hide it all from us, opening separate accounts to run the money through. We only found out because he messed up and bounced a check to a client who decided to walk into the firm on a day Howard wasn't in the office. Richard handled the walk-in, took one look at the check, and knew something was wrong."

"So why did Richard tell Sarah that he could lose everything and be disbarred?" Laurie asked.

"Because it was true. A good lawyer could have gotten all of the clients together, plus the defendants, plus their insurance companies. They would have had a tidy little racketeering case against the law firm, including punitive damages. We were his partners, which meant we'd be on the hook as well."

Laurie couldn't believe that Walter had never told the police about Howard's corruption. "Walter, don't you see how huge this is? Richard caught Howard doing something that could have sent him away for years. That's a motive."

Walter was shaking his head already. "Except I also knew what he'd been up to, and I'm still alive. And here's the important part—I was the one who wanted to report every last detail to the U.S. Attorney's Office, repercussions be damned. I thought Howard deserved to go to prison, and I told him that directly to his face. It was Richard who said we needed to think about our families. He convinced me that we could make the victims whole sooner than the government would, since they'd just be looking for jail time, and private attorneys would tie the victims up in litigation for years."

"So what did you do instead?" Laurie asked.

"We hired outside counsel to give a fair valuation to every case Howard handled and made sure every victim was compensated in full in exchange for a non-disclosure agreement. Howard left the firm without any equity, retired from the bar, and vowed never to practice again."

"You sound like you still have regrets," Laurie asked.

"It wasn't the bravest decision I've ever made," he conceded. "Trust me, if Howard were going to kill anyone at the firm, it would have been me. Richard was the peacemaker. Is there any way I can convince you to leave Howard out of this story?"

Laurie felt Grace's eyes on her. She always had a way of reading Laurie's mind, but especially at her most vulnerable moments. Laurie had gotten attached to these families and wanted to help them, but not at the expense of the truth. "Why do you care whether we expose Howard now? Hasn't the statute of limitations expired?" Laurie asked.

"You've never had a falling out with an old friend? It was painful to cut him out all those years ago, but it was for the best. I eventually started a new partnership with Dennis and Simon."

"So it sounds like they're protected legally whether Howard gets exposed or not," Laurie said.

Walter was quiet, running his thumbs up and down his glass of iced tea.

"That's right. I protected them from legal exposure. Ward and

Harrington is a separate partnership from our former firm. But if they were to find out, they might feel an ethical obligation to report Howard or even me to the bar."

"I assumed Dennis already knew," she said. "He called me last week saying that you and your wife preferred that Frankie leave well enough alone. I sensed it was related to the firm."

Walter shook his head. "Dennis is just very protective of the family. It's like he came out of the womb as our biggest defender. Even though he's the little brother, he was always looking out for Michelle. Worried about the boys she would date—that kind of thing."

"But presumably not Simon," Laurie said with a smile. "He made it clear when I first met him that he believes Simon's innocent."

Walter chuckled. "I'm talking about when they were younger. But, even now, my guess is he wanted to steer you off this case because he worries that if Simon comes off poorly, it will blow back on our family. Not to mention Frankie."

"That's funny. I got the impression from Frankie that she and Dennis weren't especially close, given their age gap and him being away for school."

"They're certainly not like siblings, but he knows how much his mother and I have come to care for that girl. I'm not sure she's strong enough to handle as much as she thinks. And if he sees us anxious about Frankie, that becomes his problem, too. Anyway, I'm rambling. My point is that there's no reason for you to get tied up in knots over Howard."

Laurie noticed Grace sit upright at the sight of headlights shining through the living room window.

"Speak of the devil," Walter said. "Dennis is here."

By the time Laurie and Grace trailed Walter into the foyer, the rest of the family was already there. Sophie and Daniel were giving Uncle Dennis high fives.

"We scared Uncle Dennis," Sophie squealed with delight. "I hid in the cabinet."

"And I was behind the curtain!" Daniel added.

Dennis tousled his nephew's wispy hair. "I'm going to get you back, you little stinkers."

"Do you know Laurie and Grace?" Sophie asked.

Suddenly aware of the newcomers' presence, he smiled awkwardly and gave them each a quick handshake. "Hey there. Laurie, I'm sorry about that call. I was just worried—"

"No need to apologize. Your dad was just telling me how you're looking out for your family. I get it."

He scooped Daniel into his arms, hoisted him on his shoulders, and then held on to Sophie's hand. "I can't believe this is your first time at the house, you guys. I have so much to show you."

Sophie bounced on her tiptoes. "Auntie Frankie showed us her hidey holes from when she was little. It's so awesome here. Did you see Auntie's new bracelet?"

Dennis's gaze shifted to Frankie's right wrist. "Very nice," he said.

Frankie ran her index finger along the fine strand of pearls. "I may never take it off. Betsy and my mother had matching ones. My mom's was lost, but Betsy wanted me to have it, so she gave me hers."

As Frankie displayed her new piece of jewelry with pride, Laurie noticed that Dennis was looking toward his mother with narrowed eyes. Betsy turned away from his gaze.

"I know," Betsy said, waving one hand. "I was planning to wait for her birthday but ruined the surprise early. I guess someone's going to get a second present in May."

Was Dennis . . . *jealous*? The unexpected addition of a third, much younger child into the family once Dennis was already away at college would have meant that Dennis was no longer the baby of the house.

Michelle placed a gentle hand on Laurie's shoulder and whispered in her ear. "Was my dad able to give you the information you wanted about Howard Carver? Is it helpful to Simon in any way?" Her eyes were pleading for hope.

"I don't know yet," she said.

Frankie grabbed Laurie's hand and led her back into the living room. "You asked for photographs. I have an entire box. Just don't lose them, okay?"

"Of course not," Laurie promised. "Precious cargo." She and Grace helped Frankie pack a bundle of photo albums into a cardboard box.

When they left, Walter offered to help them to their car. In the driveway, he asked Laurie once again to leave Howard Carver alone. "When I pushed him out of the firm, I said good riddance. I don't want to get mixed up with him again. Can you promise me you'll leave it alone?"

"The only promise I ever made was to try to find out the truth."

When the car doors were closed, she entered Howard Carver's address in the GPS.

# Chapter 38

When Grace pulled their SUV to a stop at the curb in front of Howard Carver's address, Laurie spotted Ryan Nichols across the street, looking at his phone as he leaned against a tree.

"You're here," she said, not knowing what else to say.

"Of course I am. You've abandoned me all day. You called me like an intern to email you Howard's litigation records when I was the one who figured out the pattern in the first place. I deserve to be here for the conversation."

"Ryan, it wasn't personal—"

"You're asking him about his work as a lawyer. I'm a lawyer, and you're not. If I were Alex two years ago, you'd want me to help."

"How'd you even know where to find us?" Laurie asked.

He placed his hands on his hips, clearly annoyed by the question. "You said you were going to the Wards' house first and then to Carver's. I can find an address."

"Except you didn't last time," she said.

"Very nice," he replied.

Grace coughed softly. "You guys, we don't have time for this. And for what it's worth, Ryan was the one who figured out Carver was shady."

It was the first time she could ever recall Grace siding with Ryan over her. "You're right," she said. "We'll do this together."

Laurie looked at them, steadying her will, before ringing the doorbell. As they waited, she realized how much more modest Carver's home was compared to the Wards', while the Harringtons had had the most lavish property of all. They may have been partners, but that didn't make them equals.

A moment later, the porch light turned on. When the door opened, they were met by a heavyset man with a receding hairline. He was wearing a cable-knit sweater and corduroys. As he acknowledged their presence with a nod, his gaze flickered among the three newcomers on his porch.

"Are you Howard Carver? I'm Laurie Moran from *Under Suspicion*. We spoke last week."

"I knew who you were when I opened the door." He gestured toward Ryan. "I recognized that one from the television. I already told you I'm not interested."

"We're airing the special," Laurie said, "and you'll be part of it one way or another—including the lawsuits you settled at deflated values to line your own pocketbook at the expense of your clients."

"That's defamatory," Howard said.

Ryan extended his hand. "Ryan Nichols, the guy from the TV." Howard reluctantly returned the gesture. "Since you've apparently seen our show, Mr. Carver, you must know we're very careful. We have the evidence to back up every word, so this isn't actionable. Two years of lucrative settlements. We can track down the clients to prove they didn't get their fair share. Plus, we're only asking questions for now. If you don't answer them and we go to air with our evidence, that's on you."

"For what it's worth," Laurie added, "the statute of limitations for fraud has passed. And we don't have any interest in exposing your past wrongdoings for their own sake. We just want to know what happened the night Richard and Sarah Harrington were murdered. You're the only person who claims to have seen one of the twins near the Range Rover in the overflow parking lot."

"I saw what I saw," Howard said. "What do my lawsuits have to do with anything?"

"They put you at odds with Richard Harrington," Laurie said, "who wound up dead after he discovered you were bilking your clients."

"This is offensive," Howard said. "I was friends with Richard for a quarter of a century. What exactly are you suggesting?"

Laurie put on her best smile. "Well, one possibility is that you deprived multiple clients of millions of dollars, and when your law partner caught you in the act, you found a way to silence him."

"You're so far off base," he said, shaking his head. "Fine, come on in, but you can't use anything I say on air."

Grace looked to Laurie and Ryan, expecting another argument, but Laurie and Ryan exchanged a glance and both nodded.

Howard led the way into a small living room. A sofa and wing chair were situated in front of a fireplace. He nodded toward the bench in front of an upright piano in the corner, which Ryan pulled out for additional seating.

"You're crazy if you think I killed Richard and Sarah."

"He's the one who figured out the scam you were running," Laurie said.

"He's also the one who was working to keep my rear end out of jail. Walter wanted to throw the book at me and lock away the key. Richard was furious, but he also told Walter he was being self-righteous to his own detriment. If they'd gone to the authorities, the entire firm could have been on the hook. Richard's the one who found a way to come up with the money to cover the losses with the clients and keep it all quiet."

"And how was that?" Ryan asked.

"Well, I downsized my real estate for starters. Bye-bye Beacon Hill. Bye-bye waterfront view. Hello modest little ranch house. Richard was always the rainmaker at the firm, which meant the biggest draw. He reached into his own funds to save the firm—minus me, of course. When Richard was killed, I was terrified Walter would back out of the deal and turn me in. You're barking up the wrong tree."

"You had a DUI stop around the same time," Laurie said. "According to the police officer, you seemed off-kilter. And when you were questioned the day after the murders, the investigator who spoke to you said you seemed out of it."

"I was in shock. My friend and his wife had been killed in their own home."

"Or maybe you were intoxicated," Ryan said, cracking his knuckles.

Laurie noticed Grace's eyes widen.

"You were stealing a lot of money from those clients," Laurie said, "and yet, once you were caught, you couldn't cover the losses. That means the money went somewhere. If you were drinking a lot, maybe you were also gambling? Or maybe you told police the truth that night about only having a glass of wine, and you had a different drug of choice."

Howard began to usher them out of the house, but they remained seated. His shoulders slumped. "What exactly do you want from me?"

"To talk about the night of the graduation party," Laurie said. "The evidence points to someone close to the Harrington family, but you're the only eyewitness to place one of the twins near the Range Rover after the murders were committed. Ethan and Simon both swear they stayed at the party the whole time."

"The police contacted me the next night. I think they were questioning everyone who had been at the party. They were obviously suspicious of the twins by then. I had arrived at the party late and got stuck in the overflow lot. Given my standing with Richard and Walter at the time, I was really just making an appearance, trying to keep things cordial so they didn't change their minds about helping me out of my jam. When I left, I wasn't paying close attention, but I remembered seeing the Harringtons' Range Rover, which seemed weird because presumably they would have arrived at the party early."

"But you didn't merely say you saw the car," Laurie said. "You claimed to have seen one of the twins nearby."

"Some people could tell them apart, but I never could."

"But are you absolutely sure it was one of them?"

"If I said it to the police ten years ago, then, yes, I was sure."

"No offense," Ryan said, "but ten years ago, you were telling clients you settled cases for four thousand dollars when you settled them for forty. You can't vouch for your past honesty here."

"I know this is hard," Laurie said. "You had that DUI stop. Did you have a substance abuse problem?"

Howard pressed his lips together and closed his eyes. "This is embarrassing. I thought this was all in the past."

"There's no camera here," Laurie said. "Ethan and Simon have been estranged for years over this—each of them convinced the other is the one you saw in that field. Lives are in the balance. If you were impaired that night—"

He shook his head, wiping back a tear. "It was pills. A lot of them. It's a wonder I didn't die. It started with chronic pain after a bad fender bender. My dosages kept going up and up until no legitimate doctor would write the prescriptions anymore. Then one of the quacks who was helping me get the pills asked me about representing injured patients who had viable lawsuits. When Richard figured out everything I'd been doing, I really did try to get clean. But I was stressed about having to go to that party and put on a good face—which mattered so much to Richard. I wanted to keep him happy. I took a few pills to make my way through the night."

"So did you see one of the twins or not?" Laurie pressed.

He shut his eyes, as if trying to replay the evening on a screen in his mind. When he opened them again, his gaze was distant. "It's hard to explain. When I told the police I had noticed the Range Rover, I immediately told them one of the boys had been nearby. When they asked me if I was sure, I began to doubt myself. It was common back then for me to black out, and I couldn't pull up the actual memory of seeing them. Even now, I can't really picture it."

"So how do you know it was one of them?"

"He was wearing a white shirt, white pants, white jacket, just like the two of them at the party. And I distinctly recalled seeing the

Range Rover and turning away because I didn't want my law partner's son to see me in my current state and tell his father I was using. It's like I remembered the shame and the fear of getting caught more than the person I actually saw. Does that make sense?"

It did. It also meant that Howard's perceptions could have been impaired. Laurie leaned forward on the sofa to get his full attention. "Is it at all possible, Howard, that you saw the Range Rover, knew it belonged to the Harringtons, and simply assumed the person nearby was one of the twins because of what they were wearing?"

Ryan was nodding along with her theory. "Especially if you were impaired and anxious about the possibility of being seen by them?"

Laurie had read countless articles about the unreliability of eyewitness testimony. "Your mind may have filled in the gaps. You saw the Range Rover. You saw a young guy from the party nearby. You didn't want Richard to know you were using again. And therefore you assumed that the person you saw must have been one of the twins."

Howard squinted again, struggling with fragments of a distant memory. "I guess it's possible. It was the shame that I most remembered, the threat of being caught by my law partner's son. But was it actually one of them? Maybe it's like you said, and I jumped to conclusions."

This was the break Laurie had been praying for. Maybe—just maybe—the Deadly Duo were both innocent.

# Chapter 39

Grace and Jerry were perched on two sofas, facing each other. "How pretty do we look?" Grace asked, taking a glimpse into the camera.

"Undeniably gorgeous," Laurie said, checking out the living room setup on the monitor next to the cinematographer she had hired for the shoot. "I think we need another reflector on the right side of the room, but then we should be good."

She heard the chime of a doorbell. That would be one of the twins. She took a deep breath, hoping that her last-minute decision to upend their schedule would pay off.

She had initially planned for Ryan to interview the twins separately, but the breakthrough with Howard the previous night had changed everything. After they left Howard's house, Laurie had called Randy Macintosh at the DA's Office. Within two hours, the district attorney herself had assured Laurie she'd be appointing an investigative team with the Massachusetts State Police to take a fresh look at the evidence.

Ethan and Simon were about to meet face-to-face, on camera, for the first time in years since the tragedy that had torn their family apart. Laurie wanted to capture the expression on their faces when Ryan told them the good news. After blaming each other for nearly ten years, they might finally be willing to reconcile.

It had not been easy to persuade them, but Laurie promised they had new evidence to share that would be important to both of them. She prayed it would be enough.

When she opened the front door, Frankie stepped inside, taking in the scene with wide eyes, one of her brothers trailing behind her. "Whoa, it's so eerie being back here." She gave Laurie a quick hug and waved hello to Grace and Jerry.

"Simon, right?" Laurie extended her hand for a shake.

"Well done," he said. In truth, she wasn't certain she could tell the twins apart, but had assumed Simon would be the one to arrive with Frankie since they were both staying with the Ward family. "Wow, the old place looks different, but somehow feels exactly the same. Is my brother here yet?"

"Not yet."

"Always late," Simon said under his breath. "Same old Ethan."

"Thanks again for letting me watch," Frankie said. Laurie had agreed to let Frankie join them on set, but with a promise that she would not interrupt. Ryan would sit down with her separately later in the afternoon.

"Of course," Laurie said. "And thank you, Simon, for agreeing to appear together with your brother."

She found Ryan in the Harringtons' former dining room, studying a stack of index cards. "You know you can put notes on a computer, right?" she asked with a raised brow.

He looked up from his work and winked. "Touché. Guess you're not the only one who's a little old school. I always tried my cases off note cards."

"Hey, I owe you a peace offering about last night. I had my reasons, but I shouldn't have leapt in without you. You were the one who figured out Howard was up to something back then. And I shouldn't have made that crack about not finding his address earlier."

"Well, I did mess that up. I should have checked to see if he had a house on the Cape."

"We all missed it," she said. "Anyway, I'm sorry. Are you all set for this? Simon's here and Ethan should be joining us shortly."

"Yeah, but Laurie, there's something I want to tell you. Remember when we talked in the car on the way to Southampton? And I told you I've been feeling like an empty suit?"

Was he about to start another round of complaints after she had already apologized? They both needed to be focused on the Harrington twins right now. "Of course I remember. And I've been trying to include you more as a partner. I messed up last night."

"There's more to it." He looked away from her gaze. "Those words—empty suit—came directly from my father."

"Oh Ryan, I'm so sorry."

He shook his head. "Not your fault. He and my uncle have both been riding me, saying I'm wasting my education. Pressuring me to have a more *impactful career,* as they call it. They think I'm this trivial person, a pretty face on television and in the New York gossip columns. Going through these notes, realizing the pressure Richard Harrington put on those boys to be perfect in every way—it hits a little close to home. Maybe it's impossible to be a good person if you're raised that way. Maybe you can't help yourself, like the scorpion with the frog."

She placed a hand gently on his shoulder. "You are a good person, Ryan, when you let yourself be."

He nodded in appreciation.

Laurie turned toward the sound of someone clearing their throat. It was Grace, with Jerry at her side. "Ethan's here," she said. "Spooky how much they look alike. Makeup's working on them now—in separate rooms, of course."

"Those two may hate each other," Jerry said, "but they're united on one thing: they want to know why you brought them here together, and they don't seem happy about it."

Laurie had already produced a separate segment in which Ryan laid out the evidence pointing to the twins. The use of the Range Rover. The keypad and gun safe codes. The missing nanny cam. Their motive. And most pointedly, Howard Carver's insistence that he had seen one of the twins near the Range Rover in the overflow lot.

As the cameras rolled, Ryan began with general questions to set the stage from the twins' point of view. The graduation party. The arrival of the police. The tragic deaths of their parents. The suspicions that followed. From separate sofas, Simon and Ethan were glaring at each other across the coffee table.

"You probably know the media dubbed you the Deadly Duo. How did that make you feel, Simon?"

"Angry. Obviously. I not only lost my parents, I lost my reputation."

"That happened to both of us," Ethan said. "You weren't the only person with a future to worry about."

"And is it fair to say that you each believe your brother was the person responsible for the death of your parents?" Ryan asked.

They both nodded.

Laurie's plan was to cut in an interview with an expert on eyewitness testimony to explain the reasons Howard's recollection might be unreliable.

She held up a hand and nodded toward Ryan, indicating it was time to deliver the bombshell.

"We've got some good news," Ryan announced, his voice carrying a glimmer of optimism. "The witness who once insisted to the police that he saw one of you outside the party near your car has essentially recanted his statement. We have already shared that information with the District Attorney's Office, and they will be working with the Massachusetts State Police to take a fresh look at the evidence and determine whether the Harbor Bay Police Department botched the original investigation."

"That doesn't answer the question of who murdered my parents," Ethan said.

"*Our* parents," Simon emphasized.

Ryan managed to keep his expression neutral, even though this wasn't the celebratory response they had anticipated. "It means that it wasn't necessarily either of you. That must be some kind of relief, isn't it?"

Frankie was next to Laurie, gesturing as if she wanted to join her brothers on camera. Laurie shook her head adamantly.

"Well, I've known for ten years it wasn't me," Simon said. "And if it wasn't Ethan, it was his girlfriend or his girlfriend's family. They wanted my family's money."

"That's my pregnant wife you're talking about," Ethan said, starting to rise from the sofa. "Leave her and her family out of this."

"You and our parents' money were her family's ticket out of debt, and we both know it." With lawyerly precision, Simon set forth the mounting pressure on Ethan to end the relationship. "After they were killed, you were chomping at the bit to get your inheritance, while I was the one who was willing to freeze our parents' estate so you wouldn't get a dime."

"That's not true, Simon. I didn't rush anything. You were the one trying to freeze the estate to make me look guilty and take suspicion off of you."

Ryan, determined to steer them toward alternative suspects, tried another tack. "Simon, you said a fellow college student was blackmailing you before the murders. We've spoken to that person, and he insists it never happened. We also have footage of someone spray-painting a derogatory message about your family in front of this very house. What if the same person who targeted you also committed the vandalism? Who held a grudge against your family?"

Within seconds, the twins were both on their feet, accusing each other of every possible wrongdoing. According to Ethan, Simon faked the extortion emails in a failed attempt to get money out of their father. According to Simon, Ethan might have been behind the threats in a failed attempt to get money from Simon.

The cinematographer gave Laurie a worried look. "Should we have hired security?" he whispered.

"Stop it!" The living room fell into a sudden silence, and Frankie yelled again. "Just stop! This wasn't supposed to happen." Her face was red and her lips were quivering. "Maybe it's just like the police said. The two of you did this together, but no one will ever be able to prove it so long as the Deadly Duo keeps pointing fingers at each other."

Sobbing, she turned and ran out the front door.

"Look what you did," Ethan said, shoving Simon in the chest.

"I didn't even want to do this." Simon turned to face Laurie. "This is your fault, too. I hope you're happy with your footage."

# Chapter 40

The cold, damp air was settling into Frankie's bones. She relaxed her shoulders. *Let the cold in.* Maybe if she stayed on the beach long enough, she'd eventually go numb. How glorious it would be to feel absolutely nothing right now.

Simon had managed to find her as she walked back to the Wards' house even though she had made a point not to follow the route that had once been a frequent part of their routine, back when their lives were happy and the families used to bop between the two homes as if they were one.

He tried to convince her to get into the car, but she had refused, saying she needed time alone to think. She'd been relieved to find the house empty when she returned. She found a note from Betsy on the kitchen counter. *Taking the kids up to P-town for the day. Call if you need us.*

If she had to guess, Betsy and Michelle had decided to take Daniel and Sophie away from the house to prevent them from overhearing Simon and Frankie talk about their parents' deaths, given the day's production schedule.

Grateful to be alone, she had retrieved her worn-out copy of *From the Mixed-Up Files of Mrs. Basil E. Frankweiler* from her room and then taken it outside behind the house to the spot where she now sat, her very favorite place in Harbor Bay—beneath the bluff, her back resting against a giant natural rock that had been there as long as she could remember. When she first began to live with the Wards, they were still spending frequent weekends on the Cape.

She would sit against this rock by herself for hours, pretending to bury her nose in a book, but more typically staring out onto the water, trying to live in her memories of her parents, determined to never, ever forget them.

Her phone chirped from the top of the rock she was using as a backrest. It was Ethan again. She let the call go to voicemail and then typed a quick text in reply. *Give me some time alone to think.*

As she hit enter, she replayed the words she had screamed at her brothers before storming out of the house. *Maybe it's just like the police said. The two of you did this together, but no one will ever be able to prove it so long as the Deadly Duo keeps pointing fingers at each other.*

Had she meant what she said? It was, after all, the simplest explanation—the one the police had believed from the very beginning.

When she first met Laurie at Katz's, Laurie had asked Frankie whether she truly understood where a re-investigation of the case might lead. *It means that I might find out that at least one of my brothers killed our parents.* Is that how this story would end?

When she reached the chapter where Claudia Kincaid and her brother traveled from Manhattan to Mrs. Frankweiler's home in Connecticut, she rested the book open and facedown on the rock, checking the time on her phone. She couldn't believe she had been out here for nearly three hours. She was going to be late for her on-camera interview with Ryan Nichols.

What would she even say at this point? Everything had changed since she'd first asked Laurie to help her. In her memories, her parents were always smiling at each other, holding hands and saying how happy they were. It had all been an act. Now she knew the truth about what they were like when no one else was around. And today she had seen an anger in her brothers that was unrecognizable. Maybe deep down they were as violent as their father had been.

She wondered what would happen if she simply failed to appear for her interview. Could she go back to her old ways, before Laurie

Moran ever called her—back when she had come to accept that her parents' murders would never be solved? It was so much easier then.

She realized that she had been running her index finger over the clasp of her new bracelet as her mind was wandering. She still couldn't believe what a perfect fit it was. How many times had she been told she looked exactly like her mother? Now she had a matching piece of jewelry to top off the resemblance.

*The pearls are classic and demure, as we were both raised to be. But that chunky piece of sterling silver, your mother said, was a dash of rock-and-roll rebellion—a subversive little secret right at your pulse point.*

She suddenly stopped fidgeting with the bracelet, replaying more of Betsy's words when she had given her the velvet box.

Was it possible?

She stared down at the piece of jewelry, studying its design. There was a reason it had a clasp. It was meant to fit close to the wrist, and the pearls were strung on the thin thread of silver that ran between the two halves of the clasp. She tried to slip it off without opening the clasp, but there was no give.

Something was very wrong.

She picked up her phone again to call Betsy, but stopped herself. If the fear tugging at her chest was correct, Betsy was the last person she could turn to for help. She couldn't ask Michelle either. She'd run directly to her mother.

She pulled up Laurie's number instead. She felt her grip on the phone tightening as she waited through four unanswered rings until she got a voicemail message.

"Laurie, it's Frankie. I need those photographs I gave you. Do you have them at the house for the shoot? My head's racing right now. I figured something out. Call me back."

She made her way back into the house, hoping to spot a photograph of her and her mother together. When they used to come to Harbor Bay regularly, her family would turn up in photographs hung around the Wards' house, and vice versa. But now this house was a generic vacation rental, stripped of any hint of its owners' identities.

She could feel adrenaline rushing through her system. Her ears were beginning to ring from the questions bouncing inside her mind. She was so focused on answering them that she did not notice the car parked in front of the Wards' house that had not been there three hours earlier.

*Your mother's bracelet broke during the—well, it broke later that night. The police found the pearls scattered on the living room floor.*

If her mother's bracelet had broken when she was murdered, it must be in the crime scene photos from that night. Laurie had mentioned a local prosecutor who was trying to help. He was Jenna Merrick's brother-in-law.

Standing in the kitchen, she Googled "Jenna dog walker Harbor Bay" and immediately found a matching website. Jenna picked up on the second ring.

"This is Jenna."

"It's Frankie Harrington. Do you remember me?"

"Of course I do, Frankie. How have you been? Did Laurie tell you I met her at your old house yesterday? How has the rest of the filming been?"

"Um . . . not good. I'm trying to find some crime scene photos. I need to know your brother-in-law's name, the one you introduced to Laurie."

"Randy Macintosh."

Frankie hung up without saying good-bye and searched for the District Attorney's Office covering Harbor Bay. She thought she heard the sound of footsteps on the staircase, but when she peered around the corner, no one was there. She had forgotten how these beach houses could creak. When she'd get spooked as a little girl, her mother would explain it was from the humidity and changes in temperature near the water. She called the number for the DA's Office.

"Cape Cod District Attorney's Office. How can I help you?"

She asked to be transferred to Randy Macintosh. She let out an exasperated groan when the resulting call went to his voicemail.

"Mr. Macintosh, this is Frankie Harrington. My parents were Richard and Sarah Harrington. I really need to see some of the photos from our house the night of the murders. It's important. It's about the bracelet that should have been found. It was broken. I can explain it all. Just call me."

She had a few sips of water, hoping it would calm her nerves. When that didn't work, she did the only thing she could think of and went back to her favorite spot with her book, sitting "criss-cross applesauce" as she had as a child, hoping that the story she and her mother used to read and re-read together would give her comfort.

When Mrs. Frankweiler was sharing her files with Claudia, Frankie thought she heard the sound of a stick cracking on the beach behind her. She turned to look and saw the edge of an outstretched towel coming toward her. She screamed as it landed over the top of her head, covering her in darkness.

She was swatting at the towel, trying to push it away, when it tightened around her neck. *No, please God, no.* She arched her back on instinct, preparing to gasp for air. Instead, she felt someone at the other end of the towel yanking her violently sideways.

She straightened her legs and twisted her body, coming to her hands and knees. She pulled her weight backward, trying to pull her head free from the towel that had attached her to her attacker. When that failed, she reached toward the rock with her right arm and managed to find her phone with her fingertips.

Any hope of grabbing the device was lost as she felt a hard chop against her wrist. She tried to yell for help but her voice was muffled by the terry cloth pressed against her face. She was being pulled to her feet against her will.

"Get up or I'll shoot you."

The voice was low and gruff, almost as if the speaker was trying to sound like a monster from a horror movie. She replayed the sound in her head, trying to figure out if any part of it was familiar.

Whoever had grabbed her was shuffling her down the beach. She tried to turn her head to see her abductor's face, but could only see the sandy ground beneath her feet as they moved faster than she wanted them to. She slowed down, only to get a hard shove in the back.

*Keep walking,* she told herself. *You don't want to be shot like your parents. You can't die today.* Whatever was going to happen next was better than being gunned down and left for dead.

She heard the *beep beep* of a key fob. Would anyone ever find her after she was driven away from here? She needed to stay alive, but she also needed to give herself a chance of getting help—and she had to do it now. The car that had chirped sounded close.

She thought of her book's heroine, Claudia Kincaid, following the string of clues that led her from the Metropolitan Museum of Art to the answers inside Mrs. Frankweiler's files. A smart girl with the right clues could figure out anything. Frankie had, after all.

She knew what she had to do.

She managed to slip her left thumb between the bracelet and her right wrist and pull as hard as she could.

It worked. The strand—*classic and demure, as we were both raised to be*—broke just as the ground beneath her transitioned from sand to the gravel of the access road leading to the beach.

The bracelet she had vowed to wear forever was now her only hope, broken at a crime scene just like its former mate.

Her captor let out a frustrated grunt as the pearls tumbled to the ground.

The guttural sound seemed familiar, but she couldn't quite place it.

She winced in pain as she was shoved forward, her body landing on the felt lining of a car trunk, the towel pressed firmly against her face by the palm of a hand.

After a loud slamming sound, everything faded to black.

All these years, she had been so grateful to them for taking her in.

*What other lies had Betsy told her?*

# Chapter 41

It had been three hours since the joint interview with Simon and Ethan had imploded. Laurie, Grace, Jerry, and Ryan had convened in what was once the Harringtons' dining room to strategize ways to complete the production. Their plan to convince the twins to reunite and identify alternative suspects had backfired.

As far as Jerry and Laurie were concerned, the twins had spent so many years convinced of each other's guilt that it would take overwhelming evidence to persuade them otherwise. Meanwhile, Grace and Ryan suspected Simon and Ethan of fabricating their feud, refusing to depart from their original plan to each blame the other so neither could ever be convicted beyond a reasonable doubt.

And despite two hours of debating the two scenarios among themselves, Laurie's team remained divided. She crossed her arms, ready to call it. "If we were a jury, I'd say we were hopelessly deadlocked."

"Sometimes," Grace said, "I wish we could invent some kind of voodoo magic truth serum and just start injecting people."

"Very illegal," Jerry noted.

While parsing through the explosive interaction between the twins, they had also continued sorting through the trove of photographs Frankie had unearthed from storage. Despite what they now knew from the nanny cam Sarah had hidden in Boston, the pictures seemed to portray a family life filled with joy. Ethan and Simon building competing sandcastles as Sarah and Richard looked on with pride. Frankie's fourth birthday party, her handsome teenaged brothers presenting a cake to their excited little sister. The twins posing in matching lacrosse uniforms.

Jerry was saying how much Frankie looked like a younger version of her mother when he suddenly jerked upright. "Oh my gosh. Frankie's late. She should have been back by now."

Laurie leaned over and stole a glance at his watch. "Another fifteen minutes, right?"

"No, I asked her to come in thirty minutes earlier for hair and makeup. The cinematographer has a hard stop this afternoon."

Laurie found her briefcase on the kitchen counter and slipped her cell phone from a side pocket. "She probably forgot you changed the time. Let me call her." There was no answer, so she sent a text instead. *I hope you're okay after this morning. Are you still coming for your interview? Hope to see you soon, but call if you want to talk.*

Laurie continued to leaf through the photographs, but her thoughts kept returning to Frankie. "She was so upset when she left," Laurie said.

"Because she realized her brothers really did it," Ryan said. "That would be more than upsetting."

"Maybe we should have gone after her. Ryan, can you call Simon? He said he was going to look for her when he left here. And Grace, you try Ethan and Annabeth. I'll reach out to Betsy."

Betsy answered on the second ring. Laurie heard children playing in the background. When Laurie explained she was trying to reach Frankie, Betsy said the rest of the family had taken the kids to Provincetown to give Frankie and Simon some peace and quiet at the house for the day.

"Things didn't go well this morning," Laurie said. "Simon and Ethan were arguing. It was bad. Frankie left very upset and hasn't returned for her own session."

The other end of the line fell silent and Laurie wondered if the call may have dropped. "I'm going to come back," Betsy said. "I knew this whole thing was a bad idea."

She hung up, hoping Ryan or Jerry had better luck.

Jerry looked dejected as he ended his own call. "Ethan and Annabeth haven't seen her. He's been trying to call her, but she texted him about five minutes ago to say she needed time to think."

They waited through Ryan's *okay*'s and *uh-huh*'s until he said good-bye and hung up. "Simon said she walked back to the Wards' house from here. He managed to find her but she insisted she needed time alone. That's probably why she's not picking up."

Laurie chewed her bottom lip, not satisfied with the explanation, even though it was the one Frankie had given both of her brothers.

She picked up her phone again and typed a new text. *I want you to know I never meant for the interview with your brothers to end that way. I'm so sorry. Please let me know how I can help.*

She was still holding her phone when she saw a series of dots bouncing on the screen, meaning that Frankie was composing a reply.

*I promise I'm fine. But that interview was intense. Give me some time to think. Is it possible to reschedule the interview for tomorrow?*

*No problem,* she replied. She had the house and the media company booked for the entire week. *But please call me if you want to talk.*

*Don't feel bad. I really am okay. Just need to think.*

"Okay, Frankie texted me back," Laurie reported. "She sounds okay but wants to wait until tomorrow for the interview."

Jerry rose from the table, saying he'd let the media team they'd hired for the shoot know they could leave for the day.

Laurie had tagged another family photo for use in the production when she felt Ryan's eyes on her. "What about the Wards?" he said. "The viewers might want to know something about the family that took in little Frankie after the murders."

Laurie nodded. "Good idea. There was a picture of Sarah and Betsy together in their younger years. Let's use that. And maybe one with the two families together so people can see how close they were."

"This one's perfect," Ryan said, nudging a loose photograph in her direction.

She recognized the picture's setting as the Harringtons' front yard in Boston. Ethan, Simon, and Michelle all wore caps and gowns, holding up degrees from their three different colleges. They were flanked by their parents and younger siblings, Frankie in a ruffled pink dress and Dennis in a Northeastern hockey jersey.

"The parents must have asked them to pose together for a group photo," Grace said. "This would have been within a week or two of the party in Harbor Bay. Look at how happy they all seem. There was no way to know how much life was about to change."

Tim was only a toddler when Greg was shot, an age when Laurie was snapping photos of him almost daily. Whenever she saw pictures from the weeks and months before Greg was killed, she appreciated once again the fragility of happiness and would vow never to take it for granted.

She reached for her laptop on the table. "Good find, Ryan. Let's use that one, too."

Jerry returned to the dining room, reporting that he'd worked out a schedule for the following day with the manager of the media company. "Does this mean we can take a break?" Jerry asked. "I don't know about you, but I'm starving."

Grace placed a hand on her belly. "Oh, thank the lord. I thought it was only me. I was afraid y'all were going to hear my stomach growling."

Ryan made his way to the kitchen island for the car keys. "Lunch it is."

"I think I'm going to stay here if you don't mind," Laurie said.

"I'll bring you something back?" Grace asked.

"Perfect. Thanks."

As soon as Laurie was alone, she reached for her laptop and initiated a FaceTime call to Alex. She felt herself smiling when his face appeared on the screen. She hoped she never stopped noticing how handsome he was.

"Good timing," he said. "We're on a recess. A government witness was running late. I told them they had ten minutes to swear someone in or I'd find another way to proceed."

"Did you bang the gavel?"

"Of course."

"Is it still fun?"

"A little," he said, holding his thumb and index finger an inch apart.

"What are you going to do if they're not ready?"

His shoulders shook slightly as he chuckled. "I have no idea. I just know that whenever a judge gave me that kind of a time limit, I found a way to meet it. To what do I owe this surprising chat? I thought you were slammed today."

"We were. It's been an intense day." She started to tell him why the interview with Simon and Ethan had ended prematurely, but rehashing work wasn't the reason she had called. "I just wanted to say how much I love and miss you. I appreciate you more with every day."

His eyes were locked with hers intently, as if they were face-to-face. "I feel the same. You're my world, Laurie. My everything. I knew you were the one for me from the minute we met. Where's this coming from?"

"I can't just love my husband?"

"Of course you can, but—"

"I don't usually sound like a Valentine's Day card?" she said, smiling.

"Something like that."

"Looking at some old photos of the Harrington family stirred up some feelings."

"Are you okay?" The concern on his face was palpable. "I could come up—"

"No, you can't. Nor do I need you to. I'm fine. And I'll be home in a few days. We have a birthday party for a certain young man." She gave him the short version of the explosive attempt to interview Simon and Ethan together, followed by Frankie's outburst and departure. “Maybe I shouldn’t have taken the case when she’s still so young and her emotions so raw.”

“Don’t take this on yourself,” he said.

How many times had he pointed out that she always worked so hard to fix everyone else’s problems, even at her own expense. Still, she couldn’t help but wonder how Frankie was feeling. Her brothers had been so angry, Laurie had feared that Ethan’s shove of Simon would be the beginning of something more violent.

*That’s my pregnant wife you’re talking about. Leave her and her family out of this.*

Annabeth’s family.

In the heat of chasing down Howard Carver, she had nearly forgotten about Jimmy Connolly. How had she missed it?

“I’m sorry, Alex. I just thought of something. I have to go.”

“Do what you need to do. I love you.”

“Love you too.”

She pulled up Peter Bennett’s number to call him. *Pick up*, she prayed. It would be faster to ask him her question directly than to search for the answer in the camera footage from the Harringtons’ security gate.

He answered on the third ring. “Peter, it’s Laurie Moran. You told me that a van from a local business pulled into the Harringtons’ driveway the day before the murders.”

“That’s right. He was turning around.”

“Was the business the local hardware store?” she asked. “Was it Jimmy Connolly that you spoke to?”

“Right again. His daughter’s married to Ethan now.”

The day before the murders was one day after Simon told Annabeth that his father was going to cut off Ethan financially because of his relationship with her.

“Would someone pulling into the driveway have been able to see that the security gate had a camera?” she asked.

Peter paused. “I think so. It had fallen from its mounting, but you’d still be able to see it there. Why are you asking about this?”

As the family handyman, Peter wouldn't have known about the pressure on Ethan to stop seeing Annabeth. He had accepted Jimmy Connolly's explanation at face value.

She had been waiting to approach Annabeth's father because she didn't want to risk alienating Ethan, but it was clear that ship had sailed. She sent a text to Grace, whom she knew would explain its relevance to the rest of the team. *The van that turned around in the Harringtons' driveway the day before the murders belonged to Annabeth's dad!*

She pulled up the phone number for Jimmy's store and hit enter. When the employee who answered explained the owner was out, Laurie tried her best to sound casual as she left her name and number.

As she stole another look at her phone, hoping to find a reply from Grace, she noticed that she had a voicemail alert.

It was from twenty minutes ago.

It was from Frankie. She had been so harried all day that she had missed it. She immediately hit play.

*Laurie, it's Frankie. I need those photographs I gave you.* Her voice was urgent, almost pleading, the sound of wind rushing in the background. *Do you have them at the house for the shoot? My head's racing right now. I figured something out. Call me back.*

Laurie grew more anxious with each ring as her call to Frankie went unanswered. "Come on, pick up," she said, sighing when she got an outgoing message instead. "Frankie, it's Laurie. Yes, I have the photos. But why did you say you wanted to be left alone? And I figured out something, too. Please don't let your thoughts keep racing on your own. Let me help. Call me back."

She hung up and opened her Uber app. She was going to help Frankie, whether she wanted it or not. As the car was approaching, she grabbed the box of photos.

# Chapter 42

Laurie banged her fist once again on the front door. "Frankie!" she yelled.

She set the box of photographs down on the Wards' porch and made her way through a flowerbed to get a better look into the house through the living room window, cupping her hands at her temples to block the glare. The lights and television were off.

She circled the house, peering through windows, but there was no sign of Frankie. At each stop, she would try Frankie's cell again, hoping she might at least hear it ring from inside the house. Only more outgoing voicemail messages.

When Frankie had called her about whatever she had discovered, she had raised her voice over the sound of the wind. She had been outside.

Laurie went to the back of the house and spotted a narrow path through the brush, which she followed toward the water.

She placed her hands on her hips as she scanned the beach. In the distance, she spotted a female jogger with a black Lab, but no Frankie.

Her phone vibrated in her hand. A new message from Frankie. *Please stop calling me. I went for a long run. I'll see you tomorrow.*

Laurie turned to go back to the house, but as she did, she noticed a series of footsteps and disruptions in the otherwise pristine sand. The bulk of the activity was in front of a large rock about twenty feet from the clearing in the brush, as if someone had made a temporary nesting place there, but a trail of footprints continued farther down the beach.

As Laurie made her way closer to the rock, she noticed something in the sand beside it—an open book, its pages fluttering in the wind. When she picked it up, she felt a catch in her throat. *From the Mixed-Up Files of Mrs. Basil E. Frankweiler.*

Frankie had been reading here. She would never leave this beloved book outside on the beach.

She studied the imprints in the sand more closely. It looked like two sets of footprints, extremely close to each other, led from the rock to south of the Wards' property. Laurie had a sudden image of Frankie being guided away against her will.

She created her own path parallel to the footprints, saying a silent prayer that she would find Frankie safe and sound at the end of the trail. After she'd made her way up the bluff, her heart fell when the sand ended. She was standing at a gravel access road to the beach, a literal dead end.

She looked again at her exchange of messages with Frankie.

*I promise I'm fine. But today was intense. Give me some time to think. Is it possible to reschedule the interview for tomorrow?*

*Don't feel bad. I really am okay. Just need to think.*

*Please stop calling me. I went for a long run. I'll see you tomorrow.*

She had told her brothers the same thing. How many times should she have to say it? In Laurie's own guilt for having messed up this morning's interview, had she overreacted to Frankie's desire to be left alone for a few hours? Or was she missing something?

She looked down futilely at the gravel road, hoping for some form of validation that Frankie had departed the beach from here for a run, exactly as she had said. She was about to leave when she noticed one tiny spot of pinkish white shimmering among the gray-brown pieces of gravel.

She bent down and plucked up a single, small stone. Not a stone. A pearl. She scanned the road surface for any other irregularities. A metallic glint, six inches away. She immediately recognized it as the clasp from the bracelet Betsy had given Frankie the previous night.

The discarded book. The broken bracelet.

When Frankie left her last voicemail, she said she had figured something out. She sounded desperate to see her family photographs and had pleaded for Laurie to call her back. That did not sound like a woman who wanted to be left alone.

She started to call Frankie again but composed a new text instead. *I found that lipstick you were looking for at the house. You left it on the powder room vanity.*

Bouncing dots. Frankie was replying. Or at least, *someone* was replying.

*Thanks so much! I'll get it from you tomorrow!!*

There was no missing lipstick. Something was desperately wrong. Frankie was in trouble.

# Chapter 43

Laurie sat alone on the front steps of the Wards' house, mentally replaying Frankie's phone message while frantically opening the box of photographs Frankie had retrieved from the storage unit. *I need those photographs I gave you. Do you have them at the house for the shoot? My head's racing right now. I figured something out.*

*Frankie,* Laurie thought to herself, *why did you need these pictures? What did you figure out? And did it relate to Annabeth or her father?*

The photos Laurie and the team had flagged to use in the production were the ones she had packed last into the box, so they were at the top of the pile. She flipped through those first and found herself pausing on the picture of Ethan, Simon, and Michelle in their graduation regalia, displaying their degrees from three different Boston-area schools—Simon's from Harvard, Ethan's from U Mass Amherst, Michelle's from Tufts. Frankie wore an adorably girly pink dress, while Dennis had donned a black hockey jersey from his college, only two years from graduating from Northeastern himself. Their parents next to the children. Something about the image was tugging at a memory, but she couldn't figure out how a photograph from when Frankie was twelve years old would be relevant. She had a box full of other photos to search.

She was well into a second album when her phone rang. She answered immediately, praying it was Frankie. The number on the screen was from the local 508 area code, but she didn't recognize it.

"Hello?"

"Laurie, this is Randy Macintosh from the Cape Cod DA's Office."

"I'm so glad you called. Maybe you can help me. I think Richard and Sarah Harrington's daughter is in danger."

"You mean Frankie?" he asked sharply. "That's why I was calling. She left me a very pushy message. I called her back, but she didn't answer. I was wondering how she got my name and number. I spoke to you and Ryan off the record."

"Frankie called you? I didn't tell her—" Laurie stopped herself when she realized she had told Frankie that Jenna's brother-in-law was an ADA and was trying to convince his boss to cooperate with their show. None of that mattered now. "Why did she call you? I'm at the house where she's staying out here, and she's missing. I'm really worried. I also found out Annabeth's father went to the Harringtons' house the day before the murders. I think he left when he saw the security camera. The twins got in a big fight today on set—partly over allegations Simon was making about Annabeth and her father."

"What do you mean, Frankie's missing?" Any note of irritation she had detected in his voice vanished. "She only called me thirty minutes ago. She said she wanted to see the crime scene photos from her parents' case."

"She called me around the same time asking for the photo albums she had lent me. I'm scrambling through all of them now, trying to figure out why."

"She asked specifically about her mother's bracelet—the fact that it was broken."

Laurie felt a jolt of electricity surge up her spine at the mention of the bracelet. It was happening again. A treasured piece of jewelry broken in a violent struggle. There had to be some connection between the pearl and the silver clasp she had found by the beach and Frankie's search for photographs.

"Do you have any pictures from the crime scene that show the broken bracelet that was found near Sarah's body?" she asked.

"Yes, I remember that from when I reviewed the file."

"Look, I know your boss doesn't want you working with us, despite reopening the investigation, but I won't use it for my show unless she clears it. This is important. Frankie's missing, and I need to find her."

It didn't take long for the images to land in her inbox. She used two fingers to zoom in on the pearls spilled across the bleached wood floorboards of the Harringtons' living room, shimmering in the red-brown pool of blood.

*What had Frankie been looking for?*

She found herself counting the individual pearls in the picture. Something didn't feel right.

She used her phone to pull up the Tiffany website and then searched for pearl bracelets. She immediately spotted the one she was looking for, described as a longtime classic—refined pearls combined with contrasting metal in a unique design inspired by the architecture of New York City.

*What was she missing?*

The clasp she had found on the beach was still intact and yet the bracelet had clearly fallen from Frankie's wrist. Laurie thought of her own pearl bracelet, which was elastic and slipped on and off easily. She scanned the website listing and confirmed her suspicions. The bracelet did not stretch and had to be ordered in a choice of sizes. To remove it, the clasp would need to be opened.

Frankie's bracelet had fit her to a tee, which would make sense if it had been her mother's. Frankie resembled her mother in so many ways, including her petite size. But Laurie was looking at ironclad proof that Sarah Harrington's bracelet had broken the night of her murder.

Laurie returned her attention to the photographs they had flagged for the show and pulled out the one of Sarah and Betsy when they were in college. Betsy wore wide-legged pants and a turtleneck. Sarah, nearly six inches shorter, was in a cardigan sweater and A-line skirt. Sarah's sleeves were pushed up to the middle of her forearms, before she needed to worry about anyone spotting bruises.

On their right wrists, the best friends wore matching, perfectly sized pearl bracelets. Even in this grainy photograph, it was obvious that Sarah's wrist was noticeably smaller than Betsy's.

Laurie's thoughts were interrupted by the sound of a car engine approaching the house. She looked up to see a gray SUV pulling into the driveway. Betsy Ward stepped out and rushed toward the porch, keys in hand. Laurie opened the Voice Memo app on her phone, hit the red button on the screen to record, and slipped the device in her jacket pocket.

"Is Frankie here?" Betsy asked as she unlocked the door. "She keeps texting me that she wants to be left alone and won't pick up when I call her. It's not like her to shut down this way. She must be terribly upset."

Laurie returned the photographs to the box and rose to her feet, following Betsy inside, ready to deal with the woman who had been lying about her best friend's murder for nearly a decade.

"Frankie?" Betsy called out. She yelled Frankie's name again from the base of the staircase, where she dropped her purse. "Where is that girl?"

Laurie studied the woman's face, searching for any hint of guilt. "Why did you kill them, Betsy?"

# Chapter 44

Laurie had met Betsy Ward in person for the first time only the previous night. At the time, her impression was that Betsy looked much younger than sixty-five years old. With a single question—*Why did you kill them, Betsy?*—she appeared to have aged two decades.

"Laurie, I have no idea what you're talking about. I've been trying to help you from the first time you called me nearly three years ago."

"You've certainly pretended to," Laurie said. "But Frankie and Dennis both told me you were opposed to my involvement. You didn't want anyone to know the truth—you were at the Harringtons' house when they were murdered."

"First you call me saying you're worried about Frankie. Now you're accusing me of something I don't even understand. I thought you were a reasonable woman."

If Betsy was at all worried about what Laurie had pieced together, she hid it well. She walked nonchalantly to the kitchen, poured herself a glass of water, and took a sip. "Are you coming in or not?" she asked.

"I prefer to stand here," Laurie said, lingering near the front door in the living room, ready to run outside if necessary. She realized she had let her guard down by walking inside alone, armed with nothing but a phone. Betsy might be an older woman, but anyone who killed before could kill again. Laurie eyed a heavy decorative vase positioned on the nearby console table as a backup plan.

"Suit yourself," Betsy said, making her way to the living room sofa and having a seat. "Can you please explain whatever nonsense you've come up with?"

"The bracelet you gave to Frankie wasn't yours. It was her mother's, which means the pearls the Harbor Bay police found next to Sarah's body belonged to you."

"I don't know what you're talking about. The bracelets were identical. We bought them for each other. That was the whole point."

"They were the same design, but they weren't identical. That bracelet comes in different sizes, and Sarah's was smaller than yours. It barely fit Frankie, and she and her mother are extremely petite. I saw the photos from the crime scene. You can count the number of pearls soaked with blood."

Betsy opened her mouth to speak but no words came out.

"The police will have retained every pearl they found at the crime scene," Laurie said. "I can get an expert witness from Tiffany about the sizing. We'll be able to prove you were there that night."

"Even if that were my bracelet, it doesn't mean I was at the house—just a piece of jewelry."

"Except for the fact that you gave a second bracelet to Frankie last night. Unless you have a receipt showing you purchased a new one, it's obvious that you somehow had Sarah's." Laurie was picturing the scene as she spoke. "*Your* bracelet broke that night in a struggle. There was no way you could guarantee that you'd find every last pearl if you'd tried to clean up. Even one stray jewel might have given you away. When you realized Sarah was also wearing hers, you saw the solution. You removed the bracelet from your dead friend's wrist so police would assume the broken one was hers. Why did you kill them? Was Sarah having an affair with Walter?" It was the only motive Laurie had been able to imagine. Sarah may have turned to another man—her husband's friend and law partner—for comfort from the abuse she was suffering at home.

Betsy let out a small scoff. "You're wrong about everything."

"If you say so," she said. "I have enough for a major plot twist, and the DA's Office has already agreed to reopen the investigation. My show will only increase the pressure. The Harbor Bay Police Department may have blown the investigation, but the state police won't."

Laurie was about to walk out the door when Betsy told her to stop.

She was surprisingly calm, still seated on the sofa, drinking her water. "I knew about the abuse. It had been going on for years, but Sarah only told me a few months before that night. We had gone to a spin class together, back home in Boston. By then, I had gotten used to seeing her in long sleeves, even when she worked out. She said she started getting cold all the time as she got older. But we were changing at the gym to go straight to lunch after class. She probably didn't realize how dark the bruises were because they were on her back. When I asked her about them, she said she fell down, but it didn't add up. She broke down in tears, right there in the locker room, and told me everything."

Laurie wanted Betsy to talk about the night of the murders. "You knew about the hidden cameras," Laurie said. "She was trying to get proof of the abuse, right? And you took the memory card from the device before you left the house that night?"

Betsy nodded.

"Was that a yes?" Laurie asked, hoping her phone was capturing every word.

"She wanted to leave him, but Richard said no one would believe her—that she'd never be able to prove it and he'd keep her tied up in court for years. The cameras were my idea. I kept pressing her to see whether she had evidence, and she'd tell me she was waiting until she was certain she had enough before telling him she wanted a divorce. The night of the graduation party, I asked her if she'd made any progress, and she insisted that she didn't want to talk about it. She wanted to pretend that they were still the picture-perfect family for the evening. Image was always so important to her. I think Richard ingrained that into her and the boys."

Laurie was beginning to see the connection between the trauma in the Harrington household and the tragedy that unfolded the night of the party. "But as much as Sarah tried, that night didn't remain picture perfect," she said.

Betsy's gaze grew distant. As much as Laurie had expected her to resist the truth, she almost seemed hypnotized, the words flowing from her freely.

"Richard and Howard were having a drink together and it seemed like they were getting along. But then I noticed them alone on the back deck. They were obviously arguing. I think my husband explained what was going on at the firm?" Betsy asked.

Laurie nodded. "Howard was bilking clients."

"Exactly. Richard stormed off and the next thing I knew, he had Sarah against the wall in the next room, shaking her by the shoulders like a rag doll. When he saw me in the doorway, he pushed past me and marched out to the parking lot. I followed him outside. The valets were all busy, so he just hopped in his car and drove away."

Laurie recalled Ethan saying that when he saw his father leaving the party early, he seemed upset and left alone.

"And then what happened?" Laurie asked.

"I went back inside and asked Sarah when she was finally going to leave him. I had witnessed the assault myself and could testify. She said she didn't think she was strong enough. She really wanted to believe that once Richard and Walter forced Howard out of the law firm, and once the boys were successfully out of college, Richard would stop 'taking his stress out,' as she called it."

Laurie imagined what she would do if Charlotte or another friend were in the same position. "You went to the house to confront him," she said. "But Walter had left already with Dennis so you didn't have a car. You took the Range Rover."

Betsy was nodding again. Laurie couldn't remember a time when someone had been so forthcoming with incriminating information. "I decided someone needed to stand up for my friend, and it would have to be me. Sarah tried to stop me, but I was determined. I was heading for the valet stand when I remembered that I had told Walter and Dennis to go home without me and I'd either walk or get a cab. The Range Rover was at the very front of the main lot because the twins had arrived so early. The car keys were sitting right on the driver's seat."

"How far behind Richard were you?" Laurie asked.

"Only a few minutes. I knew the gate code and used it as I always would. I rang the doorbell and Richard let me in. Once I was inside, I wasn't exactly subtle. I told him his days of controlling Sarah were over. I said he was going to grant her a divorce and custody over Frankie."

"How did he respond?" Laurie asked.

Betsy's gaze was distant as she recalled the scene. "I should have known it would be bad after everything Sarah told me, but it came out of nowhere. He grabbed me and pushed me against the wall. *How dare you speak to me like this in my own home?* I remember it like it was yesterday. I was trying to push him off me. The next thing I knew, he had a gun. I couldn't believe that this man I had known for more than thirty years was trying to kill me. I charged at him, trying to take the gun. My bracelet broke in the struggle. I probably would have died except he was distracted by the sound of the back door opening. It was Sarah. She had seen me leaving the club and figured out where I was going. She must have walked to the house on the beach."

Laurie replayed the scenario that each of the twins had depicted about the other—a confrontation with Richard that ended violently when Sarah unexpectedly interrupted.

"Richard was as surprised to see Sarah as I was," Betsy said. "I really don't think he meant to pull the trigger. It was a reflex. Sarah fell to the ground. At that point, I knew I was fighting for my life. I didn't want Richard to die. I just wanted to survive. Right when I thought I had control over the gun, he jerked the weapon away. It just went off. He fell to the ground. There was so much blood. I checked their pulses, hoping there was something I could do, but they were both dead."

There was something unnaturally flat about Betsy's account. Her best friend and her husband were dead and she was reporting the facts as if she were a neutral bystander.

"Why didn't you call the police?" Laurie asked.

"I wanted to. I was looking for evidence of Richard's abuse. But there was nothing incriminating in the camera in the hallway outside Richard's office. Sarah told me she had some evidence, but I didn't know where it was. That's why the house was torn apart. I was searching for the videos. When I couldn't find anything, I grabbed the memory card so the police wouldn't know I was there. Before I left, I realized my bracelet had broken. I was sobbing when I removed Sarah's bracelet from her wrist, vowing I would find the right time to give it to Frankie. I took the Range Rover back to the overflow lot and walked home from there."

Betsy's account of that night was checking all the boxes. The Range Rover. The keypad. The gun. The bracelet. "You're confessing," Laurie said. "And yet it doesn't add up."

"You said you wanted the truth and I'm giving it to you. I see now that I should have called the police immediately. I thought I could find some kind of redemption by doing my best to help Sarah's children. I didn't let myself see how much I had hurt Frankie, Simon, and Ethan until you got involved."

"I don't know you well, Betsy," Laurie said, "but I'm having a hard time believing that you spent almost ten years raising Frankie while Simon and Ethan were being blamed as murderers, just to protect yourself."

"I promised myself that if Simon and Ethan were ever charged, I'd come forward to tell the truth. I was never going to let them go to jail for what I had done."

Laurie was used to criminals telling half-truths. They'd concede they were present at the crime scene but blame someone else for pulling the trigger. Or they'd admit to pulling the trigger but claim they were acting in self-defense. She was certain Betsy wasn't telling the complete truth and yet she had been so quick to confess.

Why would she confess so quickly?

"There's something you're not telling me," Laurie said. "You didn't have to give Frankie that bracelet. If you hadn't, I never would have figured out you were at the house that night. Your best friend was dead and yet you didn't call the police. Her sons were suspects, and you still didn't come forward. You weren't protecting yourself. You were protecting someone else."

Betsy said nothing.

Was it Michelle? No, if anything, the murders derailed the life of Michelle's future husband.

Walter? No. He may have wanted to call cops on Howard, but Richard was the one who made up the losses and found a way to save the firm.

Which left . . . Dennis? What did he have to do with it?

Laurie pictured the two families, always together. The mothers were best friends. The fathers were law partners. Even his older sister had chosen a Harrington as her boyfriend. And by all accounts, the Harringtons were supposedly "perfect." At the law firm, Richard was the rainmaker with the bigger draw and the nicer houses. Sarah was an artist like Betsy, but Sarah was the one who had showings in Manhattan galleries. The twins were incredibly handsome, one a Harvard graduate about to go to a top-ranked law school, the other a talented musician. *How could Dennis even begin to compete?*

Laurie flashed back to Michelle telling her about the day Simon arrived at her house, confessing that he had paid another student to write his term paper. She said it was during spring break. *Why?* she had demanded to know. *Why would you have done something so wrong and reckless?* Dennis could have easily overheard the conversation. Simon began receiving the anonymous blackmail messages only days later.

Laurie thought about the graffiti spray-painted at the Harringtons' beach house. *This Family is a Lie.* Peter Bennett had found a moment in the front gate's camera footage that captured a brief glimpse of the vandal's shoe and shirtsleeve. According to Peter, Sarah had been adamant about not calling the police.

Laurie realized now why she had been bothered by the group photograph of the twins and Michelle with their graduation degrees. Dennis had been wearing a black hockey jersey from Northeastern—long sleeved with white and red stripes near the elbow, just like the sleeve in the graffiti video.

Raised in the shadow of a family that was always a little too perfect, Dennis must have been seething with resentment.

"Where's your son?" Laurie asked.

"We all went to Provincetown together. I came back when you told me Frankie was upset." For the first time since Laurie had confronted her, Betsy looked nervous. More than nervous. Terrified. Her fists were clenched and her lips were trembling.

"It will take me one phone call to Michelle to ask if I can talk to Dennis."

Betsy said nothing.

"Sarah told Peter Bennett she didn't want to call the police to press charges after the vandalism incident, even though he had video. She recognized your son, didn't she? She would have gone to you instead of law enforcement."

Betsy remained silent.

"And Simon was getting blackmailed about cheating on a paper until the anonymous emails suddenly stopped not long after the graffiti. Dennis was jealous, wasn't he? Never able to live up to the picture-perfect twins? Or the family that was always better?"

"I already told you what happened. I never should have gone to the house that night. Leave my family out of this."

"Betsy, if everything played out as you said, you would have called the police immediately after the shooting. You were defending yourself from Richard. The only reason you'd take that nanny cam footage and leave your friend to be found by someone else would be to protect your son. After he left early with Walter, he could have walked back to the Harringtons' house. Your family had a spare key. Had he already killed them when you arrived?"

"Please, I'm begging you. Leave Dennis alone. He was always in the shadow of those boys. I didn't realize how much he resented them until it was too late. If I had taken the graffiti incident more seriously, maybe Sarah would . . ." Her voice drifted off.

"Betsy, I know you want to think you can keep protecting Dennis, but look at the facts. Frankie's missing. So is Dennis. And so is his car. I found her beloved childhood book abandoned on the beach. The bracelet you gave her was intentionally broken near the access road of the beach, where I think she was abducted. Look at the trauma you've inflicted on your best friend's children. Now Frankie is in danger, and I think you know in your heart that Dennis is probably involved."

Betsy's shoulders began to quiver and then shake until she collapsed forward, her head in her hands. When she sat upright, she wiped tears away from her eyes. "He didn't go to that house to hurt them. He was feeling resentful about the lavish party and the way the boys were ignoring him in favor of their college friends. He went to the house thinking he'd move their stuff around or some other mind game. Then Richard came home and found him. When I got there, I heard screaming inside. I recognized my son's voice. The door was unlocked. Richard had his gun on Dennis so he couldn't leave. Sarah never told him that she recognized Dennis from the spray-paint incident, but he put two and two together after finding Dennis in the house. He said he was going to call the police. I tried to talk him out of it, promising I'd get Dennis into counseling to deal with his anger, but Richard refused. He was heading for the phone when I told him that if he called the police on Dennis, I'd tell them all about how he had been abusing Sarah for years. And then the rest is exactly like I told you."

"He grabbed you?"

"He smacked me so hard I fell to the ground. Dennis charged at him headfirst, trying to protect me. They were struggling over the gun. That's when Sarah walked in through the back door. She ran toward the living room. Right as she neared them, the gun went off. It's just like I said before—she was shot first, and then Richard—but it wasn't me fighting for my life. It was Dennis. I jumped in and tried to help. That's when my bracelet broke. Dennis thought he had control over the gun, but then Richard grabbed it again, and that's when he was shot, too."

"Dennis must have driven the Range Rover back to the club," Laurie said. "He's the one Howard Carver saw in the parking lot."

Howard had told the police he saw one of the Harrington twins near the Range Rover as he was leaving. But when Laurie had pressed him about the recollection, he couldn't pull up a visual image of either Simon or Ethan. *He was wearing a white shirt, white pants, white jacket, just like the two of them at the party. And I distinctly recalled seeing the Range Rover and turning away because I didn't want my law partner's son to see me in my current state and tell his father I was using. It's like I remembered the shame and the fear of getting caught more than the person I actually saw.*

The next day, in the aftermath of the investigation, he of course assumed that the "law partner's son" near the Harringtons' Range Rover must have been one of the twins.

Betsy nodded, confirming Laurie's theory. "Sarah had told me the gate camera was broken. I had no idea they'd have footage showing the Range Rover. That's why I told Dennis to take it back to the club and leave it nearby. I figured the valets would find it for the boys at the end of the night and they'd chalk it up to shuffling cars around during a busy party."

"How did you get home?" Laurie asked.

"I put poor Bacon in Richard's office and went out the back door and locked it with my spare key, then walked home on the beach. I was sobbing the entire time. I even thought about filling my jacket pockets with rocks and wandering out into the bay like Virginia Woolf, but my son needed me. So did Frankie."

"We need to find Dennis," Laurie said. "Even if what happened that night was an accident, it doesn't change the fact that Frankie is missing."

"He would never hurt her."

"You're still protecting him, Betsy. Frankie told me she had figured something out. He could have panicked and tried to stop her."

Betsy chewed her lip, obviously torn between her loyalty to her son and her commitment to caring for Frankie.

"Let me call him," she said, heading to the staircase for her purse. She made the call but soon shook her head. "Straight to voicemail. I'll try Frankie." Another disappointed shake of the head. "Their phones must be off. Hold on, let me see if I can find them."

"How?" Laurie asked.

Betsy was fiddling with her phone. "When Frankie decided to go to school in California, I made her promise to share her location with me so I would always be able to find her. Even if her phone's off, it should tell me where she was the last time she had a signal. Okay, I've got it." She read the address aloud.

"That's the storage unit I rented for her. They must be inside. There's probably no phone signal."

Laurie was certain that Dennis had been using Frankie's phone to send all those messages asking for time alone. Dennis could have both phones inside the storage unit, searching for any evidence he might want to destroy. There was no guarantee that Frankie was even alive. *Please, God, keep her safe.*

Betsy was already heading out the front door. Laurie followed, climbing into the passenger seat.

As Betsy started the engine, Laurie called ADA Randy Macintosh. "I need your help."

# Chapter 45

Frankie's eyes were beginning to adjust to the darkness of the car trunk. She had bundled the towel as a pillow beneath her head to soften the impact of sudden halts and bumpy roads, but now the car was still, the engine turned off.

When she had first landed in the trunk, she actually found herself hoping that the car would drive from the beach immediately. That would mean that her abductor had left her broken bracelet on the ground. She prayed that Laurie would get her voicemail message, go looking for her, and understand that she intended the jewelry as a clue.

But she had waited in the dark car trunk, seconds and then minutes passing. Whoever grabbed her had grunted in frustration when she broke the pearl bracelet so they must have understood its importance—proof that Betsy had been at the house when Frankie's parents were killed.

Betsy, the one who had taken her in when she'd suddenly become an orphan.

Why? Why would Betsy hurt her parents? She replayed that voice on the beach. *Get up or I'll shoot you.* The person was obviously disguising their voice. But Betsy, grabbing her and shoving her in a car trunk? No. She couldn't believe it.

She had no way of tracking time, but her best guess was that the drive lasted fifteen minutes before coming to a stop. The engine turned off, and she heard the driver's door open and shut, but no one had come for her yet. How long had it been? Another fifteen minutes?

*Is anyone even looking for me?*

Exploring the area within her reach, she felt a netting-like material lining the side of the trunk. Pulling at it with her fingertips, she realized the netting stretched. It was a storage space.

She found the opening and reached inside. She pulled out a plastic box the size of an old-time videocassette. When she snapped it open, the contents spilled onto her chest. She picked up what seemed like a small piece of paper. Holding it up, she made out the shape of a Band-Aid. It was a first aid kit. Useless.

She reached into the storage cubby again and this time pulled out some type of can. It was cool to the touch. She found a button on the top and pressed it. She immediately recognized the smell of bug spray. She held her breath and pressed her eyes shut to protect against the fumes. If he ever opened the trunk, she could go for his eyes and make a run for it if that was her only chance.

She reached in again and felt something else tube-shaped. Not a can. This was heavier. Much heavier. Fumbling with it, she found a switch. The trunk was suddenly bathed in light. She squinted, quickly turning it back off. She tapped the flashlight against the palm of her left hand and began to make a plan.

# Chapter 46

Simon was surprised to see no other cars at his in-laws' beach house as he parked his blue Subaru in the driveway. He knew Michelle had the minivan in Provincetown with the kids and that Dennis had been talking about driving to Chatham, but Michelle said Betsy was taking her and Walter's car back to Harbor Bay to try to talk to Frankie. That's when Simon had decided he had given Frankie enough time to herself. He needed to apologize to her for losing it with Ethan that morning.

An open cardboard box was on the patio. He peered inside to find the photographs Frankie had packed up from the storage unit. A copy of Frankie's favorite childhood book was tucked between the box and the house. Why would she possibly leave these outside?

He was unlocking the door when the knob turned without resistance. It was unlocked. "Hello?" he called out when he stepped inside. "Betsy? Frankie?"

The house was silent.

He took the stairs two at a time. No one was upstairs. He made his way out to the beach, hoping to find Frankie holed up in her favorite spot by what they referred to as her "reading rock." He could tell from the indentation in the sand that she had probably been sitting there earlier, but she was gone now.

He had just walked back to the house when a white Subaru, identical to his own except in color, came to a halt at the front curb. Ethan stepped out from behind the wheel, and a very pregnant Annabeth quickly followed from the passenger seat.

Simon charged away from the front door, meeting them in the yard.

"What are you doing here?" Simon demanded.

Ethan rolled his eyes. "Frankie's my sister, too. She texted me that she wasn't ready to talk, but I want to make sure she's okay. Is she here?"

Simon thought again of the book and photographs on the patio. Frankie would never leave them outside if she had any choice in the matter. "Where have you been since our interview this morning?" he asked.

Ethan looked confused by the question.

"Why do you have to be this way?" Annabeth asked, sounding genuinely hurt. "He was with me. I was having cramps, and he took me to the doctor to be safe."

The tone of her voice brought Simon back to that night at the Pizza Palace when he told her she was getting in the way of Ethan and his family. He had treated her so poorly. "And are you okay?" he asked, his expression softening. "The baby?"

She nodded. "We're fine. Thank you."

"Why were you so curious about our whereabouts?" Ethan asked.

Simon told them about the pictures and book he had found on the patio.

"She loves that book," Ethan said. "Something's not right. Since you asked us, where were *you* all day?"

Simon started to argue but realized he had demanded the same information of Ethan. "Meeting with a real estate broker. Daniel and Sophie love it here so much, I thought I'd see what we could afford. Call the agent if you don't believe me."

The implication was clear. If Frankie was in danger, it wasn't because of either Simon or Ethan. Laurie Moran had been right. All this time, they had been accusing each other while the real killer was out there.

And now Frankie could be paying the price.

"Should we call the police?" Simon asked.

"And tell them what?" Ethan asked. "That she's been texting us all day saying she needs time to herself but we found a book? Let's just find her so we can stop freaking out. Where might she have gone if she really did want to be alone?"

Simon thought about the possibilities. She didn't have any friends in Harbor Bay. And he'd seen her running shoes in her room, so she wasn't on a jog. "The storage unit. She's been going through all the stuff from our old house."

"Do you know where it is?" Ethan asked. Simon nodded. "Let's go. Come with us. You navigate. I'll drive."

Whatever their differences, they needed to work together now—for their little sister.

# Chapter 47

Betsy pointed to a black Audi sedan at the back of the lot at the storage facility. "That's Dennis. He's here." She was about to drive in that direction, but Laurie stopped her.

"The state police said to wait until they got here." ADA Macintosh had put her in touch with the detective who was going to lead the newly reopened investigation of the Harrington murders. She was sending an emergency response team to meet them.

"I need to see my son. I can get him to calm down. He'll let Frankie go and turn himself in."

"Or," Laurie said, "you'll be like Sarah walking unexpectedly into a volatile situation—and end up the same way."

"That's ridiculous. Dennis would never hurt me or Frankie."

"Guns go off, Betsy. You of all people know that."

"Dennis doesn't even own a gun."

"Are you sure about that?" Laurie asked. "You'd bet Frankie's life on it?"

That was enough to convince Betsy to tuck her SUV against the fence at the front of the storage property. From their vantage point, they could see Dennis's car, but he would be unlikely to notice them.

Betsy had just turned off the engine when the door to the storage unit next to the black Audi opened. It was Dennis.

Laurie's heart fell when she saw that he was alone. Where was Frankie?

He bypassed the driver's door and moved toward the rear of his car. She heard the faint *beep beep* of a key fob. The trunk opened.

Frankie had her plan—the risk she had decided she would have to take when this trunk finally opened. *If* it opened. She held the bug spray in her left hand, index finger ready on the trigger. She had the flashlight in her right, her fingers wrapped firmly around the base, her arm ready to swing.

Frankie couldn't believe how fast it all happened.

The silence was broken by the *beep beep* of the key fob. When the trunk sprang open, she sat upright, her left arm extended. *Aim for the eyes.* She held the trigger down hard as she rose to a standing position and jumped from the trunk. Her captor was bent over, rubbing his eyes. She dropped the can of bug spray as she raised the flashlight high, steeling herself to lower it onto his head, when she realized she recognized the car. The voice that was groaning in pain.

Dennis?

Still holding the flashlight tight in her hand, she turned toward the gate of the storage facility and began to run. She knew where the diner was. And she had always been a faster runner than Dennis.

Laurie couldn't believe how fast it all happened.

The trunk opened. Dennis slumped forward as if in pain. Frankie leapt from the sedan's trunk. She had something raised over her head, poised to strike, but then stopped herself. She began to run.

And then Dennis ran after her.

They couldn't wait for the police now. Before Laurie knew what she was doing, she was out of the car, waving Frankie toward Betsy's car. She narrowly avoided being hit by her open car door as Betsy lurched the SUV forward, heading directly toward Dennis.

Laurie pulled Frankie into a hug as Betsy took a sharp turn, cutting off her son's path.

"Oh my god, you found me. I was praying."

"You did good, Frankie. You're safe now."

She looked up to see Betsy out of her car. At the sight of his mother, Dennis stopped running, breaking down in her arms, sobbing like a child who needed his mother to protect him once again.

She heard the sounds of sirens in the distance.

# Chapter 48

The lead state police detective's name was Jessica Foster. Since the police had arrived to the scene, Laurie had laid out to her everything she knew, and detectives had taken preliminary statements. Betsy and Dennis were extremely emotional and wanted to talk to detectives about what had happened to Richard and Sarah. Frankie was deeply traumatized but was able to describe the terrifying details of her abduction by Dennis.

As Dennis and Betsy were being driven away in the back of separate patrol cars, Laurie asked Detective Foster what would happen to them.

The detective shrugged. "So far, they're being cooperative. We'll see if that continues at the station. Betsy has already confessed to taking the memory card, so that's evidence-tampering, plus the false statements she made to the police when she said she last saw them at the party. But as for the actual homicide? That'll be up to the District Attorney's Office after we do a more complete investigation, but according to both her and the son, an armed Richard Harrington assaulted her first and they were trying to defend themselves from that point on."

Laurie was raised by a cop, married to a criminal law expert, and had covered true crime cases for years. She knew the picture was more complicated than that. "And what about the fact that Richard armed himself because he was about to call the police on Dennis?" she asked.

Detective Foster squinted, processing the question. "The state could go for felony murder, but Dennis didn't actually break into the house. He had a key. And there's no proof he went there to do anything but a juvenile prank. Like I said, the DAs will make the call."

"And for kidnapping Frankie?" Laurie asked.

Dennis claims he panicked when he heard her call the ADA about the bracelet. He popped the trunk because he'd come to his senses and was going to tell her the truth about what happened the night of the murders.

The detective glanced over her shoulder in Frankie's direction. As a precaution, EMTs were monitoring her as she rested on the edge of an ambulance with the doors open. She was out of earshot.

"As of now, she's saying she doesn't want to press charges. The DAs can't prove anything in court without her testimony, but I took her statement and told her not to make any final decisions right now. With time, she may change her mind."

Laurie had a feeling she wouldn't.

Detective Foster pulled a car key from her coat pocket. "Betsy said you and Frankie would need a ride home."

"Has anyone told Walter yet?" Laurie asked. "Betsy insists he didn't know."

"ADA Macintosh asked him to come into the DA's Office. He's breaking the news to him now."

Laurie nodded. There would be no happy endings here. Betsy had been trying to protect Dennis, but if they had told the truth at the time, he would probably have been a free man by now, and all of this would have been in the past.

It was exactly as Dennis had said when he called her, trying to get her to drop the investigation. *I have this horrible feeling that opening the door to the past is going to lead somewhere really bad.*

As she waited for the EMTs to give Frankie the all clear, Laurie answered every question Frankie had to the best of her ability.

"I can't believe they knew this entire time," Frankie said. "My brothers got blamed."

Laurie started to explain that Betsy's plan was to come forward in the event the twins were ever charged, but it wasn't up to her to make excuses for Betsy's decisions. At some point, when Frankie was ready, she could hear Betsy out directly.

A white Subaru took the turn at the fence of the parking lot. An officer positioned there held up a hand, stopping it from entering. Frankie sat up straighter at the sight of the car.

The officer called out in Detective Foster's direction. "They're family."

Laurie could make out two identical faces, side by side, in the front seats.

As Frankie hopped down from the edge of the ambulance, Laurie saw her smiling.

Simon and Ethan jumped from the car, rushing past the officer toward their little sister.

"My god, we thought we had lost you," Simon cried out.

"We both love you so much," Ethan sobbed as both brothers hugged her tightly. "Nothing will keep us apart again."

Laurie's own eyes began to water. The Harrington kids were going to be all right.

# Epilogue

Two months later, Frankie was playing yet another round of ring-around-the-rosie with Daniel and Sophie. *We all fall . . . DOWN!* She would have tired of this three fall-downs ago except for the elated joy in her niece and nephew's giggles after they threw themselves to the grass.

As she rose to her bare feet, she looked at her brothers, side by side at the dining table on the back deck, smiling as they studied whatever Simon was showing Ethan on his phone. In the past two months, they had somehow started to resemble each other even more—as if the differences that had developed during their years of estrangement were dissipating.

After everything that had happened in Harbor Bay, Frankie initially had no idea what she should do next. She thought about quitting her internship at the courthouse in New York, which would mean deferring her graduation until the following semester. The dean suggested that she take a few days to make up her mind. Meanwhile, her supervising judge had found a way for her to work remotely while she finished the research component of her work from Boston.

She'd be graduating on time with her class next month.

One thing she had known immediately was that she could not continue living with the Wards—at least not yet. Dennis and Betsy had been arrested, and Walter was going to have to work through the repercussions of decisions the two of them had made without him. Walter and Frankie were both innocent victims of their deceit. Being under the same roof together would only be a constant reminder of their conflicted loyalties.

With no hesitation, Simon and Ethan had both invited her to move in. For the first ten days, she bounced between their houses, aware that she needed to make a decision if she was going to stop living out of a suitcase.

She had been leaning toward staying with Ethan and Annabeth. She could help once the baby was born. Not to mention, Michelle was Simon's wife and her sister-in-law, but she was also Betsy's daughter and Dennis's sister—literally a member of both families. Even more so than Frankie and Walter, she was torn between two families. And yet choosing either house felt to Frankie like she'd be choosing one sibling over the other.

At Ethan's suggestion, she decided to flip a coin. To Ethan and Annabeth's house she went.

As it turned out, the decision wasn't so monumental. From the moment Simon and Ethan had arrived together at the storage facility with Annabeth, there was little hint of their previous estrangement. They now knew the truth about the death of their parents, which meant there was nothing more for them to fight about. In the two months that had passed, they had shared family meals at least once a week.

Tonight's dinner was at Simon's. When Annabeth and Michelle stepped out from the sliding back door with a platter of cookies, Daniel and Sophie leapt from the grass and ran toward the deck.

"Do we have chocolate chip?" Daniel asked.

"I want shortbread," Sophie said, trailing a few steps behind.

As Frankie joined them on the deck, Michelle assured them she had both of their favorites, and Sophie asked Annabeth if she could touch her "tummy" again. Annabeth held Sophie's hand to her swollen belly, and Daniel quickly rushed to his sister's side.

"I want to see our baby cousin," he said.

"Any day now," Annabeth said.

It turned out that the thing Simon had been showing Ethan on his phone was a real estate listing—a small cottage in Harbor Bay not far from the Wards' house or Annabeth's parents. The plan was to make an offer the next day.

For now the family meals were only for the Harringtons and their spouses. Frankie had seen Betsy a few times, trying to understand the choices she had made that night and in the ten years since. Betsy had even found a counselor in the hope that Frankie might go with her. Their first appointment was the following week. She had no idea whether her relationship with Betsy could be salvaged, but she wasn't ready to shut her out of her life permanently without at least trying.

Frankie stole a glance at her phone. It was nearly eight o'clock. "You guys, we should go inside. It's almost time."

The *Under Suspicion* special was premiering tonight. It couldn't have been better timed. Dennis had pled guilty last week to the charge of involuntary manslaughter. Frankie had decided not to press charges against him for what he had done to her in Harbor Bay. It just didn't feel right. Dennis was paying the price for the death of her parents, despite her father's own role in that night's deadly events. She kept reminding herself that Dennis had been more than a year younger than she was now. There was no reason to add to Walter and Michelle's pain.

She knew that Betsy would be completing a year of community service work for her role in obstructing the original investigation, but otherwise, Frankie had made a point to avoid the specifics of either Dennis's or Betsy's plea agreement. Her focus was right here—on her family.

Two hours later, a national television audience knew the truth: the Deadly Duo were never deadly. They were two innocent young men who not only lost their parents ten years ago, but were forever cast under suspicion—by the police, the general public, and each other. The cloud hanging over their heads had finally cleared.

As they all broke into applause over the closing credits, Frankie noticed that Annabeth wasn't clapping. Her hands were on her stomach, and Ethan was rising from the sofa where he had been seated next to her.

"Is it happening?" he asked.

Annabeth nodded, taking deep breaths through her mouth.

The Harrington family was about to have another member.

Two hundred and fifteen miles away, in New York City, Laurie chewed her lower lip, hoping that her production choices for completing the special would pay off.

She had decided to focus exclusively on the Harrington and Ward families. There was no reason for the public to know that Peter Bennett had secretly fallen in love with Sarah. Or that Howard Carver was a recovering addict who had stolen from clients. Or that, as Laurie had confirmed after Dennis and Betsy were arrested, Jimmy Connolly had driven to the Harringtons' house to confront Richard but then turned around when he decided that he trusted Ethan and Annabeth to work out their relationship on their own, no matter how their fathers might feel.

On the screen, Frankie sat between Simon and Ethan in the Fisher Blake studios with a black backdrop. "It took ten years before I was ready to fight for someone to reinvestigate my parents' murders," she said. "There was never going to be a happy ending. My parents are gone and nothing can change that. But I hoped against hope that the truth would prove my brothers were innocent. I never thought it would lead to such pain for my second family, but I try to focus on the part that makes me happy. The three of us are a family again."

Ryan looked directly into the camera as it focused in on him. She and Ryan must have written fifteen versions of the closing lines before they reached a final version.

"Not all crimes are a black-and-white story of good versus evil. We've learned tonight that the perfect father can be abusive and toxic behind closed doors. The perfect sons can be struggling to meet the expectations of a demanding parent. A troubled college student's animosity can build from vandalism to blackmail to a deadly confrontation involving a gun. What we have tonight is the unvarnished truth—for better and worse. Simon and Ethan Harrington are no longer under suspicion."

The screen fell to black, with stark white text informing the audience of the final details. Both Dennis and Betsy had cooperated with police and prosecutors. Betsy was not charged with the homicides but pled guilty to evidence tampering and was sentenced to probation and community service. Dennis pled guilty to involuntary manslaughter and had begun serving a three-year prison sentence.

It was their best special yet. Even Brett had said so when he first saw the completed version. As the credits rolled, her boss was the first on his feet to offer a standing ovation. "To the finest team in true crime reporting," he said, holding up a flute of champagne. "Good job, Ryan."

Ryan raised his glass in Laurie's direction. "To Laurie. This show belongs to her, from beginning to end."

Brett had splurged and rented a private room at Le Bernardin. It was a testament to his influence that he had somehow convinced one of the most sought after fine-dining establishments in the city to bring in a television for the evening. Ramon, the usual chef for the show's viewing parties, had been looking for reasons to complain, but Laurie noticed how delighted he had seemed with every course of the meal.

Tim rushed to her side and gave her a big hug. "You're the bomb, Mom. Grandpa might be the cop of the family, but you're the real detective." He always had a gleam in his eye like a kid who had a secret, but tonight he actually did. She and Alex had told Tim and her father the news two weeks earlier.

Her father tousled Tim's hair. "Who do you think she learned it from, buddy?" he said. "How's Ranger doing?"

Tim let out a giggle at the mention of the puppy he had gotten for his eleventh birthday. Of course he had named him after his favorite hockey team. "He's so cute. Ramon and I taught him how to shake hands today. I can't wait to show you."

Once Tim ran off to continue mingling, Laurie's father wrapped his arms around her and dropped a kiss on top of her head. "I'm so darn proud of you, sweetie." He reached for a bottle of sparkling water on the table and refilled her champagne flute. For the first time, he had brought Chief Judge Russell to a family event as his plus-one. Laurie hoped it was a sign of things to come.

By the time she was done making the rounds, Tim was in the corner with Grace and Jerry, practicing a new TikTok dance in perfect time, while Charlotte filmed with her camera.

She noticed Ryan lingering nervously nearby. "Laurie, do you have a second?"

As he led the way to a quiet hallway outside the private dining room, she noticed Grace eyeing them. Laurie had spotted them together two weeks ago through the front window of Del Frisco's steak house, when she was on her way to meet Charlotte for dinner, but she hadn't mentioned it. If there was anything to report, Grace would tell her in good time.

"You're happy with the special?" he asked.

"Very. Our best yet."

"This is even harder to say than I thought, but this will be the last time I'll be hosting *Under Suspicion*. I haven't told Brett yet. I wanted you to know first."

She placed a hand on his forearm. "Ryan, no. We've had our ups and downs, but I understand now. I thought we'd been working well together."

He placed his free hand over hers. "And we have been. But TV's not for me. I'm going to run for district attorney of Manhattan."

"And this is what *you* want to do? Not pressure from your father and uncle?"

He nodded, looking more satisfied than she'd ever seen him. "Definitely. I'll be declaring next week."

"Wow. That's big. And soon."

"Sooner than I may have wanted, but my campaign manager

says to strike while the iron is hot. And I have you to thank for that. You were the one who exonerated Simon and Ethan, but I get to play hero."

"Well," she said quietly, "we're a team. We always have been. Will you please stay in touch?"

"Trust me, if things work out how I want, you'll be seeing plenty of me." He gave a sideways glance to Grace, and Laurie made a point of following his gaze.

"As the district attorney, you mean," she said with a knowing smile.

When she made her way back into the dining room, Alex was waiting for her. "What was that about? Do I need to play referee?"

"One, when have I ever needed you to protect me from Ryan?"

"True, if anything it's the other way around."

"And two, I apparently need a new host for my show. Any chance you're willing to return to the fold, Your Honor?"

He pushed a lock of her hair behind her ear and gave her a kiss. "I think your father's girlfriend would be very disappointed in me."

"I dare you to call the chief judge his girlfriend in front of them."

"Not on your life." He wrapped an arm around her shoulder. "You look happy, my love."

She scanned the room. "I am definitely very happy. How could I not be?" Her amazing son, her loving husband, the father who would always be her hero, the best coworkers she could possibly ask for, her best friend, and of course Ramon—the man who started off working for her husband but had become an honorary uncle.

She felt Alex's eyes on her and turned to face him. "This is crazy, but should we just tell them?"

"Now?" he asked.

She nodded. "It feels right."

He smiled. "I was thinking the same thing."

Their baby was due in six months. It was safe to share the news.

She took his hand in hers. "Our child will be so lucky to know everyone in this room as family. Let's do it."

# Acknowledgments

Thank you to editor extraordinaire Sean Manning, along with the entire *Under Suspicion* team (aka "Team Clark"): Jonathan Karp, Tim O'Connell, Tzipora Baitch, Anne Tate Pearce, and Danielle Prielipp at Simon & Schuster; Robert Barnett and Deneen Howell at Williams & Connelly; and the family of the beloved Queen of Suspense, Mary Higgins Clark.

And thank you, readers, for jumping into another visit with Laurie, Alex, Leo, Tim, Grace, Jerry, Ramon, Charlotte, and even Ryan and Brett. Happy reading!